Frederick T. Hodgson

Stair-Building Made Easy

Being a full and clear description of the art of building the bodies, carriages and

cases for all kinds of stairs and steps

Frederick T. Hodgson

Stair-Building Made Easy
Being a full and clear description of the art of building the bodies, carriages and cases for all kinds of stairs and steps

ISBN/EAN: 9783337387181

Printed in Europe, USA, Canada, Australia, Japan

Cover: Foto ©Andreas Hilbeck / pixelio.de

More available books at **www.hansebooks.com**

Stair-Building Made Easy.

BEING A FULL AND CLEAR DESCRIPTION OF THE ART OF

BUILDING THE BODIES, CARRIAGES AND CASES FOR ALL KINDS OF STAIRS AND STEPS.

TOGETHER WITH ILLUSTRATIONS SHOWING THE MANNER OF

LAYING OUT STAIRS, FORMING TREADS AND RISERS, BUILDING CYLINDERS, PREPARING STRINGS, WITH INSTRUCTIONS FOR MAKING CARRIAGES FOR COMMON, PLATFORM, DOG-LEGGED AND WINDING STAIRS.

TO WHICH IS ADDED

An Illustrated Glossary of Terms used in Stair-Building, and Designs for Newels, Balusters, Brackets, Stair-Mouldings and Sections of Hand-Rails.

— • ◦ • —

BY

FRED. T. HODGSON,

EDITOR OF "THE BUILDER AND WOOD-WORKER"; AUTHOR OF "THE CARPEN-
TER'S STEEL SQUARE, AND ITS USES," ETC., ETC.

NEW YORK:
THE INDUSTRIAL PUBLICATION COMPANY.
1884.

PREFACE.

———◦•◦———

Many books have been written on Stairs and Hand-Railing, but so far as my experience extends, one of two objections has prevented them from being universally adopted by the operative workman.

First, the books have been written by men who did not seem to think it necessary to begin at the beginning, and first teach the young workman how to build a stair of the humblest sort, and thus lead him, step by step, until he became able, by gradual and natural acquirement, to erect and complete stairs of a better description. This objection, I have found, by close observation and a knowledge of the wants of young workmen, to be fatal to the large sale of any work published on the subject; and though I am fully aware that to the workman who has, from practical experience in the workshop or in the building, obtained a fair knowledge of stair-building and hand-railing, some one or other of the many excellent works now obtainable is a necessity, and it is not intended that this work will replace the more advanced ones. Yet, I think, that even the advanced stair-builder will be able to find something here that will more than repay for the cost.

The second objection I have met with to the books on this subject now in the market, is their high price. Young and struggling workmen cannot afford to pay fancy prices for books they do not understand. GOULD'S AMERICAN STAIR-BUILDER, which is the lowest priced book on the subject published in this country, costs $3.00; while MONCKTON'S NATIONAL STAIR-BUILDER costs $5.00, and RIDDELL'S UNIVERSAL STAIR-BUILDER costs $7.50; and so it is with CUPPER, DEGRAFF, LOTH and other works. Doubtless, these books, every one of them, are worth the money asked for them, and the advanced workman would not be without a copy of one or the other of them if he had to pay double the market price; but while these books may be invaluable to the advanced stair-builder, they are not at all adapted to the wants of the uninitiated; and are as much out of place on the shelves of the young apprentice as a learned treatise on the lost tribes of Israel would be in the hands of a child struggling with alphabetical word-making.

I have tried to avoid both the objections mentioned; first, by presuming that the reader knows nothing about the art of stair-building when he buys this book, and must necessarily commence at the beginning, and work his way up; second, by keeping the cost of the book down to such a price that the poorest apprentice boy may be able to procure it.

This book will be followed by another on the same subject, one that will begin where this leaves off, thus enabling the student to pursue the subject to its highest domain. Of course, it is intended that each work will be complete in itself, and that both works will cover the whole ground of Stair-Building and Hand-Railing.

FRED. T. HODGSON.

New York, November 1, 1884.

TABLE OF CONTENTS.

	PAGE.
Preliminary,	9
Use of Terms,	9
Introduction,	9
General Directions,	9
Stairs Generally,	10
Staircases,	10
Treads,	11
Risers,	11
Rise and Run,	11
Strings Generally,	12
Flights, Fliers and Landings,	13
Winders, Spaces and Nosings,	13
Cylinders, Newels and Balusters,	14
Method of Setting Out Stairs,	18
Consecutive Flights,	19
Rules for Laying Out Strings,	20
Graphical Method of Laying Out Stairs,	22
Laying Out Stairs by Figures,	23
Plans of Stairs,	23
Pitch-Boards,	25
Fenced Pitch-boards	26
Uses of Pitch-board,	27
Method of Using Pitch-board,	27
Construction of Steps,	29
Another Method of Same,	30
French, German, Italian, English and American Methods	31
Line of Nosings,	31
Scheme for Strings,	33
Housing Strings,	34

	PAGE
Placing Balusters,	35
Finishing Ends of Wall-Strings,	36
Trimmers and Joists,	37
Finishing Cut Strings,	38
Lower Newel Finish,	38
Top Finish of Cut String,	39
Well-Hole Finish,	40
Three-Neweled Stairs,	41
Straight Platform Stairs,	41
Planning Stairs,	42
Dog-Legged Stairs,	43
Stairs with Four Newels,	45
Close-String Stairs,	46
Continuous Stairs,	48
Geometrical Stairs,	49
Carriages of Stairs,	53
Balancing Steps,	54
Story Rod,	55
Dancing the Treads,	56
How This is Done,	57
Double Platform Stairs,	57
Straight Flights and Winders,	58
Cylinder—How Made,	63
Elliptical Stairs,	63
Carriage for Same,	65
Method of Forming Carriages,	67
Circular Strings,	68
Elliptical Strings,	69
Radiating Treads,	70
Stretchout of Strings,	72
Solid Newels,	77
All Winders,	77
Method of Framing,	79
Built String,	80
Staved Cylinder,	82
Bracketed Stairs,	83
Plain Balusters,	84
Ornate Balusters,	85

PAGE.

Newels, - - - - - - - - - - 86
Words on Handralling, - - - - - - - - 89
Pedestal Newel, - - - - - - - - 90
Plain Newel, - - - - - - - - - 91
Miscellaneous, - - - - - - - - 93
Dancing Steps Graphically, - - - - - - - 94
Method of Obtaining, - - - - - - - 94
Reducing Brackets, - - - - - - - - 95
Mitering Cap and Rail. - - - - - - - 96
Scribing String, - - - - - - - - 97
Appliances for Same, - - - - - - - 98
Small Cylinders, - - - - - - - - 99
Gluing Up Stuff, - - - - - - - - 99
Scribing Stuff, - - - - - - - - 100
Glossary, - - - - - - - - - 103, 123

ILLUSTRATIONS, DIAGRAMS, ETC.

Oak Stair, - - - - - - - - Frontispiece.
Block Steps, - - - - - - - - - 14
Cellar Steps, - - - - - - - - - 15
Curious Block Steps, - - - - - - - 16, 17
Rough Steps, - - - - - - - - - 18
Plan of Platform Stairs, - - - - - - - 19
Diagrams of Tread and Riser, - - - - - - 21, 22
Plan of Stairs with Cylinder, - - - - - - 24
Pitch-board, - - - - - - - - 25, 26, 27
View of Stairs, - - - - - - - - 28
Plans of Strings, - - - - - - 29, 31, 33, 36, 37, 38, 39
Method of Forming Steps, - - - - - - 30
Plan and Elevation, - - - - - - - 35
Plan of Well-Hole - - - - - - - - 40
Plan of Platform Stairs, - - - - - - - 41
Plan and Elevation of Return Stairs, - - - - - 43
Plan and Elevation of Four-Neweled Stairs, - - - - 45
Closed-String Stairs, - - - - - - - 46, 47
Plan and Elevation of Continuous Stairs. - - - - 48

PAGE.

Plan and Elevation of Circular Stairs, -	50, 51
Partial Elevation of Circular Flight, -	52
Plan and Elevation of Straight Flight, -	53
Geometrical Stair and Carriage,	54
Double Platform Stairs,	57
Plan and Elevation of Straight and Winding Stairs,	58, 59
Elevations of Winding Stairs,	60, 61
Semicircular, with Platforms, -	62
Cylinder,	63
Plan of Semicircular Stairs,	64
Plan of Elliptical Stairs,	65
Stair Carriages,	66, 67, 68, 69, 71
Stretchout of Strings,	71, 73, 74, 76
Circular Plan,	77
Circular Elevation, -	78
Method of Framing,	79
Built String, -	80
Elevation of Elliptical Stairs, -	82
Balusters,	84, 85, 105, 106
Newels,	86, 87, 88, 90, 91
Dancing Treads,	93
Diminishing Brackets, -	95
Mitering Cap and Rail,	96
Scribing String, -	97
Small Cylinder,	98, 99
Stair Brackets, -	36, 106, 107, 108
Sections of Hand-Rails,	110, 113, 114

STAIR-BUILDING

MADE EASY.

———

PRELIMINARY.—The object of this work is to teach the beginner in the arts of carpentry and joinery, some simple rules for the construction of the body of stairs, so that he may be able to undertake work of this kind with some degree of certainty that satisfactory results will follow his efforts.

There are a great many terms used in the construction of stairs by professional stair-builders, many of which I shall be obliged to use in this volume; and, as the young reader is not supposed to be conversant with these terms, and as their explanation would be tedious and out of place in the body of the work, it has been deemed necessary to append at the end of the book a complete glossary or explanation of the terms used. This it is thought will add to the value of the work, and will doubtless aid the student very much to a thorough understanding of its contents.

Introduction.—Stairs are constructions composed of horizontal planes elevated above each other, forming steps, affording the means of communication between the different stories of a building.

In the distribution of a house of several stories, the stairs occupy an important place. In new constructions their form may be regular, but in the reparation or remodelling of old buildings, the first consideration is generally to make the distribution suitable for the living and sleeping rooms, and then to convert to the use of the stairs the spaces which may remain; giving to them such forms in plan as will render them agreeable to the sight, and commodious in the use.

A great variety of form in the plans of stairs is thus in a measure forced on the designer, leading to many ingenious contrivances for overcoming difficulties, disguising defects, and enhancing accidental beauties, which he might not have adopted if unfettered in his choice. These inventions, originated by necessity, are again applied in cases where the necessity may not exist, recommended by their intrinsic beauty, or by the desire for variety in design.

Being also somewhat intricate and difficult to understand, it is absolutely necessary that the designs or drawings should be clear and distinct, and that every part should be correct and true in its relations to other parts. This applies just as much to the building of bodies or carcases of stairs, as it does to the construction of hand-railing. I say this much to the student in order that he may be persuaded to be very careful when making drawings for future work, or designing stairs for his own instruction. Perhaps there is no branch of joinery that requires so much skill and careful workmanship as the building and completing of a first-class geometrical stair; and it should be the chief ambition of every joiner to be able to say he designs and executes the work in a complete and satisfactory manner.

The following terms are necessary, and the student must make himself familiar with them before he proceeds further, or his progress will be very slow and difficult :

Stairs are arrangements for conveniently ascending from one level to another. They are generally constructed of wood, and it is this kind of stairs that this volume discusses. They are sometimes built of stone, concrete, or iron.

The Body or Staircase is the room or space in which the stairs are contained. This may be a space including the width and length of the stairs only, in which case it is called a *close stair*, and no rail or buluster is necessary ; or the stairs may be in a large apartment, such as a passage or a hall, or even in a large room, openings being left in the upper floors so as to allow head room for persons on the stairs, and to furnish communication between the stairs and the different stories of the building. These are called open stairs, from the fact that they are not enclosed on both sides, one side showing the ends of the steps while the other side of the stairs is generally placed against a wall. Sometimes stairs are left open on both sides, this latter class being more common in hotels, public halls, and steamships. When these stairs are employed, the openings in the upper floor should be well "trimmed" with joists or beams, something stronger than the ordinary joists used in the same floor. The manner of "trimming" will be shown further on ; as will also the different styles of stairs.

Tread is the horizontal upper surface of the step upon which the foot is placed. In other words, it is the piece of stuff that forms the step, and is generally from 1¼ inches to 3 inches thick, and made of a width and length to suit the position for which it is intended.

Riser is the vertical position of the step. It is generally made of thinner stuff than the tread, and, as a rule, is not so wide. Its duty is to connect the treads together and to give the stairs strength and solidity. The manner of connecting riser, tread and string together will be shown in other pages.

Rise and Run.—This term is used to indicate the space the stairs will occupy, the "rise" meaning the height of the top of the lower floor to the top of the second floor, and the "run" meaning the distance from the front of the first riser to the face of the last or top riser, from which a plumb line is dropped to the floor, which point to face of first riser is the "run." In other words, it is simply the distance that the treads would make if put edge to edge and measured altogether. This, of course, means without taking in the nosings. Suppose we have fifteen treads, each being 11 inches wide, this would make a run of 13 feet 9 inches, as follows: $15 \times 11 = 165 \div 12'' = 13$ ft. 9 inches. Sometimes this distance is called the "going" of the stair; this, however, is an English term, seldom used in this country, and, when used, as often means the length of a single tread, as it does the "*run*" of the stairs.

Nosing.—This is the outer edge of the tread, and in all cases projects over the face of the riser. In most cases it is ornamented, either by taking off the corners or arrises, or by rounding the edge, or, as is sometimes done, by "sticking" a moulding on it. The nosing is said to be either chamfered, rounded or moulded, just as the case may be. When the tread projects over the "string," and the nosing is cut or wrought on the projecting end, it is raid to be a "return nosing." Underneath the nosing, on stairs that have any claims to being termed "good," there is always a small moulding of some kind; generally a small cove or other similar moulding. This moulding or cove mitres around the end of the step on to the string, when the tread is finished with a return nosing. This will be fully explained hereafter.

String.—There are two kinds of strings—*i. e.*, wall strings and cut strings. These are divided again into other strings, as housed strings, notched strings, staved strings, and rough strings. Wall strings are the supporters of the ends of the treads and risers that are against the wall; these strings may be on both ends of the treads and risers, or they may be on one end only. They may be "housed" or left solid. When housed, the treads and risers are keyed into them and glued and blocked. When left solid, they have a rough string spiked or screwed on them to support the ends of risers and treads. Stairs made after this latter fashion are generally of a rough, strong kind, and are adapted more for use in factories, shops, and warehouses, where strength and rigidity are of more importance than appearances.

Open strings are outside strings or supports, and are cut to the proper angles for receiving the ends of the treads and risers. It is over this string that the rail and balusters range; it is also on this string that all nosings return, and on this account in some localities this string gets the name of the "return string."

Housed strings are those that have grooves cut in them to receive the ends of treads and risers. Generally all wall strings are "housed." The housings are made from ⅝ to ¾ of an inch deep, and the lines at the top of tread and face of riser are made to correspond with the lines of riser and tread when in position. The back lines of the housings are left of such a shape that a taper wedge may be driven in, so as to force the tread and riser close to the face shoulders, thus making a tight joint.

Rough strings are cut from undressed plank, and are used for strengthening the stairs. Sometimes a combination of rough cut strings are used for circular or geometrical stairs, and when framed together form the support or carriage of the stairs.

Stave strings are built up strings, and are composed of narrow pieces glued, nailed, or bolted together, to form some portion of a cylinder. These are sometimes used for circular stairs, though in ordinary practice the circular part of a string is a part of the main string bent around a cylinder to give it the right curve.

Notched strings are strings that only carry treads. They are generally somewhat narrower than the treads, and are housed right across their whole width. A sample of this kind of string is shown at Figs. 2 and 3, where the housings for the treads are numbered. These kinds of strings are chiefly used in cellars, or for steps answering a like purpose.

A Flight is a continued series of steps without a landing or other resting place.

A Landing is a resting point or platform where one flight ends, and where another may start from in any direction.

A Flier is the regular step, and is of parallel width its entire length.

A Winder is a tread wider at one end than at the other. These winders are used for turning a corner or going round a curve. The small end of winders is sometimes called a *quoin*.

A Quarter Space is a landing extending half across the width of stairs.

Half Space is a landing extending right across the width of stairs. Sometimes landings are made of greater area than the foregoing spaces would permit.

The Line of Nosings is tangent to the nosings of the steps, and is therefore parallel to the inclination of the stair.

Cylinders or Well Holes.—These are semicircular or quarter-circular openings, around which the stairs are carried. The openings are formed by either building the cylinder with staves or bending stuff to the proper curve.

Newels.—These are posts or columns either turned or built up. Generally there is one of these posts at the foot of the stairs, and the hand-rail either mitres into the cap of the post or it "butts" against a square left purposely for it.

Balusters.—These are smaller posts of either turned work, square, or wrought work, and are designed to support the hand-rail, and give strength and a finished appearance to the whole work.

A number of designs for newels and balusters will be given further on.

Besides the terms given in the foregoing, there are many others I may have to use in the body of the work, and when they are not thoroughly understood, the student is advised to look for the explanation in the glossary, which will be found at the end of the book.

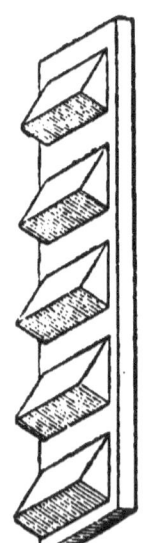

Fig. 1.

Having given these explanations, which for the present may be considered ample, I will endeavor to describe some of the more simple contrivances that have been used in various places for the purpose of getting from one plane to another.

The ladder, which is composed of two sides and a number of rungs or cleats running across the sides, may be considered the simplest form of a stair, for the

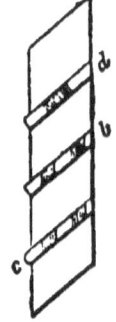

Fig. 2.

same principles are involved in the construction of a common ladder as are necessary for the building of a first-class straight flight of stairs.

That kind of stair which, after the common ladder, is the most simple, is formed of a thick plank placed at a convenient angle to form the ascent, and upon it are nailed pieces of wood to give a firm footing. This (Fig. 1) is often used in scaffolding.

The stair next in degree is composed of horizontal planks forming steps, just sufficiently wide to give a footing; the planks are tenoned on the ends and let into mortises in two raking planks; the mortises are sometimes rectangular, as at *d* (Fig. 2), and some-

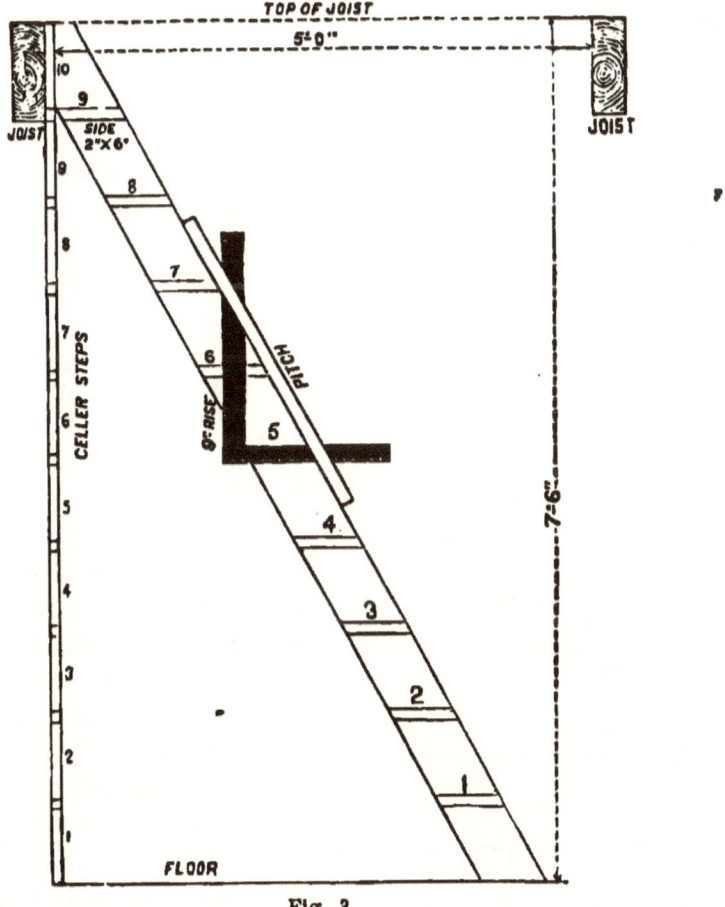

Fig. 3.

times they follow the inclination of the sides, as *b* and *c*. In the better sort the outer edge of the step has a nosing, as at *c*. The

tenons of the steps are sometimes made so long as to pass entirely
through the sides, and are secured by keys on the outside: to preserve the planks which form the steps from splitting, the sides of
the raking pieces are grooved to receive their ends. The opposite
side pieces, too, are often bound together by iron rods; one end of
each rod having a rivet head, and the other end being screwed
with a nut to embrace the side pieces. Such rods should be
placed near the middle of a step, and close to its under side.

This method of building stairs, or rather steps, will be better understood by a study of Fig. 3, where the string for the steps are
shown along with the method of getting the right angle for the lay
of the treads. In using the steel square to get the "pitch" or
angle of the tread, proceed as shown in the cut. The height of
the rise in this case is nine inches, so it will be seen that it is an
easy matter to lay off the string as the long side of the square
hangs plumb, and nine inches up its length will be the distance
from the top of one step to
the top of the next one.

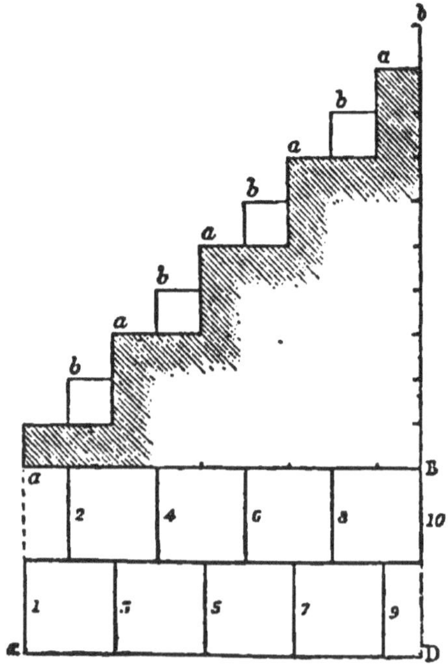

The opening in the floor
at the top of the string
shows the end of the trimming joists, which in this
case are five feet apart.

There is a contrivance
for economizing space
sometimes used, which,
perhaps, it may be well to
mention, as the ascent is
thereby made in about
one-half the space other-
wise required.

The width of this kind
of stair is divided into two
sets of steps, both of equal
length and width, but the
risers, except the first and

Fig. 4.

last, are made twice the usual height; thus, if the line a B (Fig. 4) be 72 inches, and the width C D 33 inches, and it is necessary to rise 80 inches, divide the line a B in nine equal parts, and make the step equal to two of these parts; also, divide the width in two equal parts, and the height into ten equal parts, which gives 8 inches for the tread, 8 inches for the bottom riser, and 16 inches

for the intermediate risers $a a$, etc., and 8 for the top riser b. Arrange the risers in such order that the face line of one riser shall be in the midway betwixt the face of the one next below and the one next above, as will better be seen by reference to Fig. 5. The height of the risers is so disposed that the bottom riser shall have the face of the first step 8 inches from the floor, whilst the first step on b shall be 16 inches from the floor, and the succeeding risers 16 inches each.

Fig. 5.

In using this stair, one foot is placed on a step of one flight, as at a (Fig. 4), and the other on a step of the other flight, as at b, and so on alternately. Such stairs will only admit the passage of one person at a time.

When it is required to admit of two persons passing each other, three

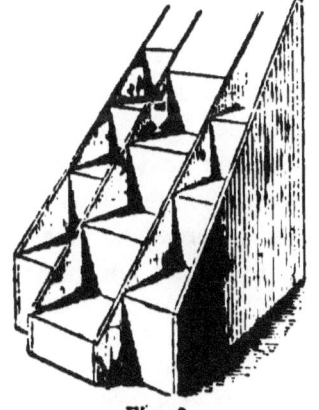

Fig. 6.

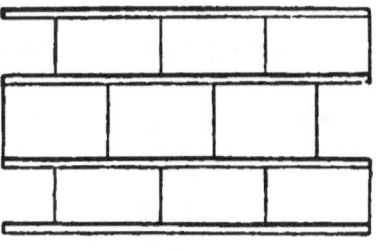

Fig. 7.

flights are necessary, the centre flight being made wider than the exterior flights (Figs. 6 and 7). This contrivance may be used in places not sufficiently spacious to admit of stairs of the usual construction.

When houses began to be built in stories, the stairs were placed from story to story in straight flights like ladders. They were erected on the exterior of the building, and to shelter them when so placed, great projection was given to the roofs. To save the extent of space required by straight flights, the stairs were made to turn upon themselves in a spiral form, and were enclosed in turrets. A newel, either square or round, reaching from the ground to the roof, served to support the inner ends of the steps, and the outer ends were let into the walls, or supported on notched boards attached to the walls.

At a later period the stairs came to be inclosed within the building itself and for a long time preserved the spiral form, which the former situation had necessitated.

Another method of forming a stair expeditiously, is to notch out the side pieces on their upper edge sufficiently to receive the steps and risers, thus: *a a* the side pieces, *b b* the risers, and *c c* the step boards or treads (Fig. 8). The risers are nailed at the ends to the sides or strings, and the steps are nailed to the risers and also to the strings. Such methods as have been described are often used in warehouses, factories, and agricultural buildings.

Fig. 8.

Where communication between the stories is frequent, the qualities necessary in the stairs are ease and convenience in using, combined with sufficient strength and durability. Economy of space in the construction of stairs is an important consideration. To obtain this, the stairs are made to turn upon themselves, one flight being carried above another at such a height as will admit of head room to a full grown person.

Method of Setting Out Stairs *where the building is already erected, or the general plan of the building is understood.*

The first objects to be ascertained are the situation of the first and last risers, and the height of the story wherein the stair is to be placed. A sketch is made of the plan of the hall to the extent of 10 or 12 feet from the supposed place of the foot of the stair, and all the doorways, branching passages, or windows which can possibly come in contact with the stair from its commencement to its expected termination or landing are noted. The sketch necessarily includes a portion of the entrance-hall in one part, and of the lobby or landing in the other, and on it have to be laid down the expected lines of the first and last risers. The height of the story is next to be exactly determined and taken on a rod; then, assuming a height of riser suitable to the place, a trial is made, by division, how often this height is contained in the height of the story, and the quotient, if there be no remainder, will be the number of risers in the story. Should there be a remainder on the first division, the operation is reversed, the number of inches in the height being made the divi-dend, and the before-found quotient the divisor, and the operation of division by reduction is carried on, till the height of the riser is obtained to the thirty-second part of an inch. These heights are then set off on the story rod as exactly as possible. The next operation is to show the risers on the plan, but for this no arbitrary rule can be given; the designer must exercise his ingenuity.

When two flights are necessary for a story, it is desirable that each flight should consist of an equal number of risers; but this will depend on the form of the staircase, the situation and height of the doors, and other obstacles to be passed over or under, as the case may be. Try what the width of the tread will be by setting off, upon the line *n a*, in Figure 9, the width of the landing from the wall A B; and dividing the length of the flight into as many equal spaces as it is intended

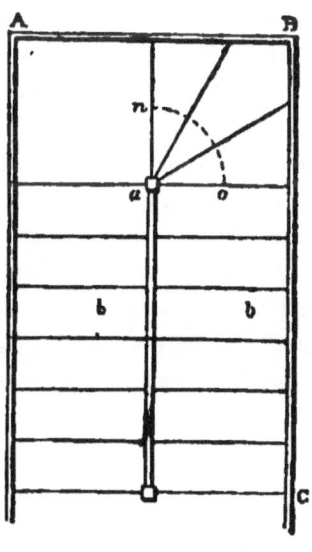

Fig. 9.

there should be steps in each flight. The landing covers one riser, and therefore the number of steps in a flight will be always one fewer than the number of risers. The width of tread which can be obtained for each flight will thus be found, and consistent with the situation the plan will be so far decided. A pitch-board should now be formed to the angle of inclination; this is done by making a piece of thin board in the shape of a right-angled triangle, the base of which is the exact going of the step, and its perpendicular the height of the riser.

If the stair be a newel stair, its width will be found by setting out the plan and section of the newel on the landing (if one newel, it should, of course, stand in the middle of the width); then, in conection with the newel, mark the place of the outer or front string, and also the place of the back or wall string, according to the intended thickness of each. This should be done not only to a scale on the plan, but likewise to the full size on the rod. Set off on the rod, in the thickness of each string, the depth of the grooving of the steps into the string; mark also on the plan the place and section of the bottom newel; the same figure answers for the place of the top newel of the second flight, the flights being supposed of equal length. The front string is usually framed into the middle of the newel, and thus the centres of the rail, the newels, the balusters, and the front string range with each other; the width of the flights will thus be shown on the rod.

It is a general maxim that the greater the breadth of a step the less should be the height of the riser; and conversely, the less breadth of step, the greater should be the height of the riser. Experience shows that a step of 12 inches width and 5½ inches rise may be taken as a standard; and if from this it is attempted to deduce a rule of proportion, substituting, for the sake of whole numbers, the dimensions in half-inches, namely, 24 and 11, then, in order to find any other width corresponding in inverse proportion,

$$\text{Say as } 24 : 11 :: 12 : 22$$
$$24 : 11 :: 19 : 13 \cdot 8$$
$$24 : 11 :: 20 : 13 \cdot 2.$$

Thus it will be seen that a step of 6 inches in width will require the riser to be 11 inches, a step of 9½ inches will need the riser to be nearly 7 inches, and that a step of 10 inches requires a riser of about 6⅝ inches.

The same thing is thus otherwise expressed. Let T be the tread and R the riser of any step which is found to have proper porpor-tion, then to find the proportion of any other tread t, and riser r,

$$\frac{R \times T}{r} = t, \text{ or } \frac{T \times R}{t} = r.$$

Take, for example, a step with a tread of 12 and a riser of 5½ inches as the standard, then to find the breadth of the tread when the given riser is 8 inches, and substituting these values for t and r in the formula, we have

$$\frac{12 \times 5½}{8} = 8¼$$

inches as the breadth of tread.

Suppose, again, the given breadth to be 13 inches, we have

$$\frac{12 \times 5½}{13} = 5 \ 1\text{-}13$$

inches as the height of riser.

This process of inverse proportion may be performed graphically as follows:

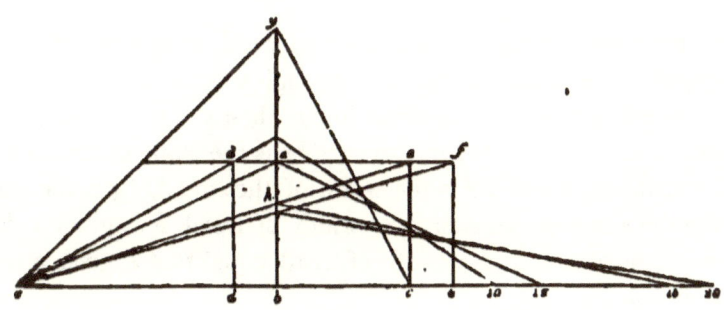

Fig. 10.

Let the tread and riser of a step of approved proportion be rep-resented by the sides $c\,b$, $6\,e$, of the triangle $a\,b\,c$, Fig. 10. Through the point *a*, draw a line *d a f*, parallel to the step line *c b*. Then to find the riser for any other step, set off on the line *c b*, from the point *c* to *d*, the required width of a step, say 10 inches, and draw *d d*; draw also *c d*, and continue it to the line *b a*, and the point of intersection there will show the height of riser corresponding to the tread *c d*. In like manner, if the width given be 18 inches, set it off in the point 6; draw 6 *e* and *c e*, and the intersection at *h* will be obtained, giving 3⅔ inches for the height of the riser. A width of 20 inches will show a height of 3·3 inches. On the right side of the figure is shown each step I have mentioned, connected with its proper riser, thus exhibiting the angle of pitch.

The same end nearly is arrived at thus: In the right-angled triangle *a b c*, Fig. 11, make *a b* equal to 24 inches, and *b c* equal to 11 inches, according to the previous standard proportion; then

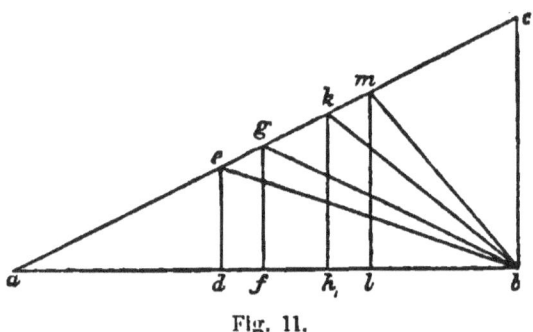

Fig. 11.

to find the riser corresponding to a given tread, from *b* set off on *a b* the length of the tread, as *b d*, and through *d* draw the perpendicular *d e*, meeting the hypotheneuse in *e;* then *d e* is the height of the riser, and if we join *b e*, the angle *d b e* is the slope of the ascent. In like manner, where *b f* is the width of the tread, *f g* is the riser, and *b g* the slope of the stair. A width of tread, *b h*, gives a riser of the height of *h k*, and a width of tread equal to *b l*, gives a riser equal to *l m*.

It is conceived, however, that a better proportion for steps and risers may be obtained by the annexed method:

Set down two sets of numbers, each in arithmetical progression;

the first set showing the width of the steps, ascending by inches, the other showing the height of the riser, descending by half inches. It will readily be seen that each of these steps and risers are such as may suitably pair together.

It is seldom, however, that the proportion of the step and riser is exactly a matter of choice—the room allotted to the stairs usually determines this proportion; but the above will be found a useful standard, to which it is desirable to approximate.

In better class buildings the number of steps is considered in the plan, which it is the business of the architect to arrange, and in such cases the height of the story rod is simply divided into the number required.

Treads. Inches.	Risers. Inches.
5	9
6	8½
7	8
8	7½
9	7
10	6½
11	6
12	5½
13	5
14	4½
15	4
16	3½
17	3
18	2½

Plans of Stairs.—Before giving examples of the various forms of stairs ordinarily occurring in practice, I will with some minuteness illustrate the mode of laying down the plan of a stair, where the height of the story, the number of the steps, and the space which they are to occupy are all given.

The first example shall be of the simplest kind, or dog-legged stairs.

Let the height (Fig. 9) be 10 feet, the number of risers 17, the height of each riser consequently 7 1-17, and the breadth of tread 9½; the width of the staircase 5 feet 8 inches.

Proceed first to lay down on the plan the width of the landing, then the size of the newel *a* in its proper position, the centre of the newel being on the riser line of the landing, which should be drawn at a distance from the back wall equal to the semi-width of the staircase, and at right angles to the side wall. Bisect the last riser *a b* at *o*, and describe an arc from the centre of the newel, as *o n*, on which set out the breadth of the winders; then to the centre of the newel draw the lines indicating the face of each riser. If there be not space to get in the whole of the steps, winders may be also introduced on the left hand side, instead of the quarter space, as shown.

The next example is a geometrical staircase.

Let A B C D (Fig. 12) be the plan of the walls where a geometrical stair is to be erected, and the line C be the line of the face of
the first riser; let the whole height of the story be 11 feet 6 inches,

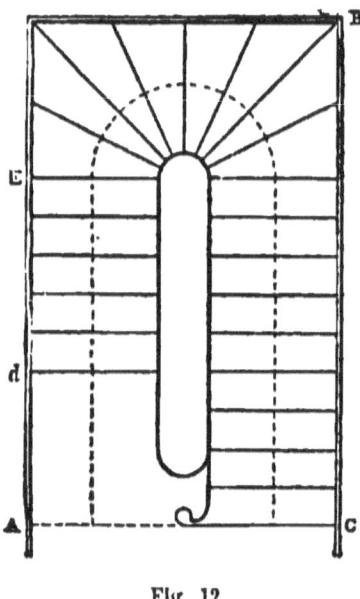

and the height of riser 6 inches,
the number of risers will consequently be twenty-three. The
number of steps in each flight
will be one fewer than the number of risers, and according to
the preceding rule the tread
should be 11 inches, so if there
are two flights there will be
twenty-one steps; or if winders
are necessary, there will be
twenty-two steps in all, from the
first to the last riser. Having
first set out the opening of the
well-hole, or the line of balusters,
divide the width of the stairs into
two equal parts, and continue
the line of division with a semi-
circle round the circular part, as

Fig. 12.

shown by the dotted line in the figure; then divide this line from
the first to the last riser into twenty-two equal parts, and if a proper
width for each step can thus be obtained, draw the lines for the
risers. This would, however, give a greater width of step than is
required; take, therefore, 11 inches for the width of step, and this,
repeated twenty times, will reach to the line *d*, which is the last
riser. There is in this case eight winders in the half space, but
four winders might be placed in one quarter space, the other quarter space might be made a landing, and the rest of the steps being
fliers, would bring the last riser to the line A C. The usual place
for the entrance to the cellar stairs is at D, but allowing for the
thickness of the carriages, the height obtainable there will be only
about 6 feet, which is not sufficient. At E, in this example, would
be a better situation for the entrance to the cellar steps.

In a straight flight of stairs it is hardly necessary for the young workman to make a drawing of the plan of the stairs, as the steps are all alike, and if a proper division of the height or "rise," and the length or "run" is made, and a "pitch board" made to suit these dimensions, this will be quite sufficient to enable the workman to lay out the strings correctly.

It is now in order to explain what a "pitch-board" is, how to make it, and what are its uses.

A Pitch-Board, properly speaking, is a thin piece of wood—generally pine or sheet metal—and is a right-angled triangle in shape. One of its sides is made the exact length of the *rise;* at right angles with this line of *rise* the exact width of the *tread* is measured off, and from this point to the point forming the height of the riser, a line is drawn, and the material cut at this line forms the third side. Further on I will show, by illustration, the shape of the tool—for it is a tool—and the method employed in making it ready for use.

Perhaps the simplest way of making a *pitch-board* is by making

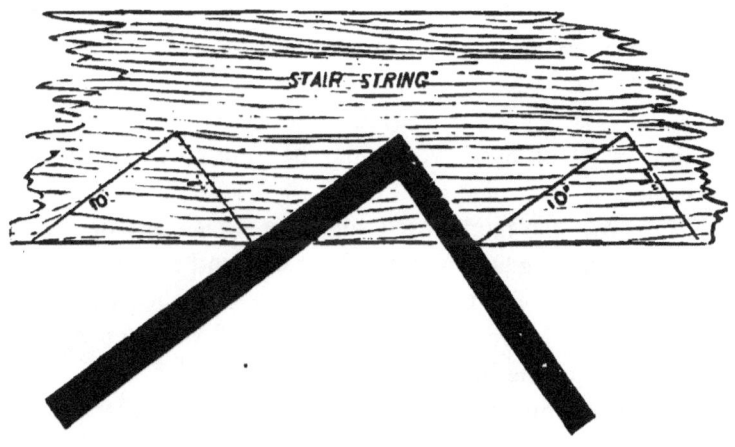

Fig. 13.

use of a steel square, which, of course, every carpenter in this country is supposed to possess. To show him how the *pitch-board* may be made by using the square, or how the stair-string may be *layed out* by the square, I give the following, which is taken from the

"Steel Square and Its Uses," a very valuable work. Fig. 13 shows a part of a stair string with the square laid on, showing its application in cutting out a pitch-board. As the square is placed it shows 10 inches for the tread and 7 inches for the rise.

To cut a pitch-board, after the tread and rise have been determined, proceed as follows: Take a piece of thin, clear stuff, and lay the square on the face edge, as shown in the figure, and mark out the pitch-board with a sharp knife; then cut out with a fine saw and dress to knife marks, nail a piece on the largest edge of the pitch-board for a fence, and it is ready for use.

The next thing to be considered is what is the manner of using the pitch-board? Before showing, its use, however, I wish the learner to have a thorough conception of what the pitch-board is, and with that object I show and explain the following illustrations. Fig. 14 shows the pitch-board pure and simple; it may be half an

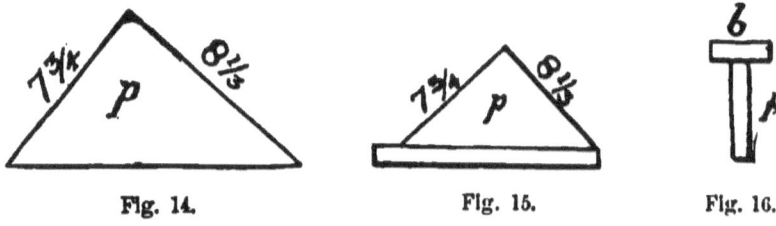

Fig. 14.   Fig. 15.   Fig. 16.

inch thick, or if of hard wood may be from a quarter to an half an inch thick.

Fig. 15 shows the pitch-board after the gauge or fence is nailed on. This fence or gauge may be about one and a half inches wide, and from ⅜ to ¾ of an inch thick. Fig. 16 shows a sectional view of the pitch-board with the fence nailed on as at *b p*, which shows the edge of the board.

At Fig. 17 the manner of applying the board is shown. R, R, R, R is the string, and the line A shows the jointed or straight edge of the string. The *pitch-board, p,* is shown in position, the line 8⅓ represents the step or tread, and the line 7¾ shows the line of the riser. These two lines are of course at right angles, or, as the carpenter would say, " they are square." This string shows four complete cuts for treads, and a part of a fifth one, and five complete cuts for risers. The bottom of the string at w is cut off at the line of the floor on which it is supposed to rest. The line c is the line of the first riser. This riser is narrower than any of the other risers, because the thickness of the first tread is always taken off it; thus, if the tread is 1½ inches thick, the riser in this case would only require to be six and a quarter inches wide, as 6¼ and 1½ inches together make seven and three-quarter inches. Another thing to be considered is the string, which must be cut so that the line at w will be only six and a quarter inches from the line at 8⅓, and it must be parallel with it. The first riser and tread having been satisfactorily dealt with, the rest may be easily marked off by simply sliding the pitch-board along the line A until the line 8⅓ on the pitch-board strikes the line 7¾ on the string, when another tread and another riser are to be marked off. The remaining risers and treads are marked off in the same manner.

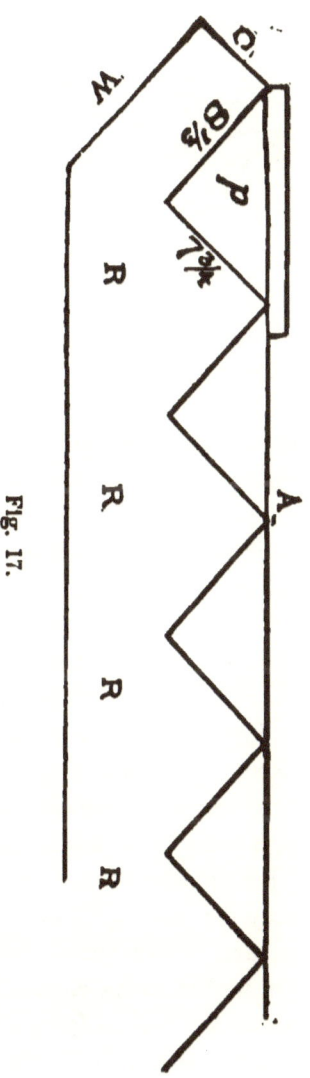

Fig. 17.

Sometimes there may be a little difficulty in fitting the string at the top of the stairs to the trimmer or joists, but, as I first desire the student to become expert with the pitch board before I give him anything that he will not readily understand, I will leave the subject of trimming the well, or attaching the cylinder to the string until other matters have been discussed.

Fig. 18 shows a portion of the stairs in position. s, s show the strings, which in this case are cut square; that is, the part of the string to which the riser is joined is cut square across, and the

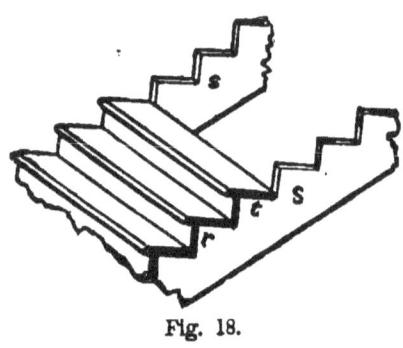

Fig. 18.

"but" or end wood of the riser is seen. In this case, also, the end of the tread is cut square off and flush with the string and riser. Both strings in this instance are open strings. Usually in stairs of this kind the ends of the treads are rounded off similar to the front of the tread, and the ends project over the strings the same distance that the front

edge projects over the riser. If a moulding or "cove" is used under the nosing in front, it should be carried round on the string to the back edge of the tread, and cut off square, for in this case the back edge of the tread will be square. The riser is shown at *r*, and it will be noticed that it runs down behind the tread on the back edge, and is either nailed or screwed to the tread. This is the American practice, though in England the riser usually rests on the tread; it is much better, however, for general purposes, that the riser go behind the tread, as it tends to make the whole stairs much more strong and rigid.

Fig. 19 shows the customary way American workmen put their risers and treads together. T, T show the treads; R, R the risers; S, S the string; O, O the cove moulding under the nosing X, X. B, B show the blocks that hold the tread and risers together. These blocks should be from four to six inches long, and made of very dry wood. Their section may be from one to two inches square. On a tread three feet long, three of these blocks should be used at about equal distances apart, putting the two outside ones about six inches from the strings. They are glued right in the angle. Warm the blocks, then coat the two sides with good strong glue; then put in position and "rub" the block to-and-fro, pressing it close into the angle until you cannot move it any further; let it stand a day or two until quite dry and hard, and the work so far will be complete. It will be noticed that the riser has a lip on the upper edge which enters into a groove in the tread. This lip is generally about ⅜ inch long, and may be ⅜ or ½ an inch in thickness. Care must be taken in getting out the risers, that they are not made too narrow, as allowance must be made for the lip.

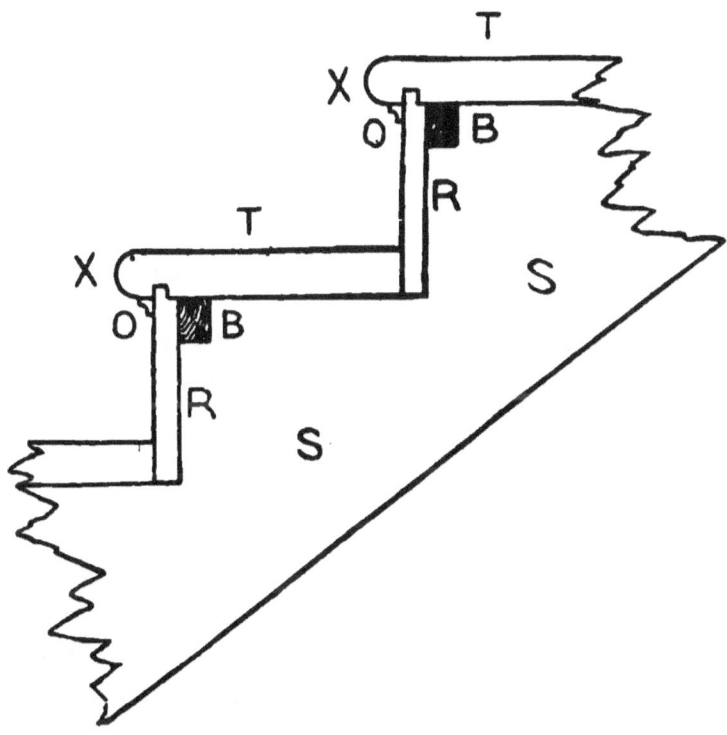

Fig. 19.

If the riser is a little too wide it will do no harm, as the overwidth may hang down below the tread; but it must be made the exact width where it rests on the string. The treads must be made the exact width required before they are grooved or the nosing worked on the outer edge. The lip or tongue on the riser should fit snug in the groove and "bottom." By following these last instructions, and seeing that the "blocks" are well glued in, a good solid job will be the result.

At Fig. 20 a scheme for the construction of the tread and riser is shown. The tread *a* has a lip worked on it at the back edge, which enters a groove ploughed in the riser. The riser also has a

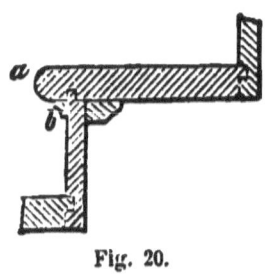

lip left on the upper edge, which goes into a groove made in the tread similar to the method shown at Fig. 19. The cove is shown at *b*, and the angle block is also represented. This makes a very solid step when well put together, and, where the stairs are to be of the better kind, this method of constructing the step may be adopted with advantage. This method is

Fig. 20.

a favorite one with English stair-builders, and has proved to be a substantial one, though it costs a little more than the American method.

I show another scheme of putting the tread and riser together at Fig. 21. Here it will be seen neither the tread or riser is "lipped,"

but the cove or "scotia" is let into the tread and the face of the riser is brought close up to it. It is claimed for this method that the tread is not weakened by being grooved so far away from the point of nosing, and thus rendered less liable to split away. For my part I see no advantage in this method over either of the methods shown, and I know, from experience, that the chances of rupture or separation, at the junction of tread and riser, is much greater than when constructed on

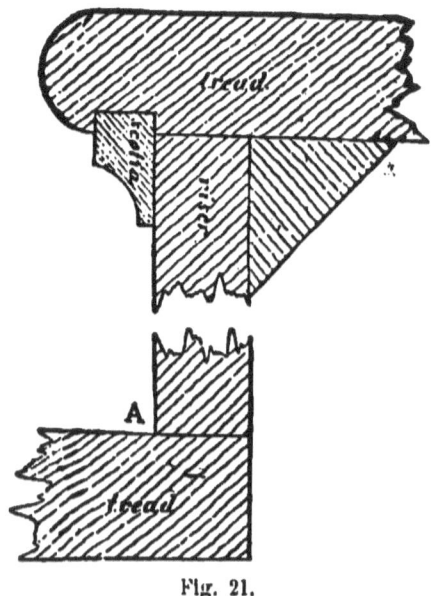

Fig. 21.

either of the methods shown at Figs. 19 or 20. It will be seen at A that the riser rests on the tread, which in this is decidedly bad construction. This method of building the step is quite common in France, Italy, Germany and other parts of Europe, but is seldom used in England or the United States. The angle block in this illustration is represented as being a right-angled triangle; this is unnecessary, and seems to me a waste of time; a square block answers the purpose, and is much easier made and applied.

I have now, I think, pretty clearly explained the methods of building a common open stair, such as may be used for stoops, verandas and cellars, or other places where strength and convenience are of more importance than appearances, so for the present I will leave this class of stairs or steps and endeavor to explain the way " housed strings " are laid out and prepared to receive the ends of riser and tread.

If it is desired to build a flight of stairs where the riser is 6¼ inches, and the tread 10½ inches, and wish to have housed strings on both sides of the flight, the proper way will be to build up all the treads and risers first, putting a tread and a riser together until we have the number required. The blocks should all be glued in place, and the risers and treads made the proper width and thickness, and put together exactly at right angles or square with each other; then cut off to the exact length and square up the ends. This done, lay the separate steps carefully aside until you are ready to put the stairs together.

The nosings on the treads, as shown in Fig. 22 are semicircular or " half-round," as the workmen say; and this is the best form of nosing, as it is neat and easily wrought, and the recess in the " housed " string may be formed for its reception by using a centre-bit or augur the proper size. Let me here suggest that Clark's patent expanding bit is perhaps the best tool for this work.

Gauge lightly a line from the upper edge of the string, the distance in-

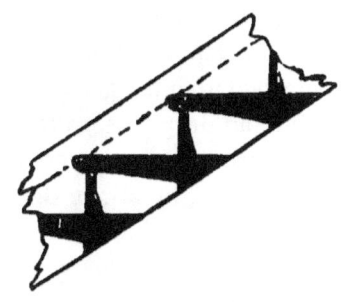

Fig. 22.

tended to stand above the treads as shown in the dotted line. On this line apply the pitch-board as explained on previous pages. In laying out housed strings it is as well to take the fence off the pitch-board, as it can be handled much better without it, as the long side will have to be kept close to the gauge line, to insure good work. The top lines for treads, and the face lines for risers, are the lines that define the step, and cannot be changed; but the back line of the riser and the lower line of the tread should be made to run so that the housing or groove will be wider at the under side of the string than at the junction of the riser and tread at the nosing, where the grooves will be the same width as the riser and tread are in thickness separately. The nosing projects over the riser, as will be seen, and to mark this portion out it is usual to make a template or pattern for the purpose. Indeed, it is best to make a template to lay out the whole housing of the tread, and in shape like the shaded part shown in the illustration.

The reason the grooves are left wider at the back edge of tread is so that a wedge can be driven between the tread and the lower edge of the groove, to force the top side of the tread close to the upper edge of the groove, thus making a tight joint and insuring strength and rigidity to the whole structure. The risers are also wedged in place, as will be shown in Fig. 23. After the treads and risers are *laid out* on the string, a sharp-pointed knife blade should be used to mark the lines for the face of the riser and the top of the tread, then a fine tenon saw should be used to saw down to the exact depth. This will not be difficult to perform when the hole forming the nosing recess has been bored to the proper depth. A gauge line should be made on the back edge of the string to indicate the depth of the housing. Care should be taken in removing the wood from the grooves that too much is not taken or the grooves made too deep. A gauge for trying the depth may be made out of a piece of hard wood, say about four inches long and three inches wide, by about one-half inch in thickness. Make a tenon on the centre of one end, about three-quarters of an inch in width, and cut the shoulders back sufficiently far enough to admit the tenon being long enough to touch the bottom of the groove or housing, when the shoulders rest on the face of the string.

At Fig. 23 I show a sectional elevation through the steps. The treads, *t, t,* and the risers, *r, r,* are shown in position. These are secured, as will be seen by means of the wedges, *x, x,* and *y, y,* which are to be well covered with glue before they are inserted and driven home. Stairs made after this manner are strong and perfectly solid under foot.

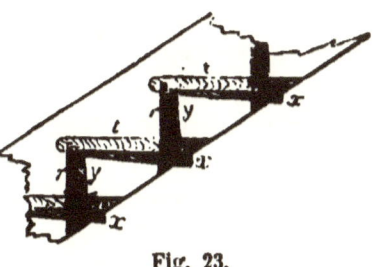

Fig. 23.

I have now shown you the way to make an open string, and how to make a housed string. There are several other methods of making a stair string than those shown you already; one way is to form two tenons on the end of the tread, which fit into mortises cut through the string. This method makes a very strong stair if the string is sufficiently wide enough to allow for the loss of strength caused by making the mortises.

At Fig. 24 several ways of forming an open string are shown.

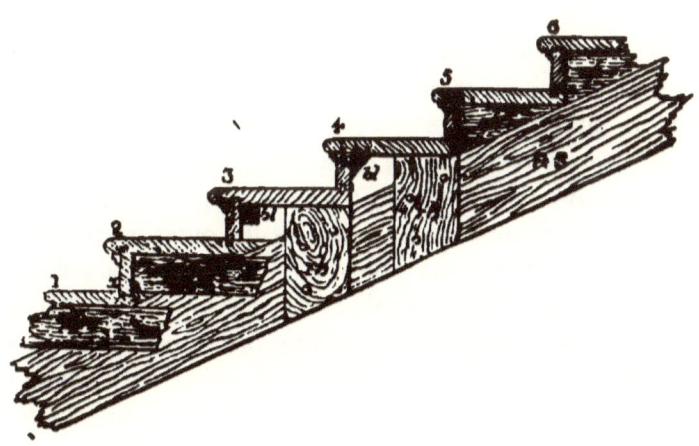

Fig. 24.

Different methods of uniting the risers and treads are shown. They may be grooved and tongued, as in steps 5 and 6, or feathered as in step 4, or rabbeted as at step 3; in every case the joint should be glued and blocked. Sometimes the riser is housed into the tread as at *x*. The tread is also sometimes tongued into the riser, but this is not good construction, and should be avoided. R, S show a rough string or scantling, having pieces, *r*, *b*, steps 2, 3 and 4 nailed or screwed on to it to support the treads. Triangular pieces may be nailed on the top edge of the scantling to support the treads as shown at steps 5 and 6. A rough string, corresponding to the open string, may be used in place of any of the foregoing methods. The under edge of all rough strings should be made to coincide with the lower edge of the furring or cleat nailed on the inside lower edge of the outside cut string, and so arranged that the lathing will nail on the furring, the rough strings, and the lower edge of the wall string.

I have now described several methods of dealing with strings, but there still are a few other things connected with strings, both housed and open, that will be necessary to explain before you can proceed to put up a fair flight of stairs. The connection of the wall string to the base of the lower and upper floors, and the manner of affixing the outer or cut string to the upper joist and to the newel, are matters that must not be overlooked, and I intend to show how these things are accomplished, in due time. I will proceed now to describe the method of finishing the tread and riser at the end of the step that rests on the outer string.

Fig. 25 gives two views of a portion of a better-class stair, a stair with *cut and mitered string*, or open string stair. In referring to the plan, W S shows the wall string; R S the rough string placed there to give the structure strength; and O S the outer or cut string. At *a, a* the ends of the risers are shown, and it will be noticed they are mitered against the vertical or riser line of the string, thus preventing the end wood of the riser from being seen. The other end of the riser is in the housing in the wall string. The outer end of the tread is also mitered at the nosing, and a piece of stuff made or worked like the nosing is mitered against, or *returned* at the end of the tread. The end of this returned piece is again *returned on itself* back to the string, as shown in the upper portion of the cut,

· at *n*. The moulding, which is a ⅝ cove in this case, is also *returned* round the string and into *itself*.

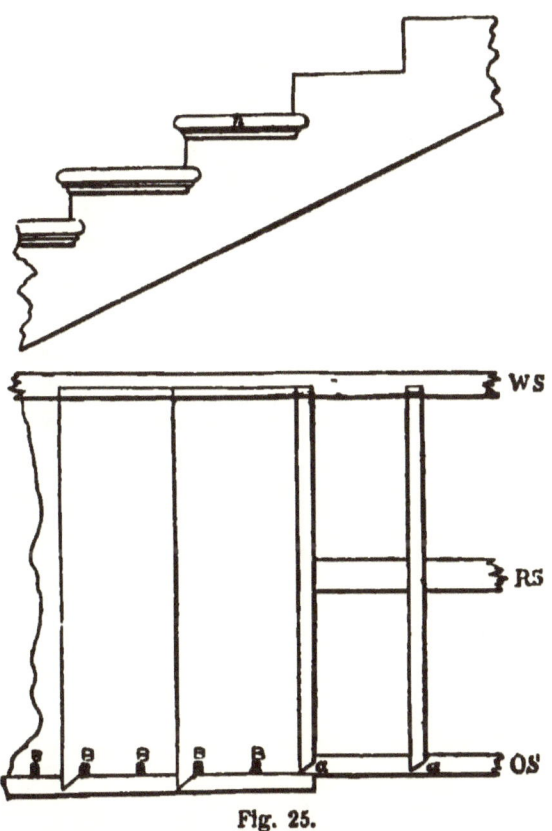

Fig. 25.

The mortises shown at the black points, B, B, B, etc., are for the balusters. It is always the proper thing to saw the ends of the tread ready for the balusters before they are attached to the string, then when the time arrives to put up the rail the back end of the mortise may be cut out, when the tread will be ready to receive the baluster. The mortise is dovetailed, and, of course, the tenon in the baluster must be made to suit. The tread is finished on the bench, and the *return nosing* is fitted to it and tacked on so that it may taken off to insert the balusters, when the rail is being put in position.

At Fig. 26 I show the end of a step on a cut and mitered string, which is bracketed. B shows the bracket and the manner in which the end is finished. Brackets on stairs are generally about ⅜ of an inch thick, and may be of almost any design that is in keeping with the surroundings. When a stair is bracketed, the point of the riser on its string end should be left standing past the string the thickness of the bracket, and the end of the bracket mitres against it, thus avoiding the necessity of showing end wood or joint. The

cove should finish inside the length of the bracket, and the nosing
should finish just outside the
length of the bracket. When
brackets are employed they
should continue along the cylinder, and all around the well
hole and trimmers, though they
may be varied to suit conditions when continuously running on a straight horizontal
facia. A number of designs
for brackets will be shown
further on.

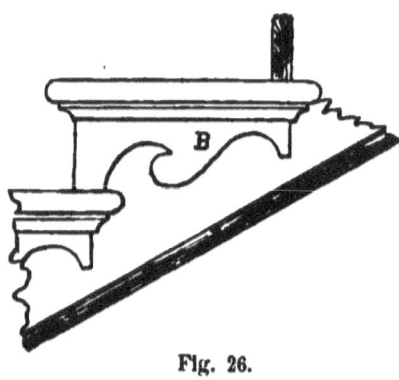

Fig. 26.

Fig. 27 shows the manner in which a wall string is finished at
the foot of the stairs.   s shows the string with a moulding wrought
on the upper edge.   This moulding may be a simple ogee, or may

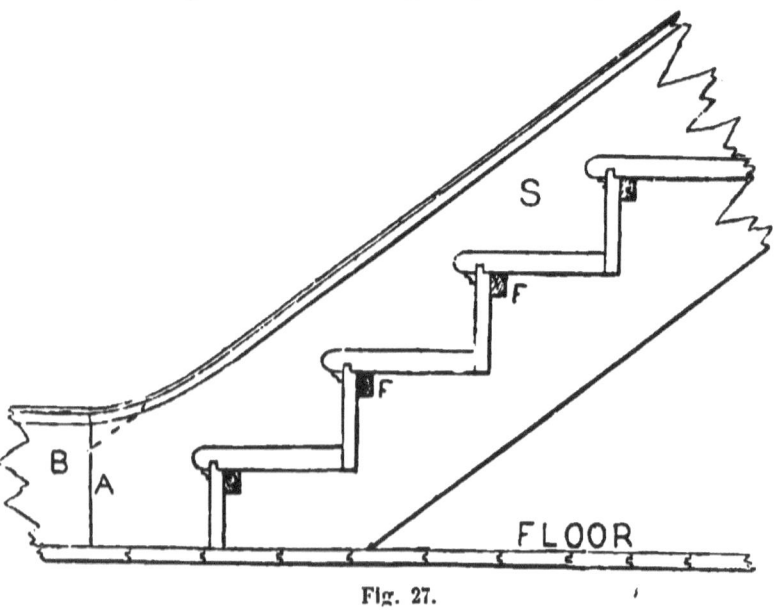

Fig. 27.

consist of a number of members, or may be only a bead, or the
edge of the string may be left quite plain; this will be regulated in
a great measure by the style of finish in the hall, or wherever the

stairs are placed. B shows a portion of the baseboard, the top edge of which has the same finish as the top edge of the string. B and A together show the junction of the string and base. The dotted line shows when a piece of stuff has been glued on to the string to make it wide enough at the junction to get the *ease-off* or curve. F F, show the blocks glued in the angle of the steps to make them firm and solid.

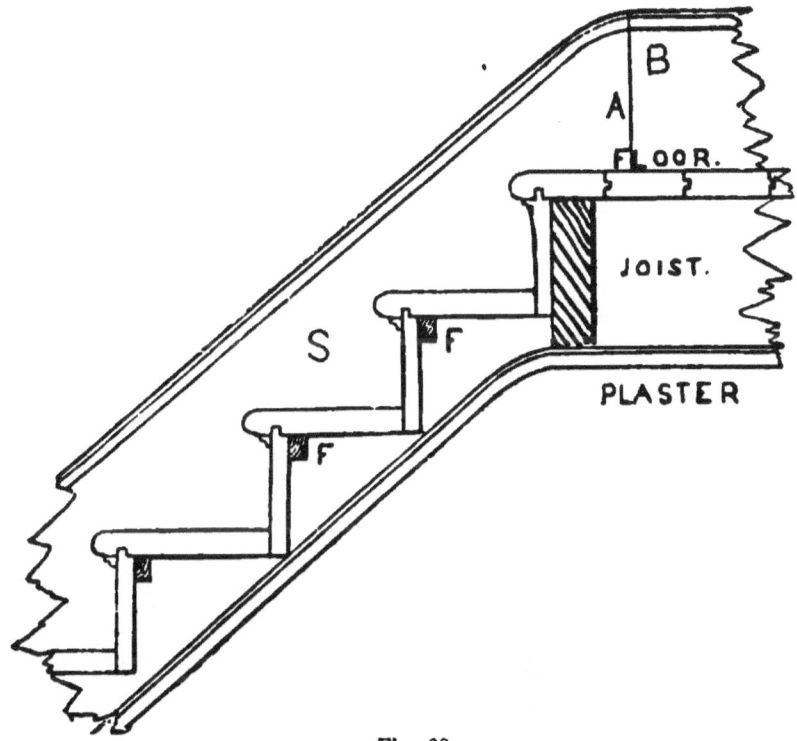

Fig. 28.

The Figure 28 shows the manner in which the wall string S is finished at the top of the stairs. It will be noticed that the moulding is worked round the ease-off at A to suit the width of the base at B. The string is cut over the floor horizontally and vertically or plumb against the joists. The plaster line under the stairs and on the ceiling is also shown.

Fig. 29 shows the cut or open string at the foot of the stairs, and the manner of dealing with it at its junction with the newel post K. The point of the string should be mortised into the newel two, three, or four inches, as shown by the dotted lines, and the mortise made in the newel should be made near the centre, so that the centre of the baluster will be directly opposite the central line of the newel post. The proper way to manage this is to measure the central line of the baluster on the tread, and then make this line correspond with the central line of the newel post. By a careful attendance to this matter, much trouble will be avoided where a turned cap is used to receive the

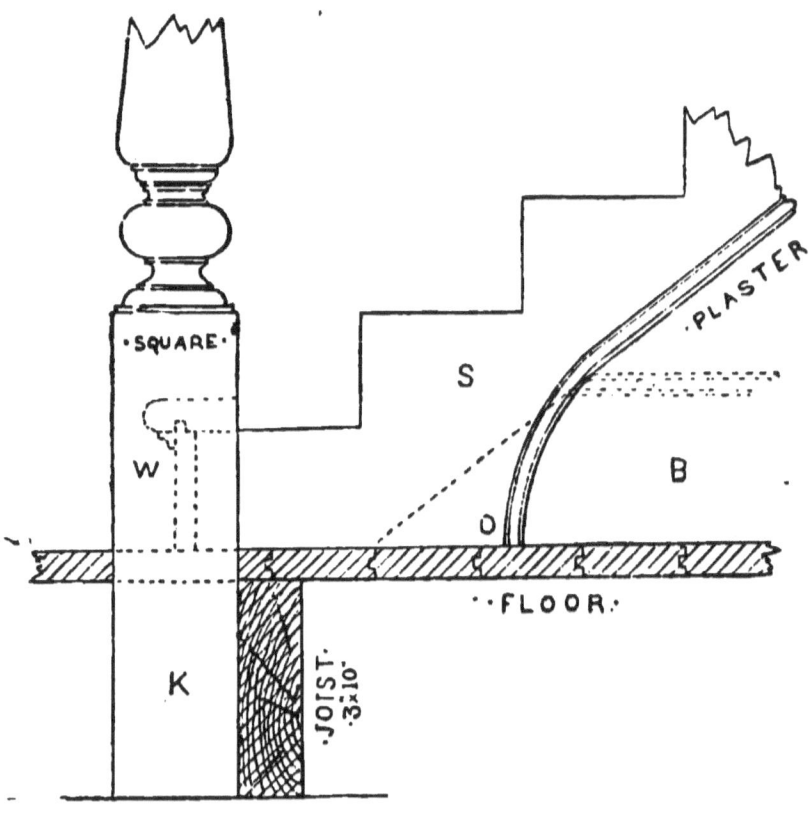

Fig. 29.

lower part of the rail. The lower riser, in a stair of this kind, will be something shorter than the ones that follow it, as it must be cut between the newel and the wall string. A portion of the tread, as well as the riser, will also "butt" against the newel, as shown at w.

If there is no spandril or wall under the open string it may run down to the floor, as shown at o. The piece o is glued on to the string, and the moulding is worked on the curve.

If there is a wall under the string s, then the base B, shown by the dotted lines, will finish against the string, and it should have a moulding stuck on its upper edge the same as the one on the lower edge of the string, if any, and this moulding should mitre into the one on the string. When there is a base the piece o is dispensed with.

The square of the newel should run down by the side of a joist, as shown, and be firmly secured to it by iron knees or other suitable devices. If the joist run the other way, try and get the newel post against it, if possible, either by furring out the joist or cutting a portion off the thickness of the newel. The solidity of a

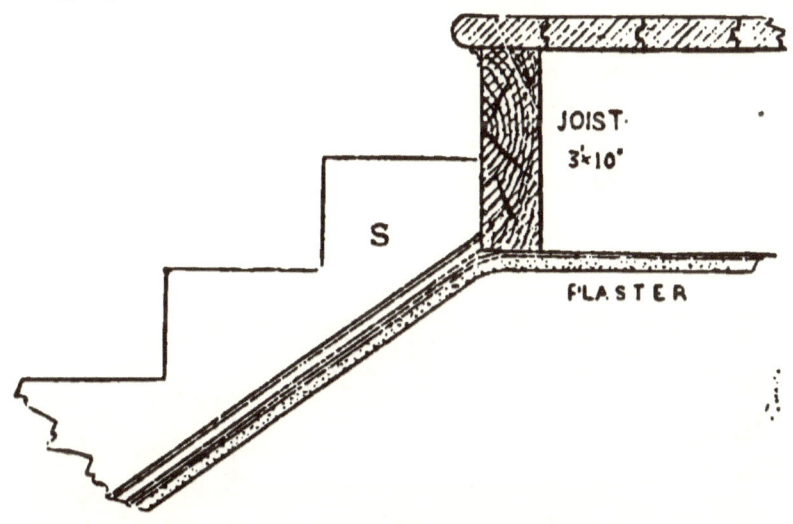

Fig. 30.

stair, and the firmness of the rail, depend very much on the rigidity of the newel post.

Fig. 30 shows how the cut string is finished at the top of the stairs. This illustration requires no explanation after the foregoing has been examined.

So far I have dealt with those stairs having a newel at the bottom only, but it is just as well here to let the reader understand that there are many modifications of straight and return stairs, that

have from two to four and six newels. When any of these conditions arise, the treatment of strings at their finishing points may
necessarily be somewhat different than that described, but the general principles, as shown and explained, will hold good. I do not
intend, however, to leave the subject here, as I want to make
everything as clear to the student as possible, so will give a few
examples of stairs having more than one newel.

Before proceeding to describe and illustrate neweled stairs, it will
be proper to say something about the " well," or opening in the
floors through which the traveler on the stairs ascends and de-
scends from one floor to another.

Fig. 31 shows a well-hole, and the manner of trimming it. In
this case the stairs are placed against the wall, but this is not necessary in all cases, as the " well-hole may be placed in any part of
a building.

The arrangement of the trimming varies according as the joists
are at right angles to or parallel to the wall against which the stairs
are 'built. In the former case the joists are cut short and tusk-
tenoned into the heavy trimmer T T, as shown in the cut. This

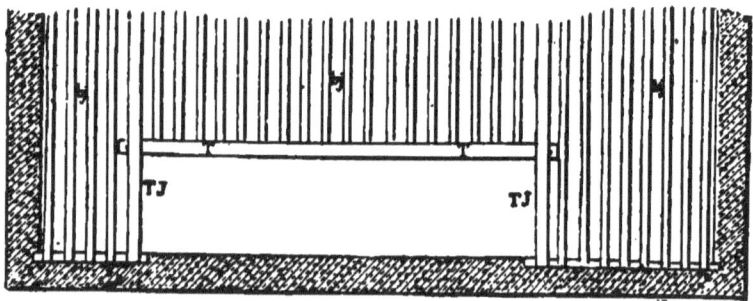

Fig. 31.

trimmer is again tusk-tenoned into two heavy joists, T J, T J, which
form the ends of the " well-hole." These heavy joists are called
trimming joists, and as they have to carry a much heavier load than
other joists on the same floor, they are left much heavier. Sometimes two or three joists are put together, side by side, and are bolted
or spiked together to give them the desired unity and strength.

If the opening runs parallel with the joists, the timber forming the side of the "well-hole" might be left a little heavier than the other joists, as it will have to carry short trimmers, T J, T J, and the joists running into them. The method shown here is more particularly adapted to brick buildings, but there is no reason why the same system may not be applied to frame buildings. Usually, in cheap frame build-

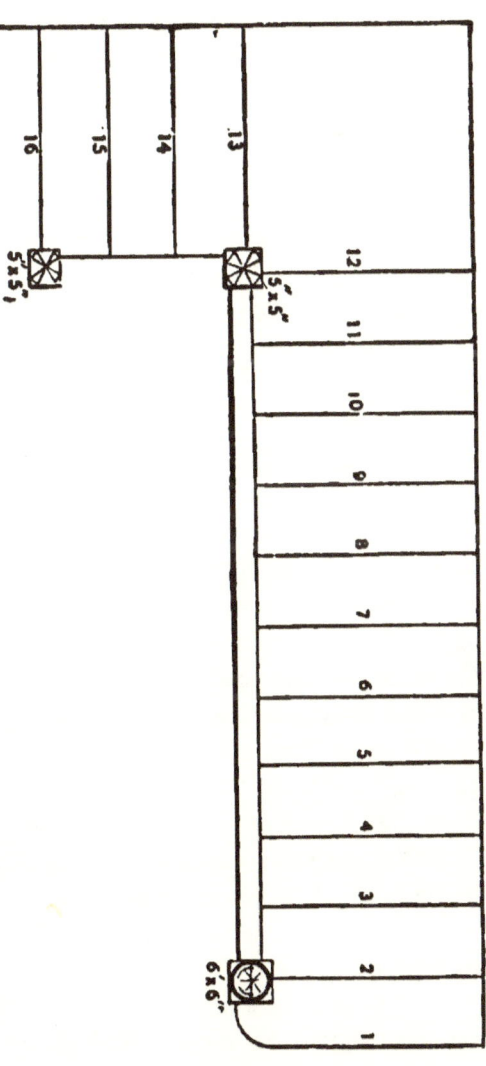

ings, the trimmers are spiked against the ends of the joists, and the ends of the trimmers are supported by being spiked to the trimming joists T J, T J. This is not very workmanlike, or very secure, and I would advise its discon- tinuance, as it is not nearly so strong or dur- able as the old method of framing the joists and trimmers together.

I show at Fig. 32 a stair with three newels and a platform.

In this example the first tread, No. 1, stands forward of the newel post two-thirds of its width. This is not ne- cessary in every case, but is sometimes done to suit conditions in the hallway. The second newel is placed at twelfth riser, and sup-

Fig. 32.

ports the upper end of the first cut string, and the lower end of the second cut string. The platform, 12, is supported by joists framed into the wall and fastened against a trimmer, which runs from the wall to the newel along the line 12. This is the case only when the second newel runs down to the floor. If the second newel does not run down to the floor, the framework supporting the platform will need being built on studding. The third newel stands at the top of the stairs, and is fastened to the joists of the second floor, or to the trimmer, something after the fashion of fastening as shown at Fig. 29. In this example the stairs have sixteen risers and fifteen treads—the platform or landing, 12, making one tread. The figures 16 show the floor in the second story.

This style of stair will require a well-hole in shape about as the plan shown, and, where strength is required, the newel at the platform should run from floor to floor, and act as a support to the joists and trimmers on which the second floor is laid.

Perhaps the best way to go about building these stairs by a new beginner will be to "lay out" the work on the lower floor in the exact place where they are going, making everything full size. There will be no difficulty in doing this, and if the position of the first riser and the three newel posts are accurately defined, the building of the stairs will be an easy matter. Plumb lines may be raised from the lines on the floor, and the positions of the platform and each riser easily determined. Not only is it best to line out on the floor stairs having more than one newel, but it is perhaps the safest way for a new beginner *to line out in exact position on the floor the points over which the treads and risers of any kind of stairs should stand.* By adopting this rule, and seeing that the strings and riser and tread lines correspond exactly with the lines on the floor, many cases of annoyance will be avoided.

At Fig. 33 I show a stair with a half-space landing. The treads in the lower flight are omitted, so as to show the strings and risers. A portion of the steps of the upper flight is broken away in order to expose to view the construction of the flight below.

In this stair the wall string w s, and the outer string board o s, are constructed as shown in Figs. 29 and 30, with intermediate

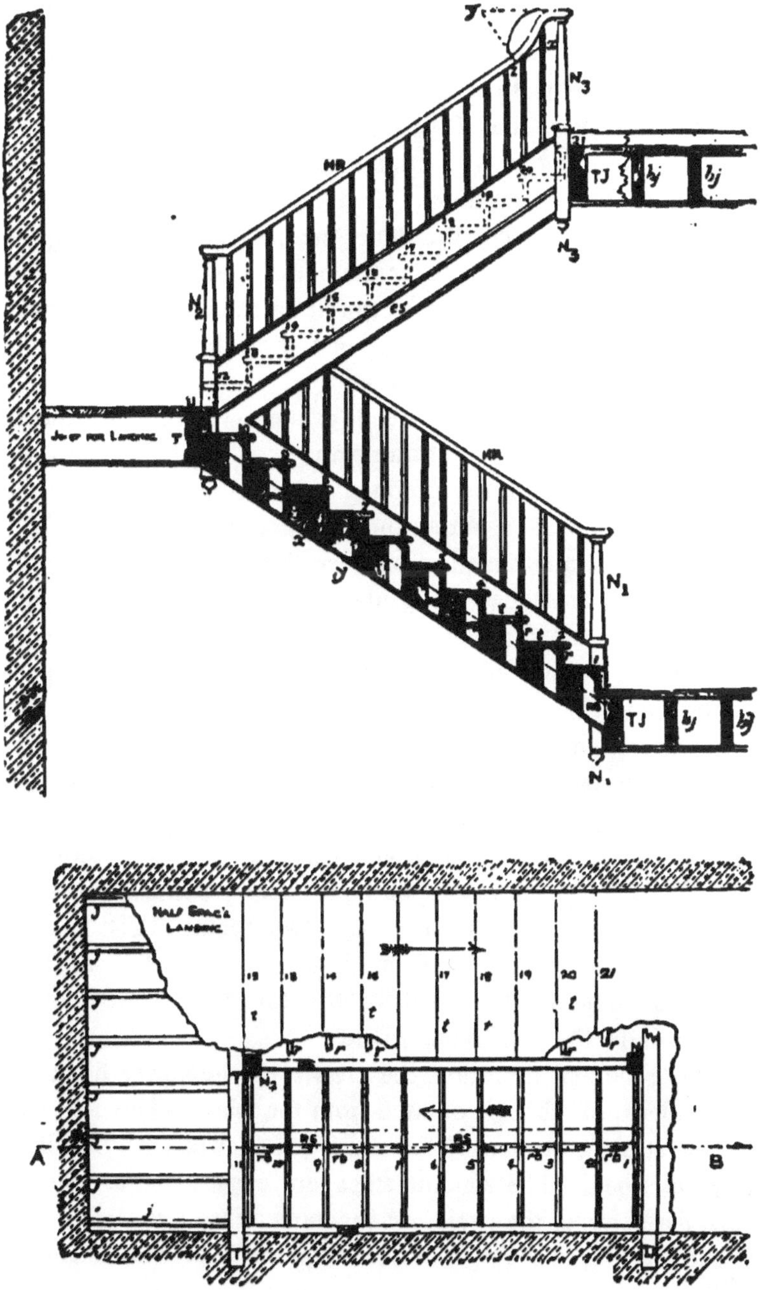

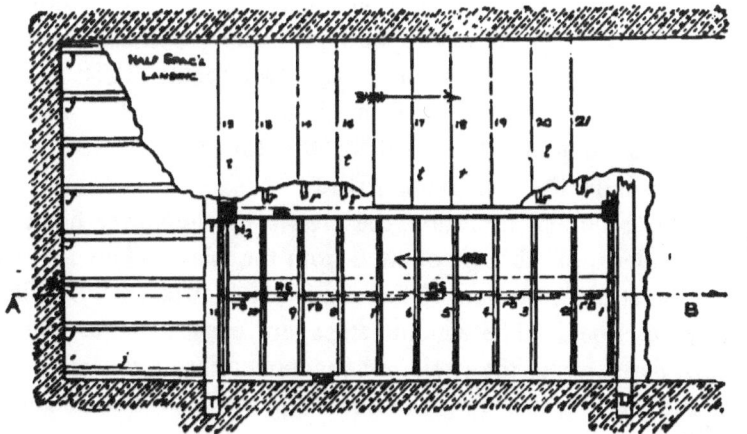

Sectional Elevation.

Plan.

Fig. 33.

rough strings, if deemed necessary. The outer strings are tenoned into the newels, and so are the first and last risers of the flight. The outer strings of the upper flight and that of the lower flight are on the same vertical plane, or, in other words, they are directly one over the other, so that if the plan of the upper flight was complete the outer string of the upper would overlap and hide the outer string of the lower flight. In the same way, if the number of steps in each flight were the same, the newel N_3 of the upper flight would in plan exactly cover the newel N of the lower flight, being immediately over it. The hand-rail on the plan is not shown, but in the upper part of the illustration I show the hand-rail and a sectional view of the stairs in position.

In the sectional elevation the treads of the lower flight are shown in section, though omitted from the plan.

The newels are fixed to trimming joists, $T J$, provided in the floors, and to trimmers, T, across the staircase at the landing. The rough strings, $R S$, are framed in between these trimmers, and rough brackets, $r b$, $r b$, are nailed alongside of them to support the steps. The tread of the top step is frequently united to the boarding of the landing by a rabbeted joint. This is advisable if the space below the steps, known as the spandril, is to be made use of as a closet, or as an entrance way to the cellar. In such a case the landing and the parts of all the steps should be matched stuff, and the joints made perfectly dust tight.

Fig. 34 shows a plan and sectional elevation of a stair with four newels. This is termed an "open newel stair," because there is a square well-hole at the junction of the two flights. The plan of this stair shows a quarter-space landing. The boarding or flooring of the landing, and the treads of the lower flight, are omitted, in order to show the construction below.

On the sectional elevation the treads of the lower flight are shown in elevation, though omitted from the plan. The construction of the straight portion of the stairs is similar to what has been already described. The winding steps are constructed as follows: Bearers, $b b$, carrying the risers, $r r$, are framed into the newels, their outer ends resting in the wall of the staircase. Between them are

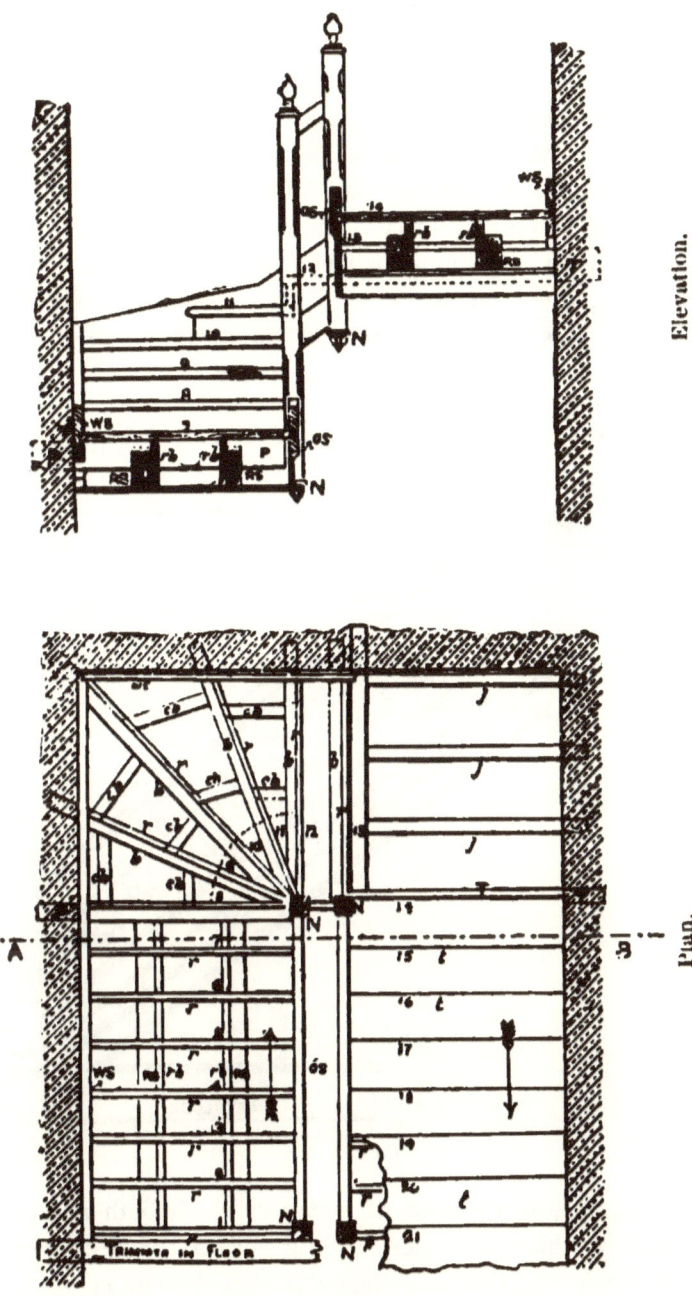

Fig. 34.

fixed cross bearers, *c b*. These would not be necessary if the stairs were narrow, but are inserted here for the sake of illustration. In this example four winders are introduced to show the defects of such an arrangement. Four winders should never be placed in a stair of this kind where it is possible to avoid such an arrangement, as it will be seen in the cut that the width of the treads at eighteen inches from the newel can never be more than seven inches. Thus, the treads of the winders must be narrower than those of the fliers, and, therefore, often inconvenient. Four winders, however, are often employed, as they are sometimes necessary in order to gain the height required within the space available.

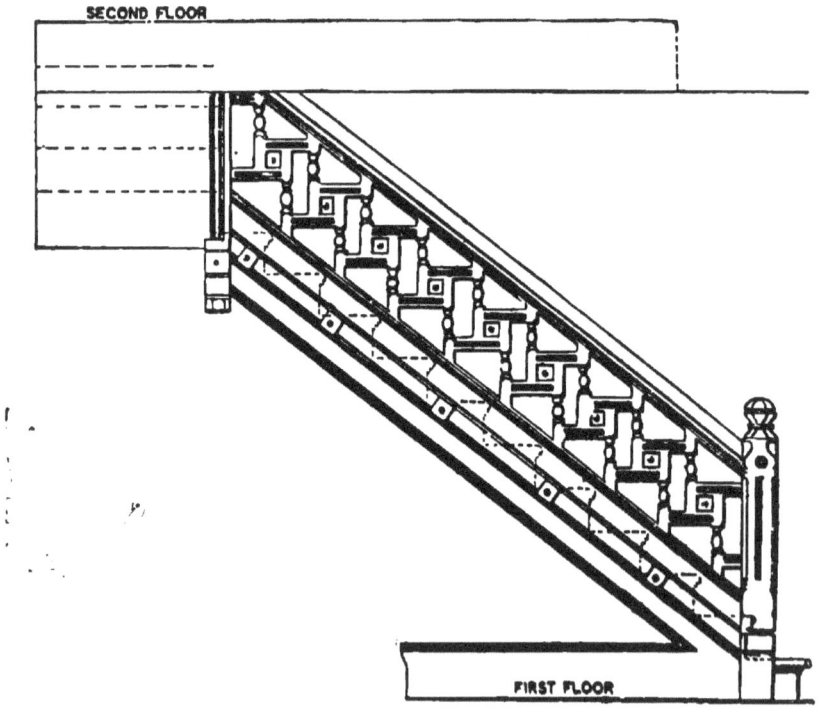

Fig. 35.

At Fig. 35 I show a portion of a stair in which both strings are housed, and in which the outer string is finished between newels. This style would suit the stairs shown at Figs. 33 and 34.

The hand-rail and style of balusters, and method of putting them in, are also shown. As the rail is straight, and the newel and balusters turned, and not difficult to work, it was deemed proper to insert them here as examples of a neweled stair finished.

Again, at Fig. 36 I furnish another example of a portion of finished stairs at its foot. In this case the balusters and newel are simply made from square stuff, dressed and chamfered. The strings are housed and closed in, and the balusters on the outer string simply rest on it, only having a dowel or small tenon on their lower ends.

Fig. 36.

The ball on the top of the newel is turned separately, and is fastened by means of a pin which is glued into the newel; this pin should be turned on the ball. The upper ends of the balusters fit into a groove made the right width and about half an inch deep on the under side of the hand-rail.

At Fig. 37 I show a portion of a straight stair having landings and newels, but still running only in one direction. In this case there is, in the first flight, eleven steps, then a landing, j T, of greater or lesser dimensions; then a second flight begins and continues until the next floor is reached. Sometimes, when the stories are more than ordinary height, there are two or more landings or "rests," and there may be only seven or nine steps between the landings. The mode of construction is shown quite clearly in this cut, and the positions of strings, carriages, newels and joists are all represented. The letters and figures exhibited, both on plan and elevation, are self explanatory.

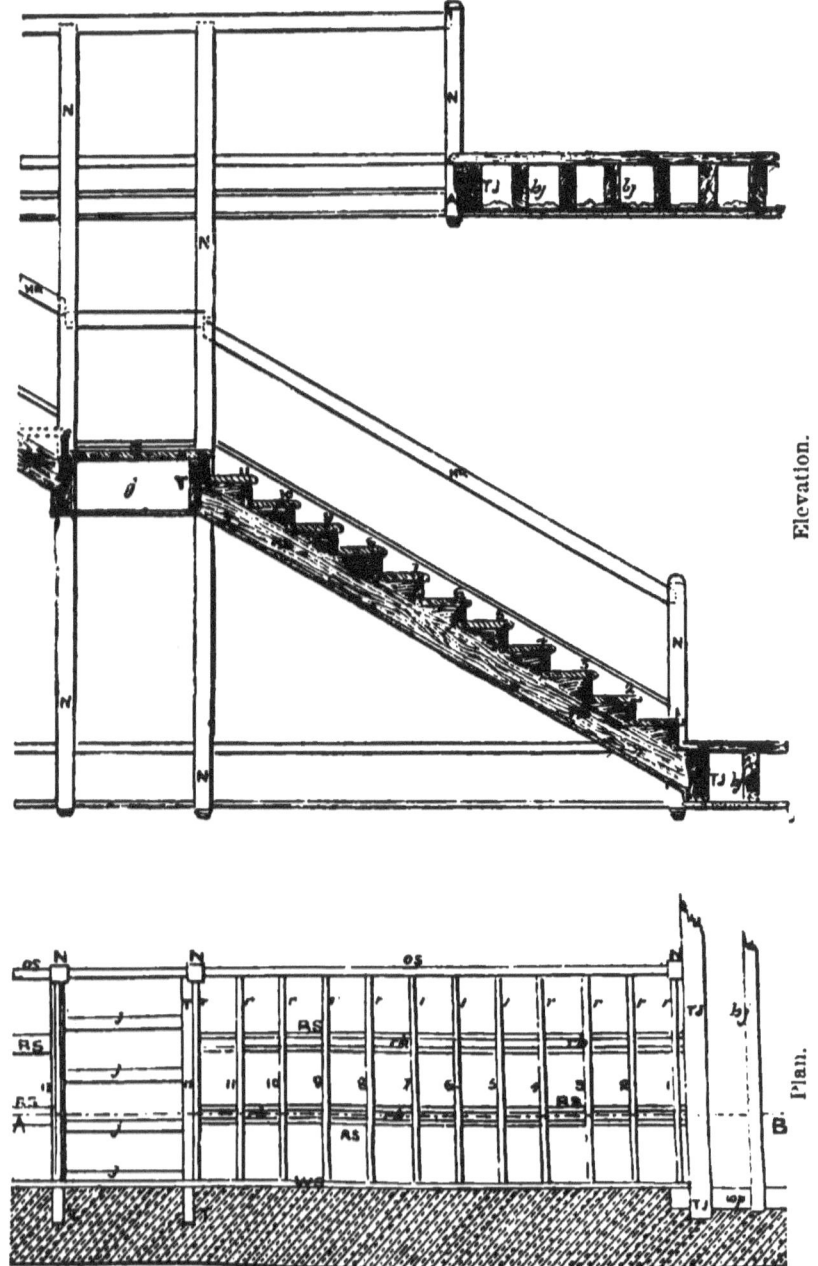

Fig. 37.

With regard to laying out the strings and carriages for dog-legged and winding stairs, I may say that I will explain all about this a little further on, or after the student gets a little more familiar with the method of laying out the stairs on plan. It is in order now, however, to describe and explain the manner of dealing with the bodies and carriages of geometrical stairs; but before entering into the subject largely, it may be as well to make a few preliminary remarks:

A geometrical stair has no newel posts. The flights are arranged around a well-hole in the centre, sometimes called an "*open newel*" or a "*cylinder;*" and each step is secured by having one end housed into the wall string, the other end resting upon the outer string, but partly deriving support from the step below it.

The rail of a geometrical stair is uninterrupted in its course from top to bottom,

The treads of these kind of stairs should be strong and substantial, and the risers and tread should be put together in a thorough workmanlike manner. Nowhere on a building is the best kind of workmanship more necessary than on the stairs, and more particularly is this the case with geometrical stairs than with straight or dog-legged stairs.

The cut strings of these kind of stairs should have a flat bar of iron screwed on their inner edges after being bent to the proper shape.

Figs. 38 and 39 show the sectional elevation and plan of a geometrical stair with winders. The portion of the staircase shown in Fig. 39 consists of six fliers, then eight winders, then seven more fliers, making twenty-two steps, leading to a half-space landing on the floor above; from this the stairs again rise, commencing with the step marked 23, the remainder being broken off to show the first flight.

The treads of the lower flight and winders are also omitted, in order to show the supports below.

The steps are formed in the way described in previous pages, with—in this case—feather-tongued joints between the treads and risers.

The treads and risers are well housed into the wall string, the outer ends resting upon a cut and mitered string, and intermediate support is afforded by a rough string, to the side of which is nailed a rough notched bracket or string, cut to fit the under side of the steps, and to serve like an ordinary string.

Fig. 38.—Elevation.

The strings themselves are framed in between the trimming joists provided in the floors, and pitching pieces, P P, projecting from the wall at the level of the first and last winders; one of these latter is shown at P P, but the other is covered by the fifteenth step.

The trimming joist, just below No. 1 step, extends, of course, right across the whole width of the stair—but it is in the plan (Fig. 39) supposed to be broken off just under the outer string in order to avoid confusing the plan of the first step.

The winders are supported throughout their length by bearers, *b b*, the inner ends of which are built and wedged into the wall of

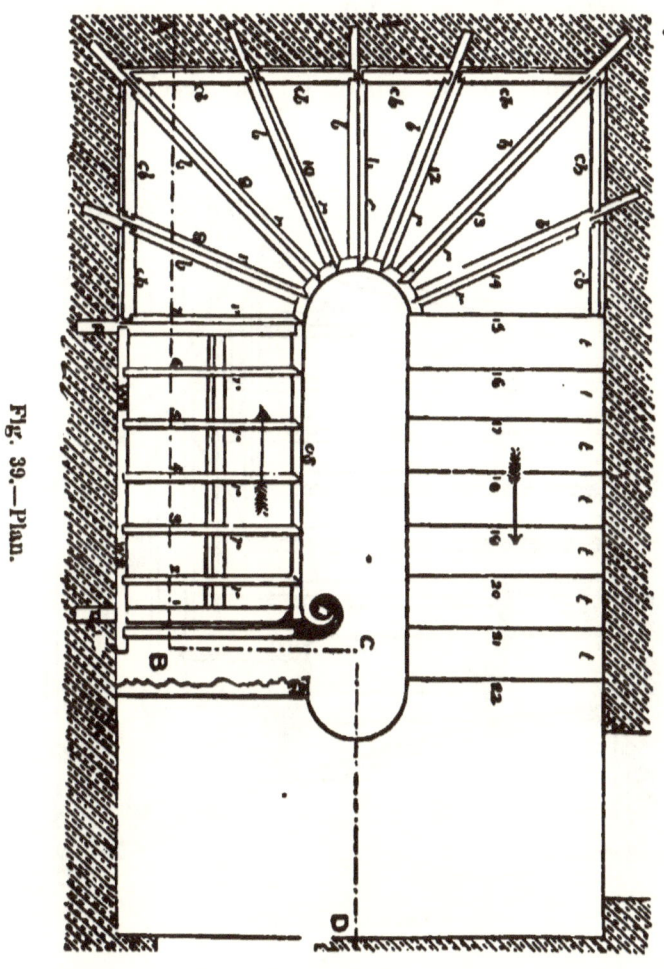

Fig. 39.—Plan.

the staircase, the outer ends being tenoned into the circular wreathed portion of the outer string.

The inner side of the staircase is finished and embellished by a skirting notched on the under side to fit the steps, and—if the wall is brick—it is secured on grounds fastened on to plugs in the brickwork. If the walls are of wood, the string may be secured quite easily.

In some cases two crown bearers are provided for each winder, one being framed in between longitudinal bearers in the centre as well as at the wide end.

If very thick treads are used the bearers and rough strings may be omitted altogether, the steps being wedged into the wall and projecting without further support till they reach the outer string.

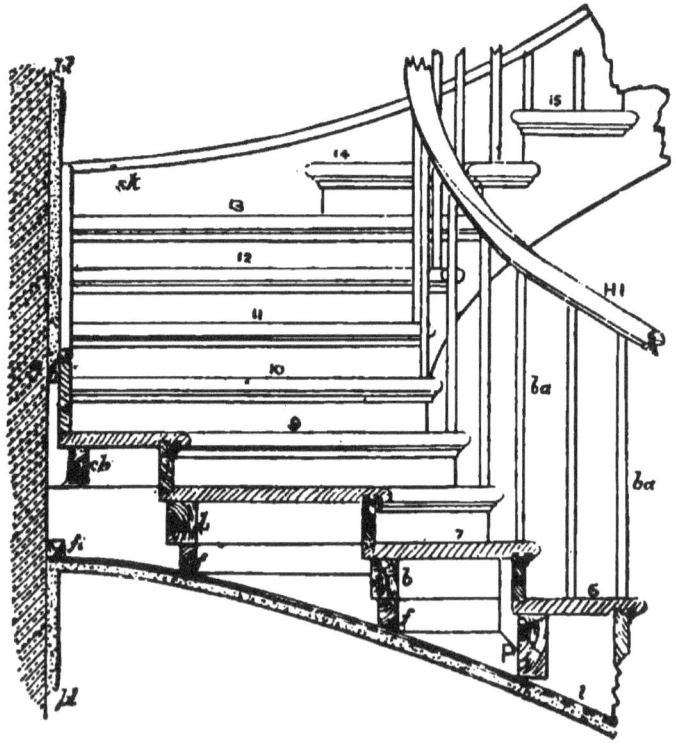

Fig. 40.—Elevation.

Fig. 40 is a portion of a stair somewhat similar to that shown at Fig. 38, but with different description of joints between the treads and risers, enlarged so as to show the plaster and other details, which could not be made clear upon a very small scale.

At Fig. 41 I show a plan and elevation of a stair having a cir-

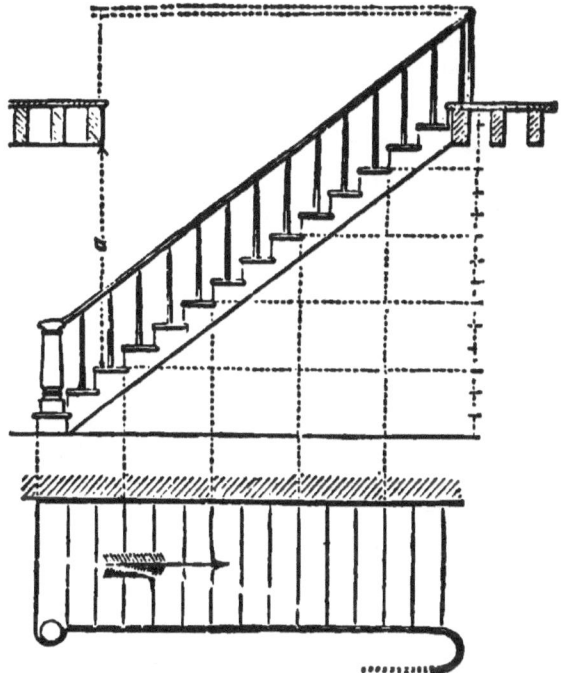

Fig. 41.—Plan and Elevation.

cular well-hole, but having no winders. This is the common straight stair with a newel at its foot, and a continuous rail from the newel to top of stairs, and by aid of a wreath around the whole well-hole and up through the upper stories of the house when there are two or more floors.

This is the most common kind of stairs, and for an ordinary dwelling, is the most convenient. The manner of building them is easily acquired, and no workman of any pretensions should rest satisfied without having a thorough knowledge of the way in which they are constructed and put up. Indeed, every country carpenter who has skill enough to superintend the building of a good farm house should be able to build a stair of this kind, rail and all complete.

In Figs. 12 and 39, I show plans of stairs, the lines of risers of which are drawn from a common centre, which is also the centre of the circle that forms the cylinder or well-hole. In a stair of this kind it is found very difficult to build a graceful rail, and in order to avoid the ungracefulness in the shape of the rail that usually occurs when the plan of the stair is laid out this way, an expedient is adopted, which, I believe, was first introduced by the French, and which is called "*balancing*" or "*dancing*" the steps around the well, that is, they are drawn so as not to converge to the same point, but so that each is directed upon a different point— formed in a manner somewhat intricate, and which will be described further on.

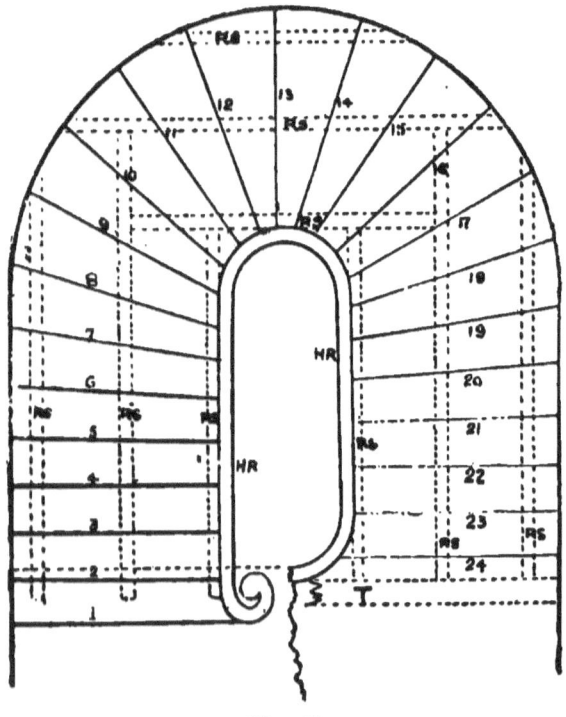

Fig. 42.

In Fig. 42, the first four and the last four steps are parallel, but the remainder "*balance*" or "*dance*" as described above. The treads are numbered in this illustration, and the line of hand-railing H R, H R, is clearly shown. The trimmer T at the top of the stairs is also shown, and the rough strings, R S, R S, R S, or carriages, are represented by the dotted lines.

This plan represents a stair with a curtail step, and a scroll hand-rail resting over the curve of the curtail step. This kind of stair is not much in vogue now in this country, though it is adopted occasionally, in some of the larger cities. The use of heavy newel posts instead of the curtail steps, is the prevailing style at present.

In laying out geometrical stairs, the steps are arranged on the principles as described in the foregoing. The well-hole in the centre is first laid down and the steps arranged around it. In circular stairs with an open well-hole, as in Figure 12, the hand-rail being on the inner side, the width of tread proportioned to the use of steps should be set off along the dotted line, 18 inches in from the hand-rail, for the reasons given in the foregoing. In stairs with the rail on the outside, as sometimes occurs, it will be sufficient if the treads have the proper width in the centre of their length.

When laying out stairs practically on the building itself, the height to be gained should be carefully marked out upon the "*story rod*," as before described, on which are marked divisions corresponding to the number and height to the risers; a similar rod is marked so as to show the treads; and from these rods the steps should be carefully marked upon the walls of the staircase.

A rod should also be prepared having marked upon it the exact width of the stairs, the length of steps, the position and size of newels, and also the size of the wall and outer strings, showing the thickness and depth of the housings.

The expert stair-builder, of course, may dispense with some of these precautionary measures, and will in many cases, build his stairs in the "shop," putting them all together ready to "set in position" before they leave his work-bench. To be able to do this, and have stairs "fit" without further "cutting" or "paring," after it leaves the shop, is an achievement that any workman may be justly proud of. The young workman, however, should follow the directions I give in the foregoing, and though it may take a little more time at the commencement, much chagrin, trouble and time may be saved· in the end, and, let me say right here, that in no place in a building will a "botched" job be more apparent than on a stair which every one belonging to the household, and every friend and visitor of the family, see and use every day; and a stair badly constructed or "botched" by bad workmanship or carelessness in the laying out, is sure to bring a bad and unenviable reputation to the men who design and build them.

With regard to having the steps "dance" around the well this may be accomplished either by calculation or graphically. By the first method, the step which is in the centre of the circular arc is regarded as a fixed line, and the divergence from parallelism has to be made between it and the extremes either way. But it is not necessary to begin the divergence at the first step, nor indeed is it advisable, and in general the first and last three or four steps are left unaltered, so that they may be perfectly parallel to the landing. Suppose then that the divergence is fixed to commence at the fourth step, it becomes necessary to distribute eight spaces along the centre of the string, commencing at the centre line of the stairs, which, from the centre line to the fourth riser, shall follow some law of uniform progression, say that of arithmetical progression, as being the most simple. The progression then will consist of eight terms, the sum of which shall be equal to the length from the centre to the fourth step. Suppose that its development is 66 inches, a length composed of the breadth of three fliers, 3, 4, 5, namely, 36 inches, and the sum of the widths of the ends of the five winding steps, 8, 9, 10, 11, 12, namely, 30 inches,

Subtracting from..................... 66 inches.
The width of eight steps of the same
    width as the winders.............. 48   "
                                  ——
There is obtained the difference...... 18   "

from which is to be furnished the progressive increase to the steps as they proceed from the centre to riser No. 4. Suppose these increments to follow the law of the natural numbers 1 2 3 4 5 6 7 8, etc., the sum of which is 36, divide the difference 18 by 36, and the quotient, 0.5 inches, is the first line of the progression, and the steps will increase as follows:

$$
\begin{array}{rcl}
\text{The end of step No. } 11 & = & 6.5 \\
\text{“ \quad “ \quad } 10 & = & 7 \\
\text{“ \quad “ \quad } 9 & = & 7.5 \\
\text{“ \quad “ \quad } 8 & = & 8 \\
\text{“ \quad “ \quad } 7 & = & 8.5 \\
\text{“ \quad “ \quad } 6 & = & 9 \\
\text{“ \quad “ \quad } 5 & = & 9.5 \\
\text{“ \quad “ \quad } 4 & = & 10 \\
\hline
\text{The sum of which is} & & 66
\end{array}
$$

These widths, taken from a scale, are to be set off on the line of balusters, and from the points so obtained lines are to be drawn through the divisions of the centre line. It is easy to perceive that

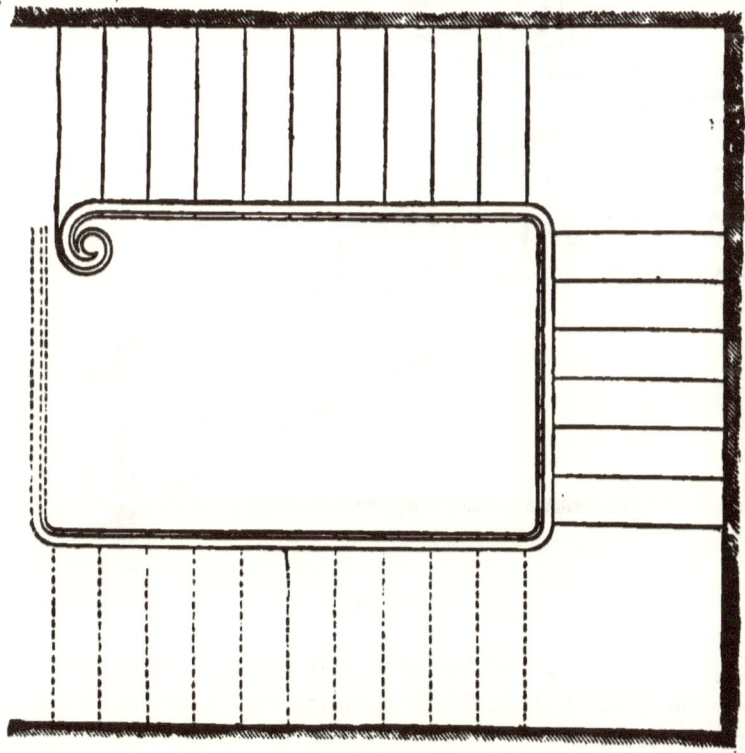

Fig. 43.

by this method, and by varying the progression, any form may be
given to the curve of the string.

The graphic method, however, yet to be described, is preferable to the method by calculation, seeing that it is important to
give a graceful curve to the development of the string, and we will
fully explain this method a little further on.

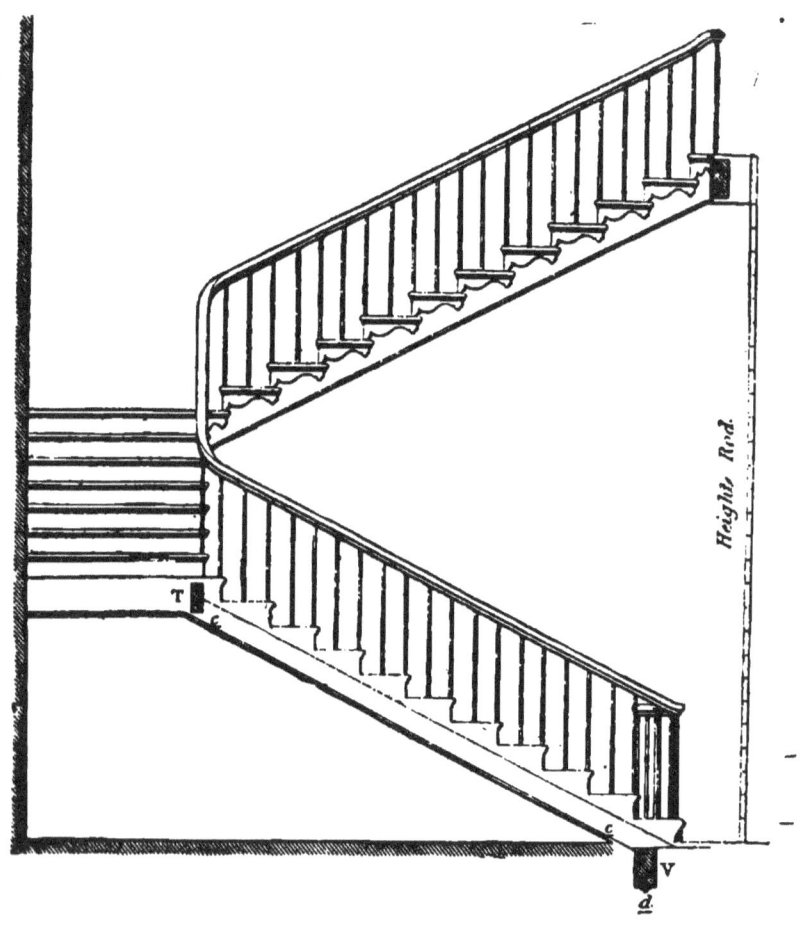

Fig. 44.

Figs. 43 and 44 are the plan and elevation of a geometrical
stair, composed of straight flights, with quarter space landings, and
rising 15 feet 9 inches.

The first flight is shown in Fig. 44, partly in section, exhibiting the carriage *c c*, т the trimmer joists for quarter space, and v the trimmer joists of the floor below, with the lower end of the iron baluster fastened by a screw and nut *d*, at the under side of the trimmer joist v.

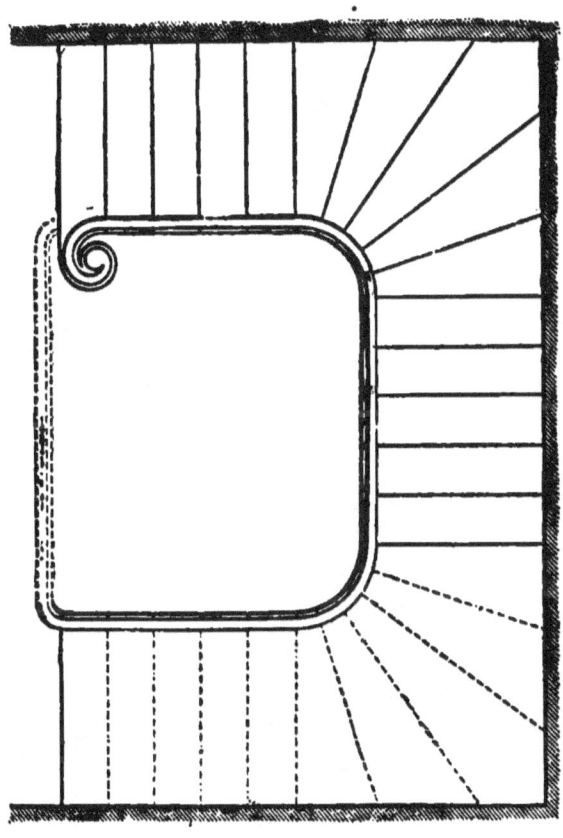

Fig. 45.

Fig. 45 exhibits the plan and Fig. 46 the elevation of a geometrical stair with straight flights connected by winders on the quarter spaces.

Fig. 47 shows the elevation and Fig. 48 the plan of a stair having a landing at the centre of the cylinder.

The strings for these stairs may be steamed, and bent over a cylinder; or they may have grooves cut into them parallel with

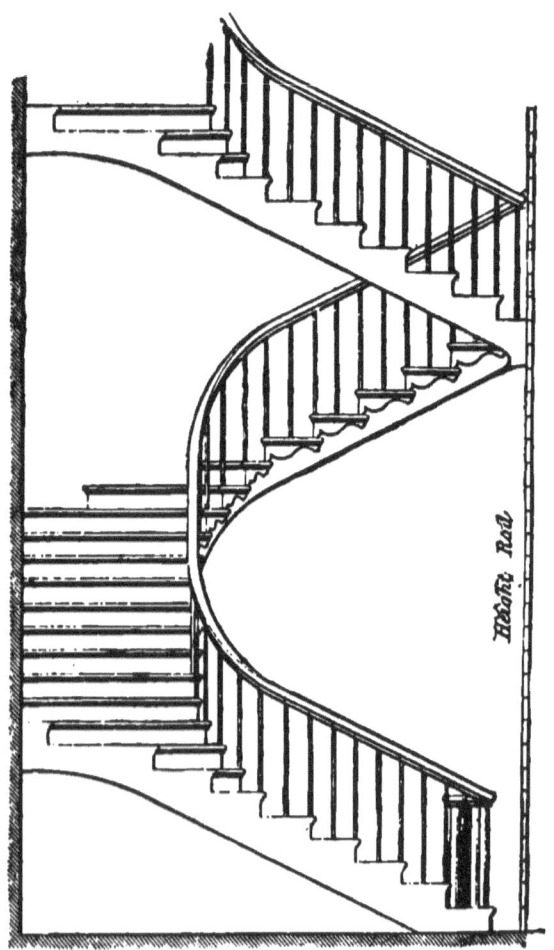

Fig. 46.

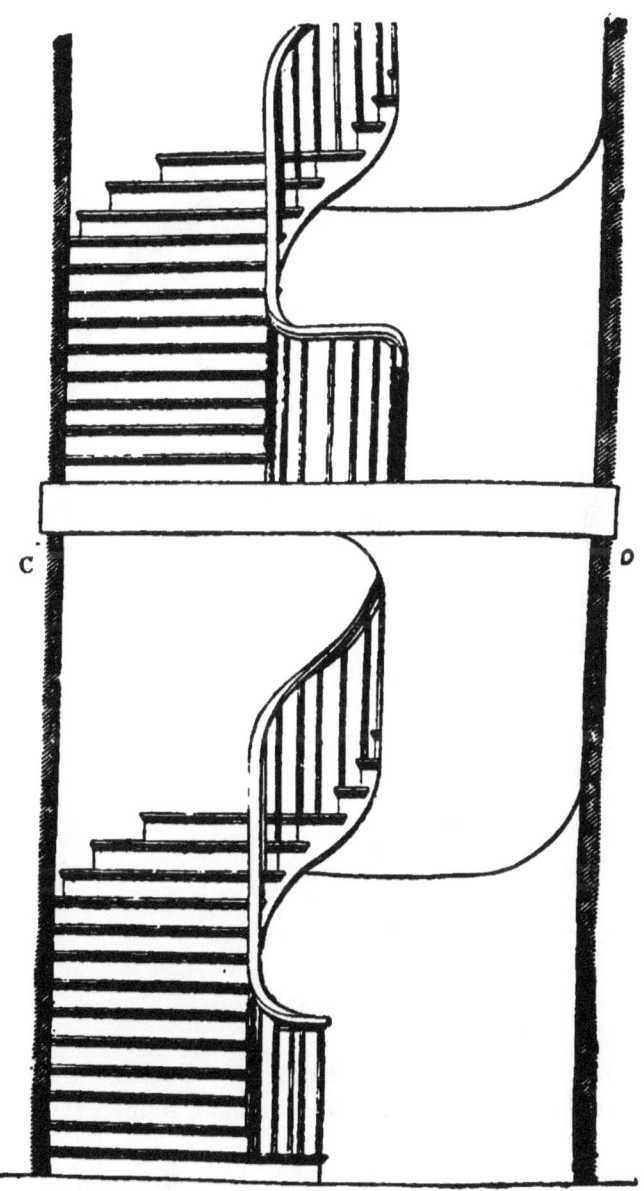

Fig. 47.

the axis of the stair, and the grooves filled up with bars of wood carefully glued in, and the whole left to dry when bent to the proper shape.

Another method in making stairs hollowed in the face to the curvature of the well-hole, and setting out as much of the string

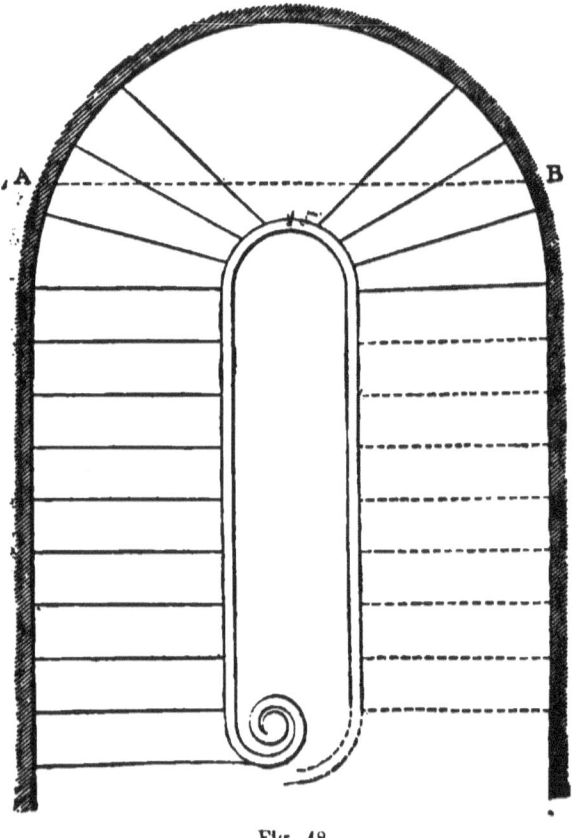

Fig. 49.

on each piece as will cover its width, then glueing the staves, edge to edge, without any veneer. This method, though expeditious, is not safe.

I show a cylinder at Fig. 49 which shows the manner of building the staves edge to edge, with keys of wood dovetailed into the backs of the staves at the joints,

Another method is sometimes practiced, when the curved surface is of great
length and large sweep, as in the back
strings of circular stairs. In this a portion of cylindric surface is formed on a
solid piece of plank about three or four
feet in length; and the string being set
out on a veneer board sufficiently thin to
bend easily, is laid down round the curve,
with such a number of pieces of like thickness as will make the required thickness of
the string-board. In working this method

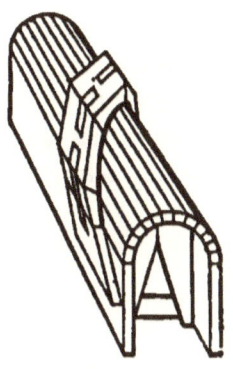

Fig. 49.

the glue is introduced between the veneers with a thin piece of
board, and the veneers quickly strained down to the curved piece
with hand-screws. A string can be formed in this way to almost
any length by glueing a few feet at a time, and when that dries,
removing the cylindrical curve and glueing down more, till the
whole is completed.

Several other ways will suggest themselves to the workman, to
build up a good solid circular string-board.

At Fig. 50 I show a plan of a semi-circular stair having winders
radiating from a common centre. The dotted lines show the carriage or rough strings, *g, h, e, i,* and *f.* c and d show the trimmer
at the top of the stair, and e and *g* show the central or main supports. These carriage, or string pieces, are of course cut out, like
an ordinary string.

Fig. 51 shows a plan of an elliptical stair, and in which is shown
the method of building the carriage for same.

Fig. 52 is the longest carriage, A B, shown in the plan; it is
formed of one pine board, 11 inches wide by 3 or 4 in thickness;
its length of bearing betwixt the walls is about 15 feet. To find
the best position for the carriages, lay a straight edge on the plan,
and by its application find where a right line will be divided into
nearly equal parts by the intersection of the risers. The object of
this will readily be understood if it is considered that in a series of
steps of equal width and risers of equal height, the angles will be

in a straight line, whereas in a series of unequal steps and equal risers, the angles will deviate from a straight line in proportion to the inequality in the width of steps. Notwithstanding the inequality in the width of steps which thus often occurs, it seldom happens that carriages may not be applied to stairs, if their situation be carefully selected by the means above mentioned. The double

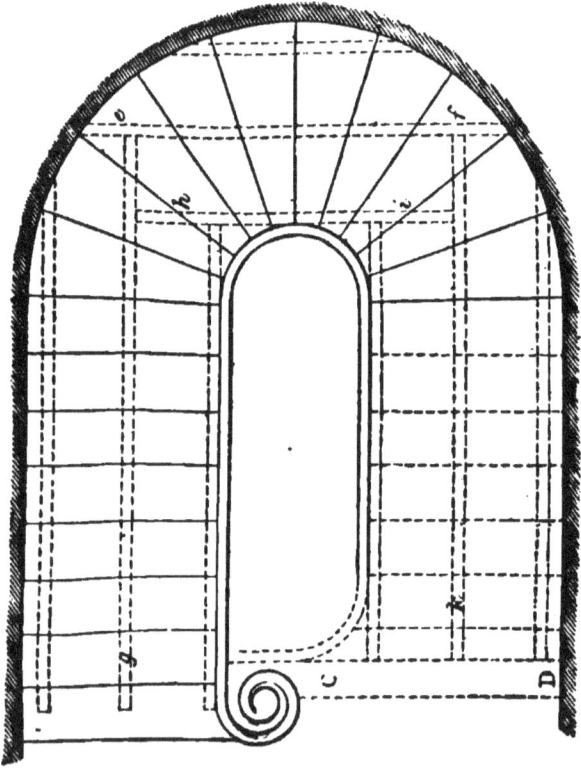

Fig. 50.

line, A B, is taken from the plan with the lines of risers crossing at various angles of inclination. These lines represent the back surface of each riser, according to the number on each. The double line, A B, will therefore be understood as representing the thickness of the piece. Lines drawn from the intersections of each of the risers perpendicularly on A B, Fig. 52, will present the width of

bevel which each notching will require in the carriage at the junction of the wall.   No. 8 crosses very obliquely; No. 9 with somewhat less obliquity; No. 10 with still less, and the obliquity continually diminishes, till at 13 the crossing is at right angles, pre-

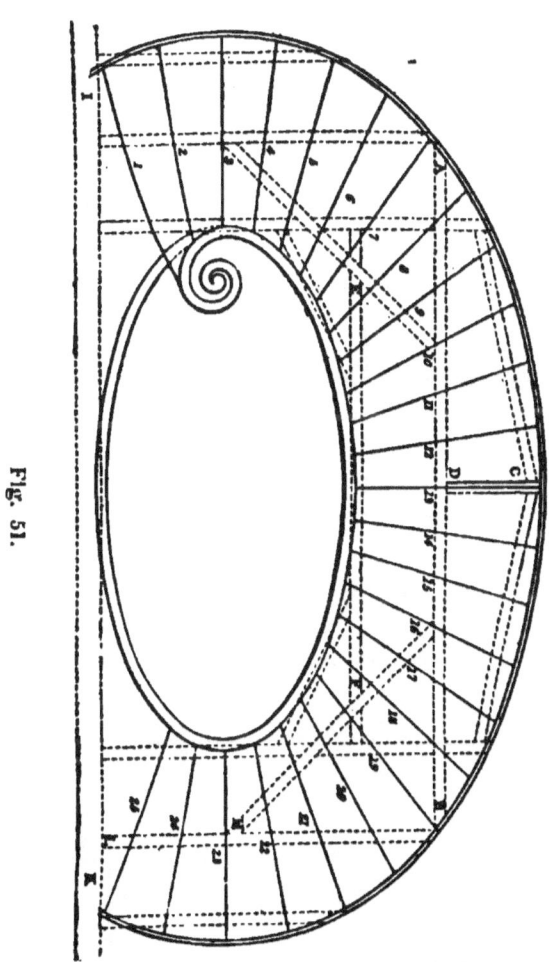

Fig. 51.

senting only one line.   The remaining numbers are bevelled in the
reverse direction, gradually increasing to No. 19, where the carriage enters the wall.   The complete lines show the side of
the carriage next the well-hole, while the dotted lines represent

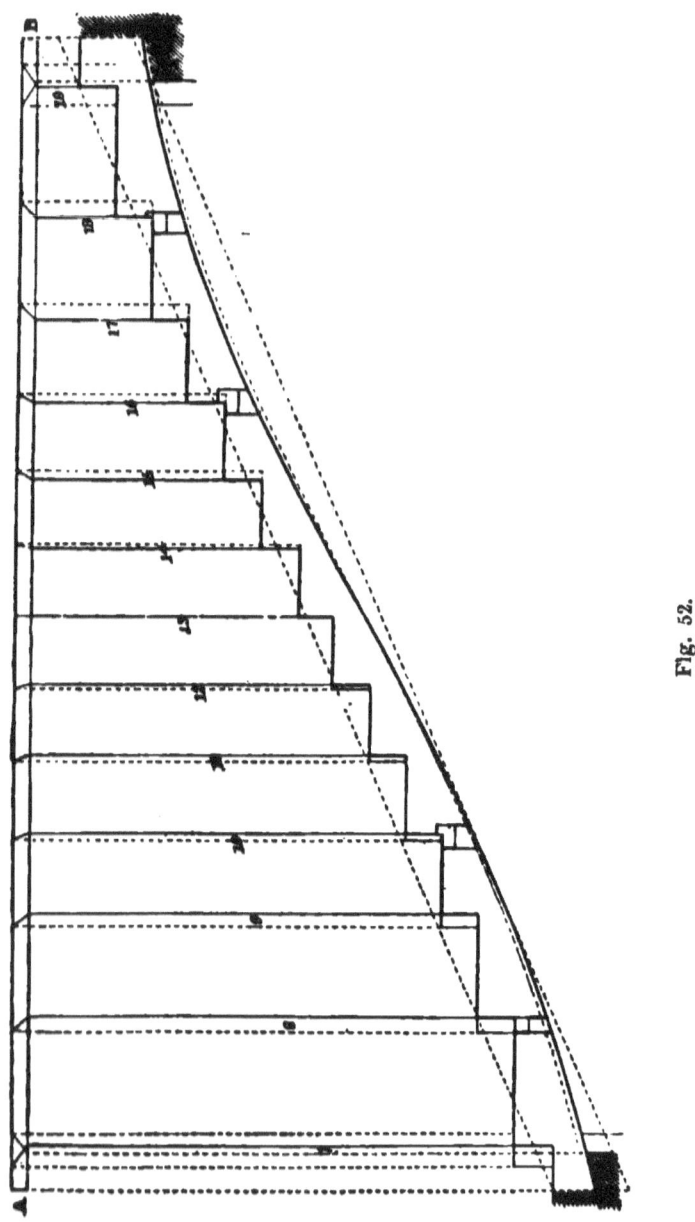

Fig. 52.

the side next the wall. The most expeditious method of setting out such carriages is to draw them out at full size on a floor.
Having first set out the plan of the stairs at full size, take off the
width of every step, in the order in which it occurs, marking that
width, and at right angles thereto draw the connecting riser, thus
proceeding step by step till the whole length of the carriage is
completed; next set out one side of the carriage as a face side and
square over to the back, allowing the bevel as found on the plan;
then, with a pair of compasses prick off to the under edge at each
angle, for the strength; this will define the curvature for the under
side with its proper wind, to suit the ceiling surface of the stairs.
The bearer, c D, Fig. 51, is a level piece wedged in the wall, with

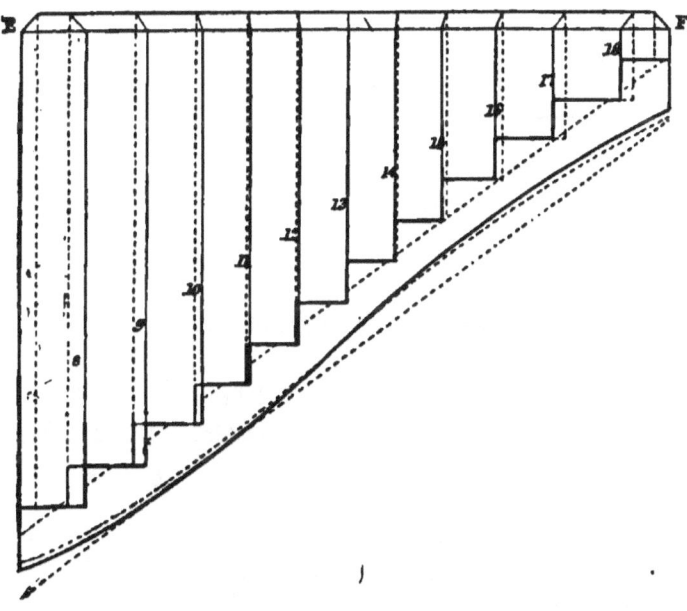

Fig. 53.

its square end abutting against the side of the carriage, A B; the
dotted line on the upper side of the carriage, Fig. 52, and the
straight dotted line on its under side, are intended to show the
edges of an 11-inch pine board previous to its being cut; the
shaded part at each end shows its bearing in the wall; at the riser

18 is shown a corpsing, to receive the lower end of the carriage,
Fig. 54, C L; and at the riser 16, a similar corpsing to receive the
carriage, Fig. 55, G H; Fig. 53 is the carriage, E F, Fig. 51, parallel with A B, Fig. 51, against which the front string is nailed; each
of the last mentioned is formed in the same manner as the one
already described. The carriages, Figs. 53, 54 and 55, have the
number of the risers figured on them.

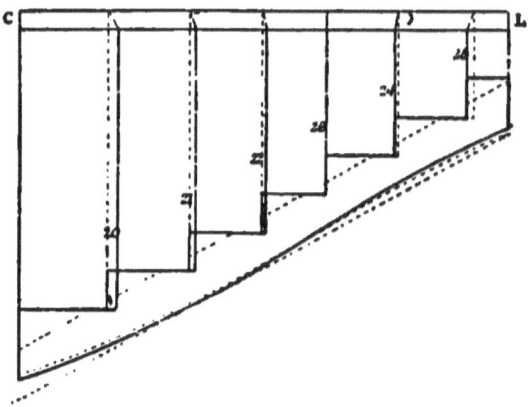

Fig. 54.

This method of framing the carriages of stairs is not yet much
practiced. It was introduced more than forty years ago, and has
given greater satisfaction than the more laborious process of framing for every step which is not only weaker from the greater number of joints, but is also more expensive. It is now gradually
coming into use.

In circular strings the string board for the circular part is prepared in several different ways. Each of these will now be described, the first being that adopted in veneered strings.

One indispensable requisite in forming a veneered string, is
called by joiners a cylinder; it is, however, in fact, a semi-cylinder
joined to two parallel sides. An apparatus of this kind must first
be formed of a diameter equal to the distance betwixt the faces of
the strings in the stairs.

Take some flexible material, as a slip of paper, and measure the exact stretch-out of the circular part of the cylinder, from the springing line on one side, to the springing line on the other. Lay this out as a straight line on a drawing-board; then examine the plan of the stairs, and measure therefrom the precise place of each riser coming in contact with or near to the circular part of the well-hole as it intersects on the line of the face of the string, and also the distance of such riser from the springing lines. These

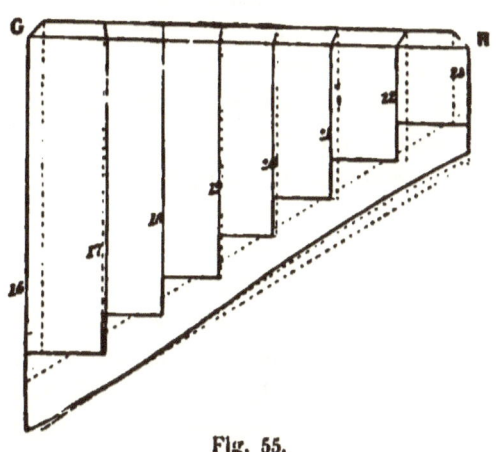

Fig. 55.

distances should all be carefully marked on the slip of paper and transferred to the drawing-board; then, with the pitch-board, set out the development of the line of steps, by making each step equal to the width found, and connecting with it at right angles, its proper height of riser. When the whole development has been set out on the drawing-board, mark from the angles of the steps downwards the dimension for the strength of carriage; by this means it will be seen what shape and size of veneer will be required. The whole of the setting out must now be transferred to the face of the veneer; then with the point of an awl prick through the angles of the steps and risers, and trace the lines on the back as well as on the front; the veneer must now be bent down on the cylinder, bringing the springing lines and centre lines of the string to coincide as exactly as possible with those of the cylinder; the whole string must then be carefully backed by staving pieces glued on it, with the joints and grain parallel to the axis of the cylinder; the lines on the back of the string will serve to indicate the quantity of the veneer to be covered by the staving; the whole must be allowed to remain on the cylinder till sufficiently dry and firm; it is next fitted to the work by cutting away all the superfluous wood, as directed by the lines on the face of the veneer, and then being perfectly fitted to the steps, risers and connecting string; it must be firmly nailed both to the steps and risers, and also to the carriages; each heading joint in the string should be grooved and tongued with a glued tongue.

There is another method of gluing up the strings sometimes practiced. In this the string is set out as before described, but instead of using a thin veneer, an inch board is taken, on the face of which the development of steps, risers, springing and centre lines must be carefully set out as before; the edge of the board must be gauged from the face, equal to the thickness of a veneer, which would bend round the cylinder; the string must then be confined down on the workbench, and grooves made by a dado plane on its back in the direction of the riser, and at about half an inch distant from each other, till the whole width of the cylindric surface is formed into a series of grooves; these grooves are then filled with keys of wood which are placed in as the string is bent round to the right curve.

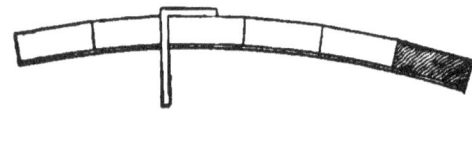

Fig. 56.

For wall strings having large or long curves a saw kerf in the direction of the riser, or in other words, the kerf should be plumb when the string is in position. The manner of cutting these kerfs is shown at Fig. 56. It will be noticed that the kerfs stop at the gauge line, which is about a quarter of an inch from the face of the stuff, the square is placed there to show that the lines on the edge of the string should point towards the common centre of the cylinder.

At Fig. 57, I show a plan of a stairs with winders radiating from different centres, and show the strings both for inner and outer bearers, with the lines for carriage timbers, which are all shown in position. On the lines a^1 b^2 and c^1 d^2 are marked the width of the treads. From the line b^2 d^2 in the plan the elevation of the front string is constructed; $b\,a$ is the stretchout of the starting cylinder, $a\,c$ is the straight part of the string, and $c\,d$ the stretchout of the land-

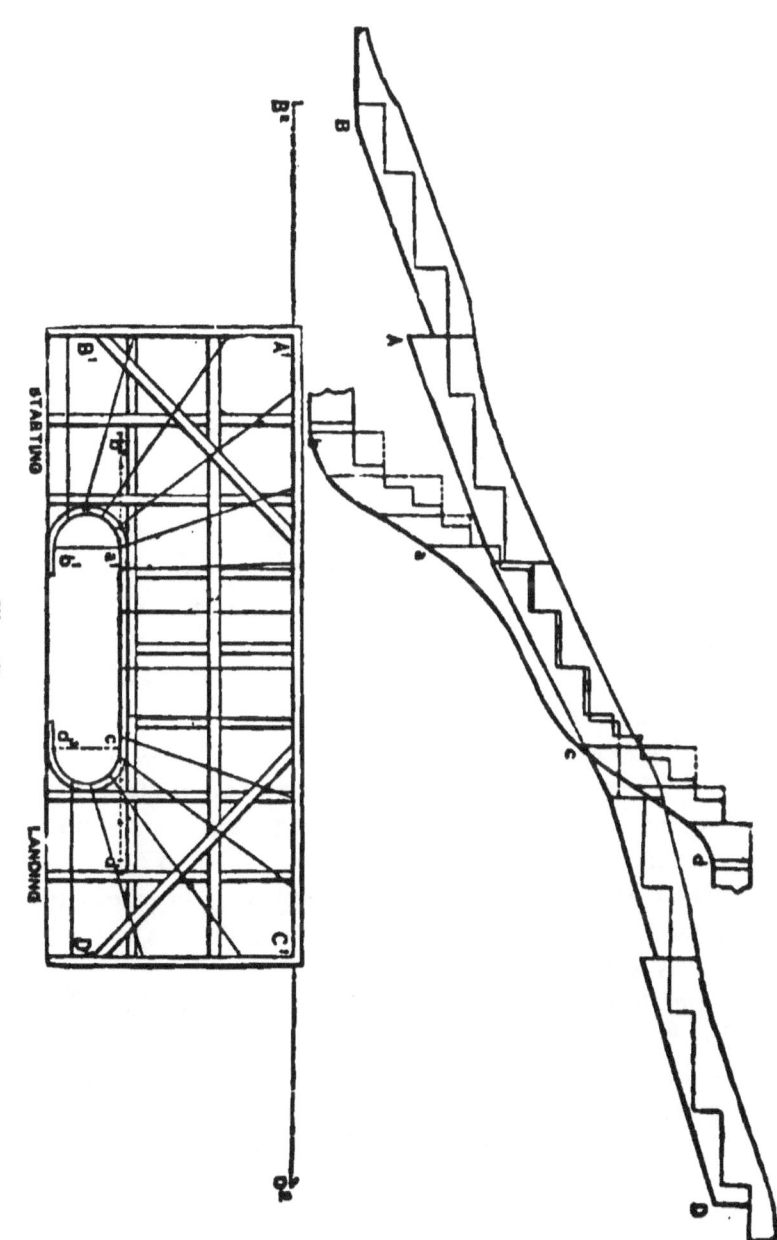

Fig. 57.

ing cylinder. After laying out the steps and risers in the elevation, the curved line representing the lower edge of the string is drawn. This line should be so located as to maintain the width of the string about alike at all points measuring square across. Easements are required at top and bottom, and must be obtained in such a manner as to preserve the average width of the string. In order to complete the easement within the string itself, it is often necessary, as shown in this figure at *d*, to glue two or three inches of straight wood on to the cylinder where it joins the facia. This may be avoided by making a part of the easement on the straight facia. Among workmen both of these methods are employed, some giving preference to one and some to the other—some using them interchangeably, depending upon the particular circumstances of the case. The dotted lines shown in the elevation of the front string, in those portions corresponding to the cylinders in the plan, show the lengths of the several pieces of cylinder stuff before the steps and risers are cut out. In making the string-piece, the line of its lower edge is drawn partly by hand, as shown at *b* and *d*, partly by marking with a flexible straight-edge bent into the cylinder, and on the straight part by bending a strip of wood to suit the curve required and marking along the side of it.

Referring again to the plan, $B^2 D^2$ is the stretchout of the wall string, and from this line in the plan the elevation of the wall string is to be constructed, as shown in the engraving. B A is the first, corresponding with $B^1 A^1$ in the plan. From A to C is the second piece corresponding with $A^1 C^1$ in the plan. The easements run to a level at the corners A and C; likewise at the top and bottom, where they join the base.

At Fig. 58, I show a plan of a stairs with sixteen risers and the winders "dancing" around the well-hole. The wall-strings are shown both prepared and in position at A A, B B, and C C. The butt of B joins to the top of A, and the butt of C joins to the top of B. The connections of the strings will be easily understood by a careful examination.

The newel, N, in this case is of large diameter, say from 10 to 12 inches. The treads are ten inches wide, and the well-hole is ten inches in diameter.

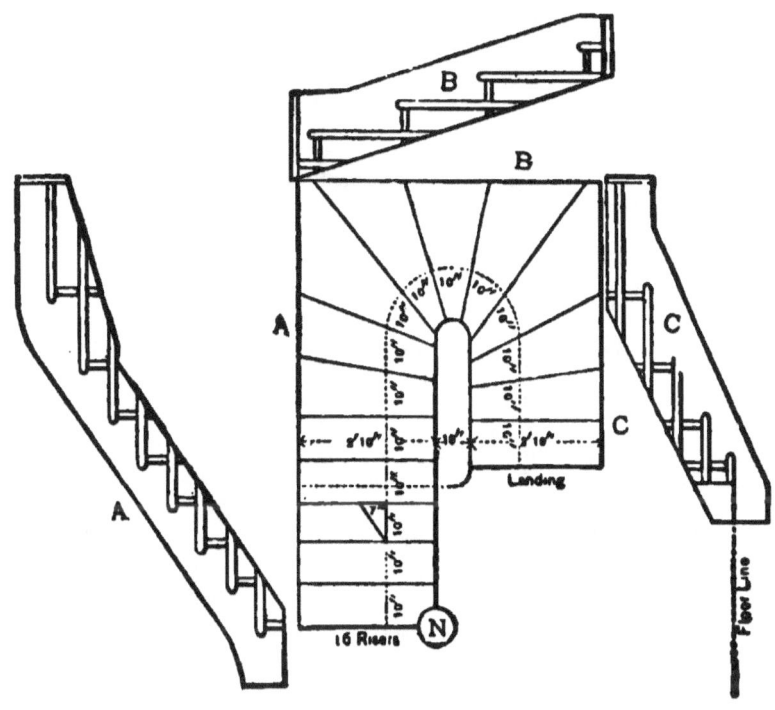

Fig. 58.

At Fig. 59, I show a stair with winders radiating to a common centre. In this stair there are thirteen treads and fourteen risers. The first wall string is omitted, but the second and third, B and C, are shown. After mastering the details of Fig. 58, there will be no difficulty in understanding this with the aid of the following instructions:

B is the cross-string. Always glue up cross-strings for stairs of this description, 10 12 14 or 16 inches wide, as the case may be, then make a line, *a b;* from that line square off the end of your string. After squaring the end from the line you must set in the thickness of the other wall string, and set out the groove (to receive the tongue of A); then set on the other half of kite-winder; then set up a riser square with the winder; set up the other winders, and the half-winder square with the half-winder; allow tongue, etc., as before described. There will be enough stuff to form all easements, etc.

c is the other wall-string, having half a winder, one winder, three flyers, and up. The up is a riser that takes on to the landing. This string will be set out similar to the first, only you must

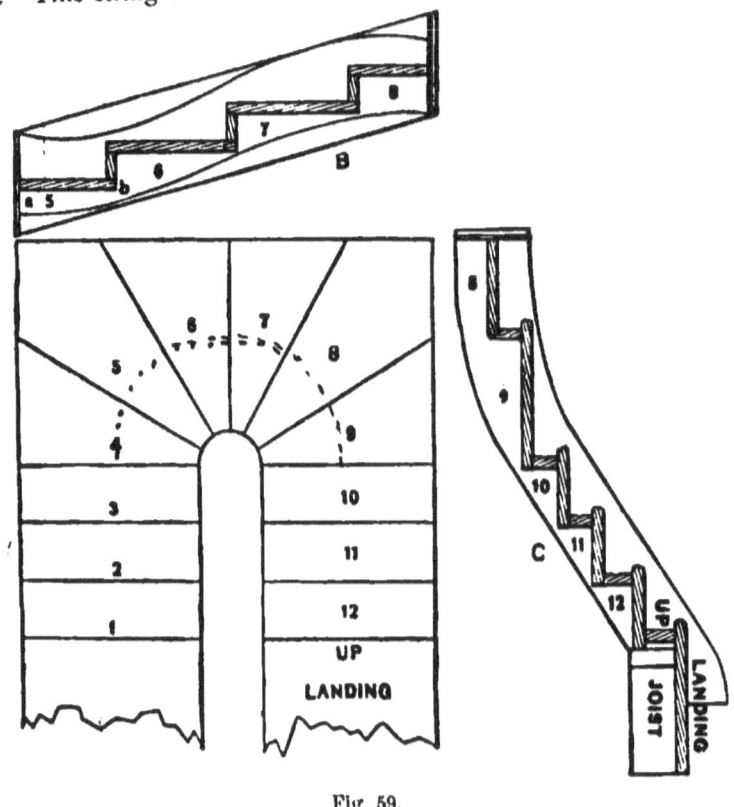

Fig. 59.

not forget the up. You must groove the winder end of string to receive tongue of cross-string; also glue a piece on to carry out your winder and form the easements. When you are setting out strings the pitch-board is the face of riser and top of tread; so you allow the thickness of the riser in and thickness of tread down, and a little more for wedging. The general depth for housing is half an inch. In all cases you must plow and tongue, glue joints, etc.

In A I have not shown the string finished, but in C it is done. The strings are prepared as in A, and after the steps are glued up, rounded and the hollow worked, they are then marked as shown in C.

I now show how the outside or cut-string and well are prepared. In getting out the cut-string I suppose you to have a board, say 10 inches wide, the pitch-board being 9 inches on the going and 6 inches on the riser. Then, by squaring the pitch-board across from the raking side to the angle of the tread and riser, you willl have 5 inches, thus leaving 5 inches. Then make a template 5 inches wide, and apply it to the bottom of the string, and the pitch-board to that, and mark off your steps. Cut the going square. The risings are mitered. The back edge of step 3, and the front edge of step 10, are the springing lines of the well-hole. The string must be left longer for tenoning or halving to the well-string. Before applying the veneer on the cylinder, you must stretch out your well, and when marking the springing line upon the veneer, set up your steps before bending it on the cylinder, so that when you have properly blocked and glued and the work is set, it can be taken off the cylinder and the steps cut. It is then ready to be fitted to the other strings.

Fig. 60 shows a plan, d, of a stairs with a quarter turn, and four winders. The strings, with their ease-offs, are also shown at a and c. A portion of the inner string, c, is shown at b.

The outer, or wall string, is shown at a, with portions of the fliers, and the wide ends of all the winders. At c, portions of the upper and lower strings are shown, with a sectional view of a few of the fliers, and all the narrow ends of the winders in the cylinder. This illustration is clear and requires no further description.

Fig. 61 shows the plan of a stairs which turn around a central post. This kind of stair is frequently used in large stores and in club-houses and other similar places.

Fig. 62 shows the elevation of the stairs complete, with rail and central newel. Stairs of this kind have a very graceful appearance if judgment is used in planning them. They are not very difficult to build, as the following details will show.

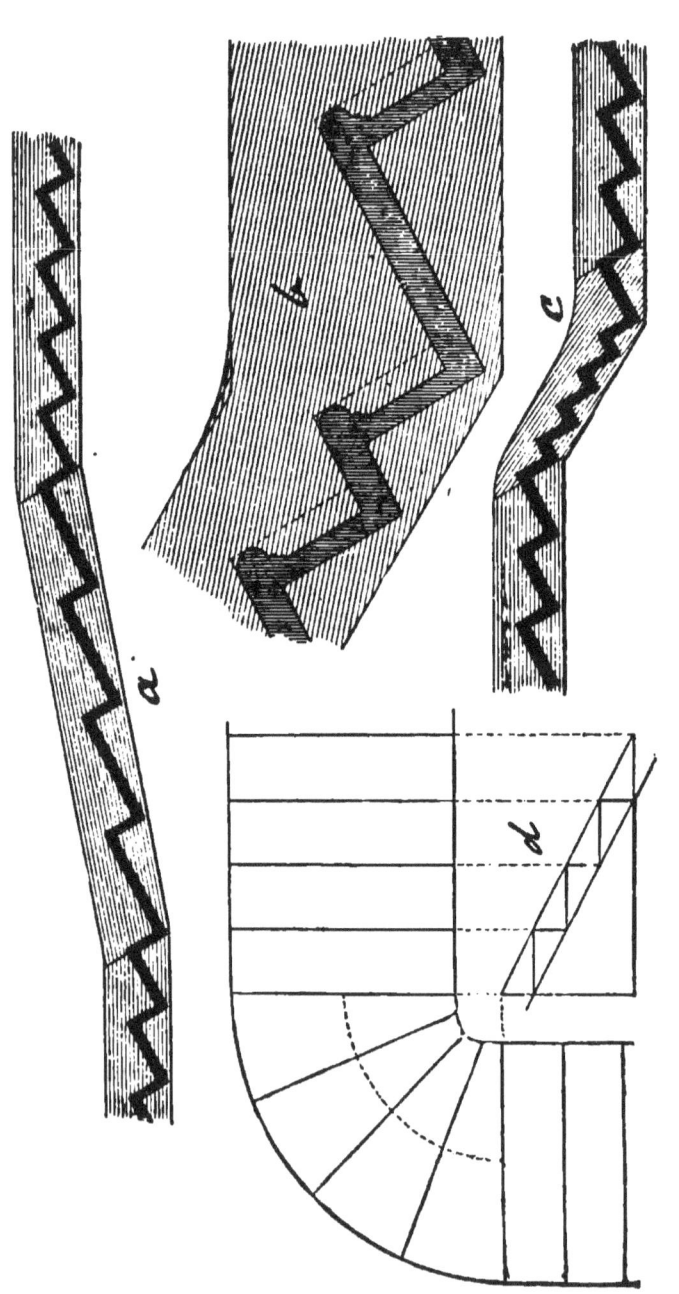

Fig. 60.

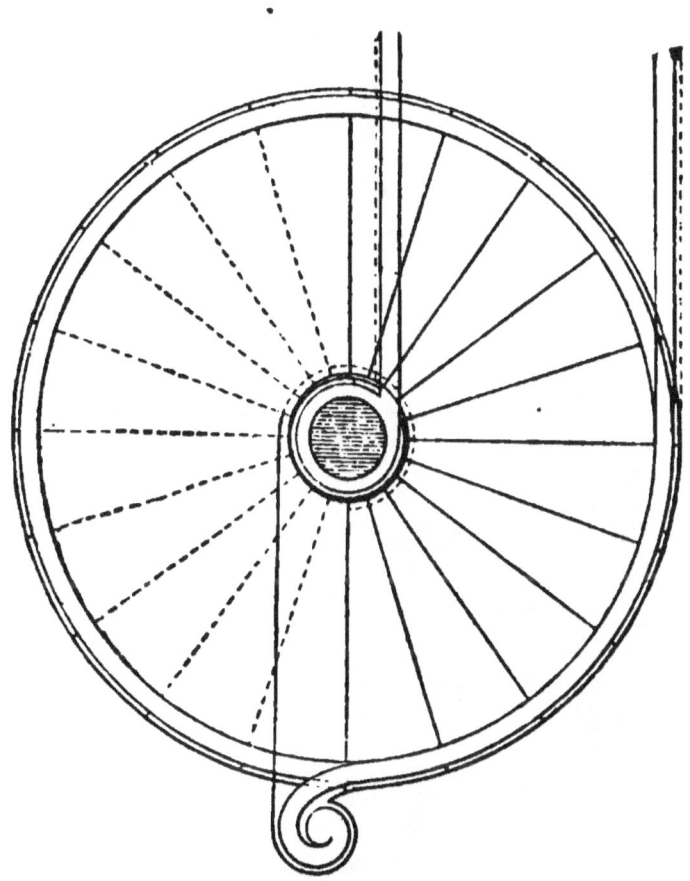

Fig. 61.

Fig. 63 exhibits the manner of framing the carriage. The pieces on the ends of the risers are dovetailed strongly into the rough risers, and the supports under the treads are also well secured into the riser and to each other. The staving, which forms a kind of barrel around the lower portion of the post, form resting points for the rough risers, which are secured strongly to post and staves on both sides of the barrel. The manner of securing, notching and arrangement, is clearly shown in the engraving.

Fig. 64 shows the manner in which the ends of the rough riser

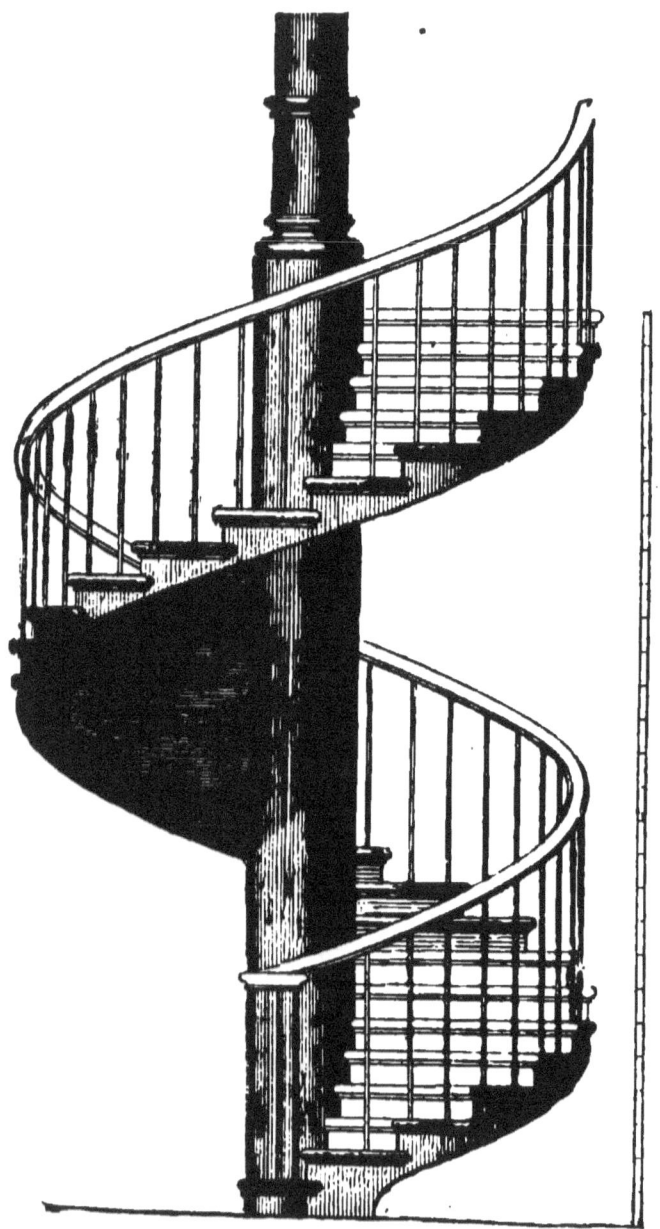

Fig. 62.

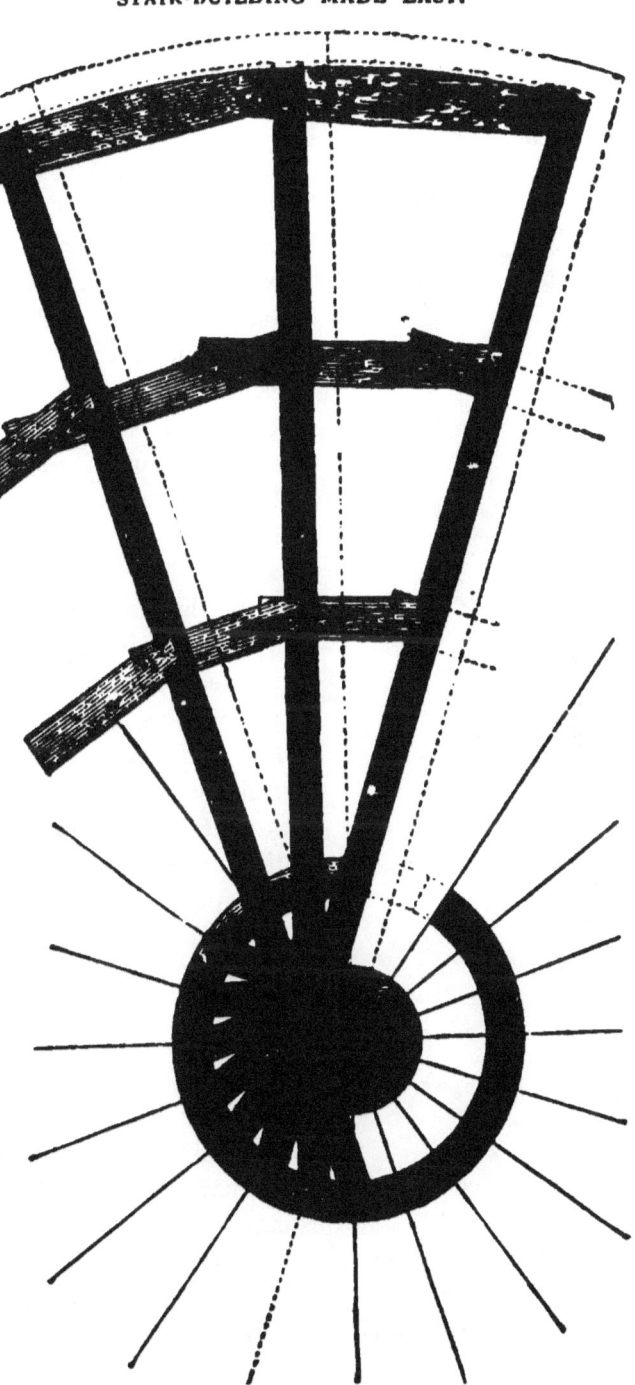

Fig. 63.

are finished, showing the dovetailed ends, joints and a flat iron bar screwed to the built string. This iron bar should be about a quarter of an inch thick, and not less than three inches wide; the screws should be heavy and not less than one and three-quarters of an inch long. A thin veneer should be bent over the outside string, and notched nicely under the tread. This veneer should be fastened with glue and screws. Furring should be used over and below the iron bar, so as to bring the face of the wood work a little more than flush with the face of the iron. When well made, these stairs are very strong, and it is surprising how much of a load they will bear without visible deflection.

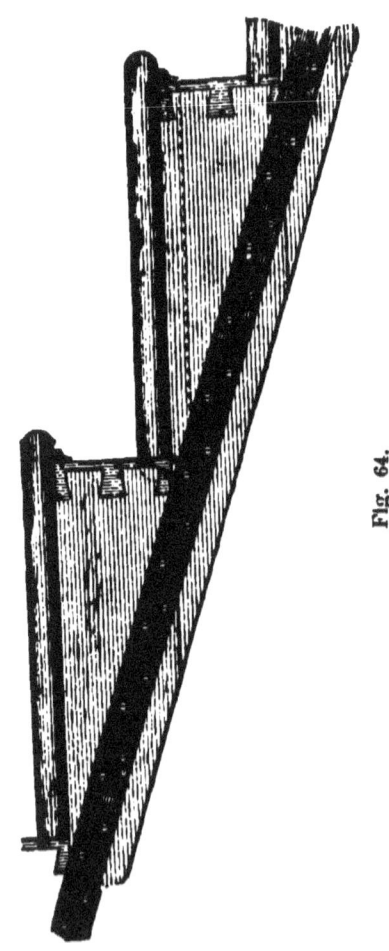

Fig. 64.

At Fig. 65 I show an elevation of the stairs shown on the plan at Fig. 50. The well-hole of this stair is semicircular; the student will notice how gracefully the lines sweep up to the third floor. This kind of stair looks very well, notwithstanding the fact that the winders converge towards the common centre, which, as I have before stated, should be avoided when possible, and this may be in almost every case.

Fig. 66 shows the elevation of the elliptical stairs, the plan of which is shown at Fig. 51. This style of stairs is perhaps the handsomest and most costly that can be built. The manner of

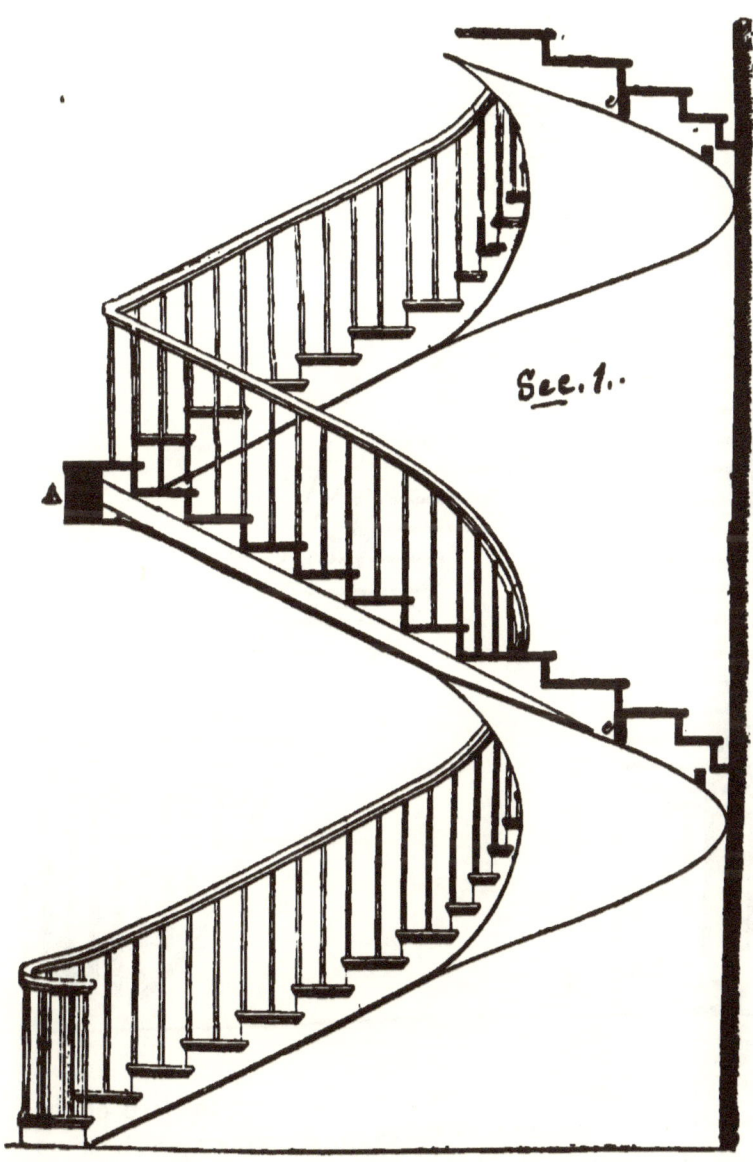

Fig. 65.

constructing it is similar to that of building a semi-circular stair.
The strings may be "built up" over a semi-ellipse form made for
the purpose, and glued together the same as described in previous

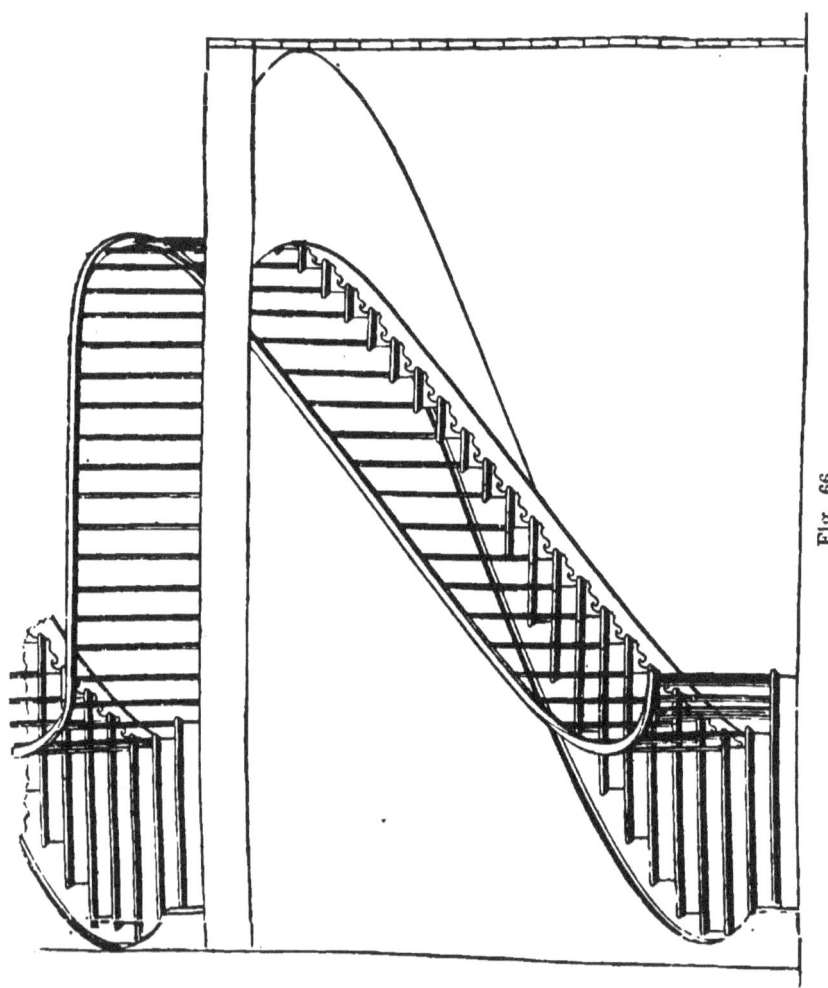

Fig. 66.

pages. Veneers should, of course, be glued over the face of the
strings if they are built up with staves ; if the strings are built up
with long thin pieces glued together, plenty of time should be
given them to dry and harden after gluing before they are used or
cut for treads and risers.

It will be noticed that on this stairs the ends of the steps are bracketed. The bracket in this case is of very simple form, but is one that has been very much used by stair-builders in times past. Further on I will give some examples of brackets that are in more common use now. In many good houses the stair bracket is dispensed with, as some architects think their use is in bad taste. Such men, however, as Wren, Inigo Jones, Downing, Hatfield and Mullet have used them freely and with complete success, and for my part, I do not think a main stairs in any building worth living in, is properly finished, if the exposed outside string is not bracketed.

I have now pretty well covered the whole ground of building the cases, carriages and bodies of stairs, but there will be cases and conditions arise in practice that I may not have provided for, and which will have to be worked out by the ingenuity and skill of the workman. Indeed, there are many things in stair-building that cannot well be foreseen, but which will not present any insurmountable difficulty to the workman of ready wit and expertness after what has been said in the foregoing pages.

While a goodly portion of the matter and illustrations in this work are original, and published for the first time, I take pleasure in acknowledging that a large portion of both text and illustrations are taken from quite a number of sources that are recognized as authoritative on the subject discussed. Chief among the sources drawn from, I may mention: "Building Construction," vol. 2; "Newland's Carpenters' and Joiners' Assistant;" "Tarbuck on Stairs;" "Hatfield's American House-Joiner;" "Builder and Wood-Worker;" "Carpentry and Building;" etc., etc.

In most cases, the position and general plan of the stairs are decided upon by the architect, where one is employed, but the arrangement, *in detail*, of the treads and risers is generally left to the joiner who builds them. The arrangement of the risers in and to the well-hole requires some study, for the "fall" of the hand-rail depends upon their position.

This has been partly explained before and should not be lost sight of, for many stairs, easy, elegant and graceful in themselves,

BALUSTERS

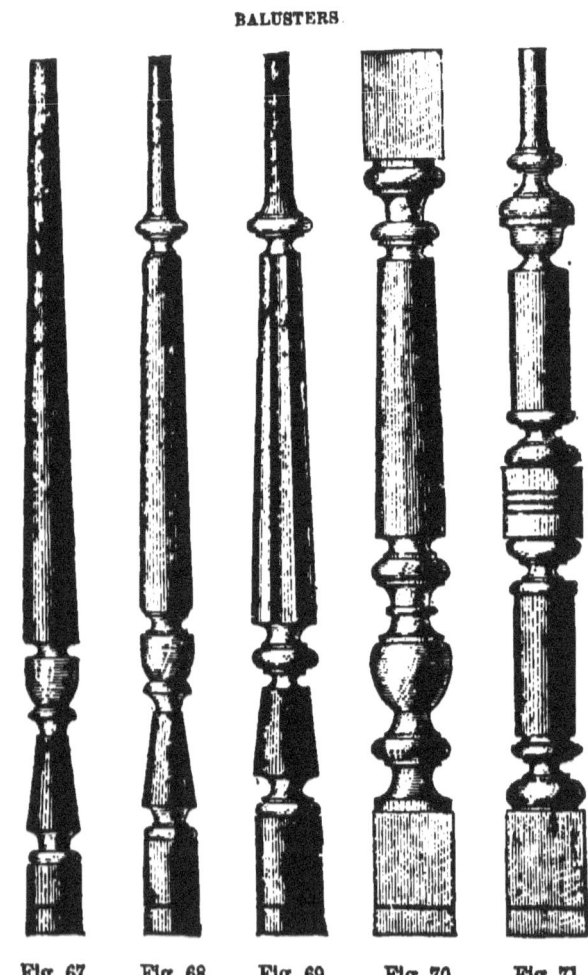

Fig. 67.   Fig. 68.   Fig. 69.   Fig. 70.   Fig. 71.

BALUSTERS.

Fig. 72.

Fig. 73.

Fig. 74.

Fig. 75.

Fig. 76.

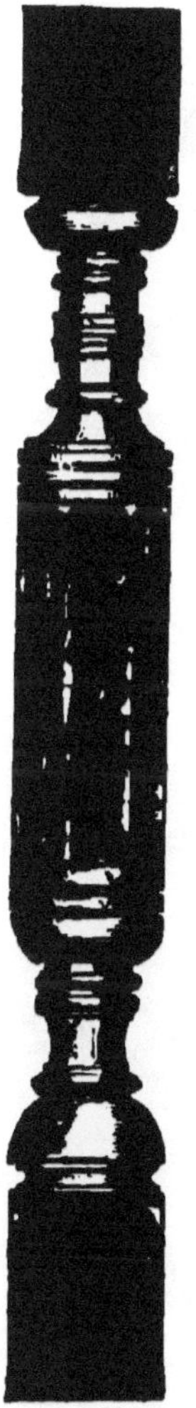

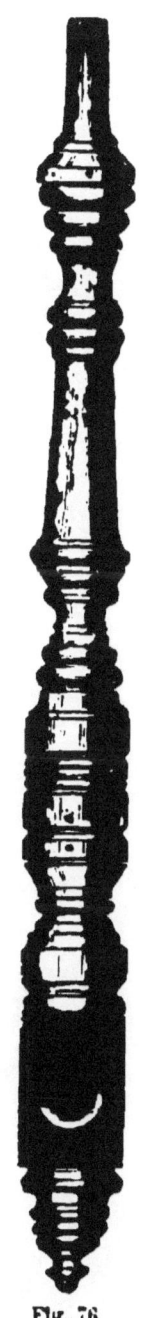

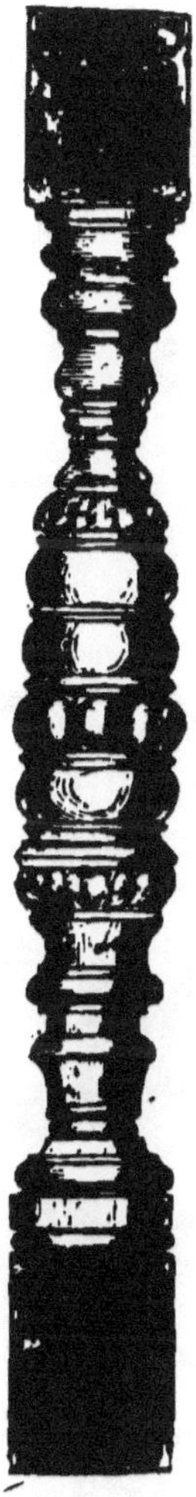

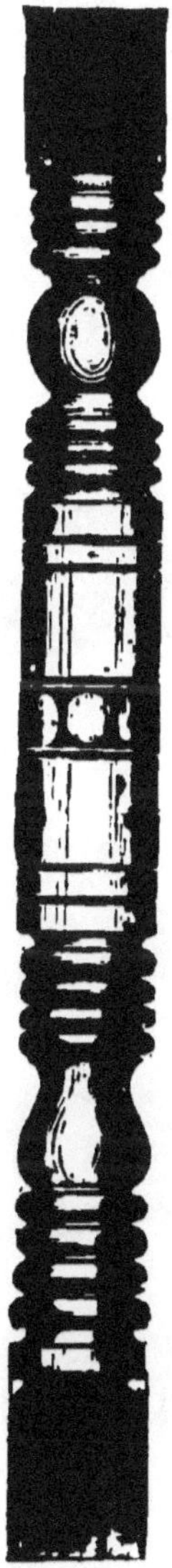

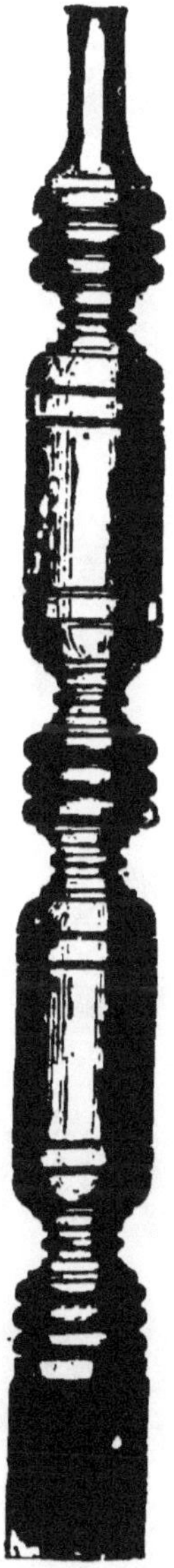

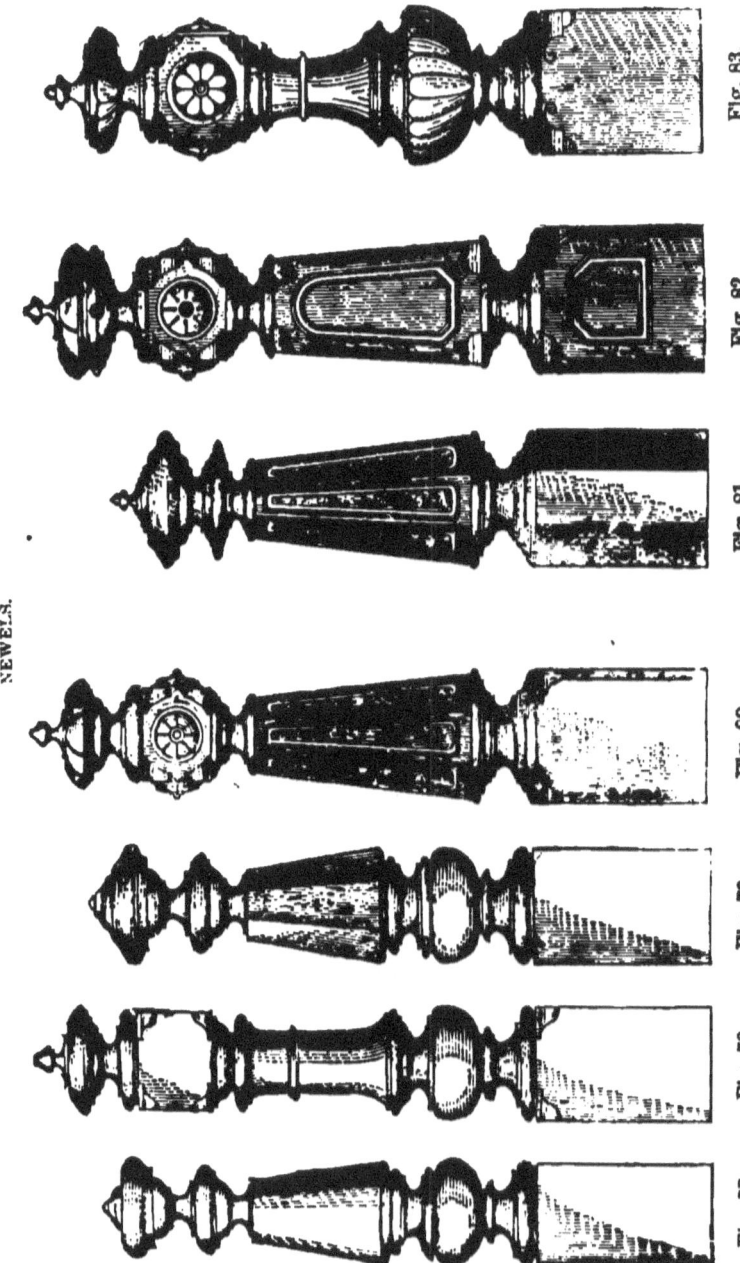

NEWELS.

NEWELS.

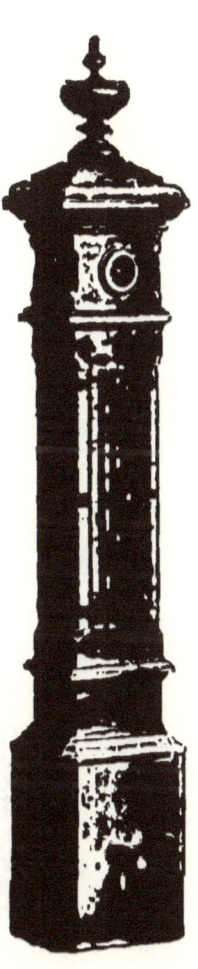

Fig. 84.   Fig. 85.   Fig. 86.

NEWELS,

Fig. 87.

Fig. 88.

require hand-rails of an inconvenient form and such as cannot
be made to look well, and which require much more labor and
material to make, than the rails would have done if the risers and
treads had been properly arranged. To provide for this, I would
suggest that the student would again read and study that portion of
this work that relates to *dancing* or *balancing* the steps around the
well-hole. A little experience in hand-railing will enable the student to avoid awkward rails.

The student should cultivate the useful habit of observing the
stairs and rails around him, and should carefully note the positions
of the risers of those which appear or feel awkward, asking himself
why they are inconvenient; should he ever fail to find a satisfactory answer, he will have learned the positions which he should
avoid, and will better understand the method of arrangement when
he comes to consider it practically.

In determining the size of a well-hole, its length must be well
considered, and ample provision made for height from the tread
directly under the trimmer, and in no case should this height be
less than six feet six inches.

Frequently, the man who builds the stairs will be called upon to
decide on the style of rail and design of balusters and newel. To
enable him to meet this emergency with intelligence and satisfaction
to himself and the proprietor, I present for his consideration a number
of designs for both balusters and newels: Figs. 67, 68, 69, 70 and
71, show a number of plain balusters that may be used in a variety
of stairs; Figs. 67 and 68 are adapted for the more common sorts of
stairs; while Fig. 69, which has an octagon shaft, is better adapted
for a stairs of some pretensions. Fig. 70 is especially adapted
for stairs with closed strings and heavy rails. Fig. 71 may be used
in almost any stairs. Figs. 72, 73, 74, 75 and 76, show a more
ornate class of balusters than those mentioned. Figs. 72, 73 and
74 are designed for stairs with closed strings and heavy rail. Fig.
75 is intended to be *bored* in the rail and dovetailed into the step.
Fig. 76 is intended for a close string stair, and is intended to be
fastened to the outside of the string. This system of attaching the
baluster to the outside of the string has obtained considerable pop-

ularity of late, and is really a very
good method of placing the balusters.

Figs. 77, 78, 79, 80, 81, 82 and 83
show seven popular examples of newels suitable for almost any kinds of
ordinary stairs. Fig. 79 has an octagon shaft and turned members and
cap. Figs. 80 and 81 have octagon
shafts panelled, with carved rosettes
and cap. These are adapted for the
better kinds of stairs in city and town
houses. Figs. 82 and 83 show more
elaborate posts; these may be used in
the better class of villas and cottages.

The five examples of "*built newel
posts*" shown at Figs. 84, 85, 86, 87
and 88, are intended for first-class
residences or hotels. These newels
are "built up" of costly woods, or are
veneered, and as a rule are very
costly. The good workman will have
no difficulty in building any of these,
if the cost is only allowed him. Most
of the examples of these balusters and
newels may be obtained from regular
dealers, and we would advise the
young stair-builder to purchase these
newels and balusters already made at
the factory rather than attempt to
make them himself, or allow even
the country turner to make them for
him. Where these things are manu-
factured there are means and appliances at hand that enables the manufacturers to make them so cheap that
the everyday workman would starve

Fig. 89.

on the prices. Then again, the large manufacturer always has a large amount of material of good quality to draw from, and can insure good work, which are advantages the country workman rarely possesses.

Fig. 89 shows a newel post adapted for gas-lights. The same design of post may be used for a kerosene lamp. The lamp may be held in a basket made of brass, iron wire, or other suitable mate-

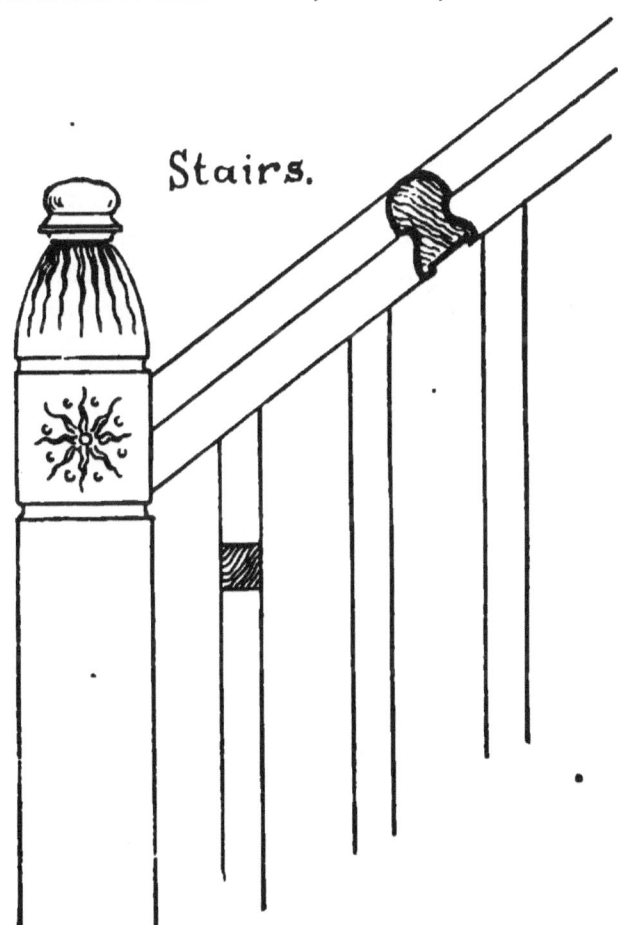

Stairs.

Fig. 90.—Newel and Rail.

rial; or it may stand on a guarded platform prepared for the purpose, or by other device which the cunning workman will have no trouble in perfecting.

There are many other kinds and styles of balusters and newels than the ones shown.

Fig. 90 shows a portion of a square newel with a carved top, incised panels and turned cap. The balusters in this case are square, because that form is in keeping with the style of newel and rail shown in this example.

A section of the rail is also shown, which, it will be noticed, is rather peculiar in shape; this style of newel baluster, and rail is well adapted for small cottages in rural districts, or for seaside cottages.

By referring to Figs. 35 and 36, pages 46 and 47, several other designs for balusters and newels will be seen. At Fig. 35 the arrangement of balusters is worth examining and studying, as the system pursued may be varied to almost any extent.

At Fig. 36 the newel and balusters are very plain but very effective. The taper chamfers on the newel and the parallel chamfers on the balusters are easily wrought, and may be often adopted with gratifying results.

MISCELLANEOUS.

N this chapter I propose to say a few things concerning stairs that may be useful to the workman, in aiding him to work out some little things that have not been mentioned in the main body of the book.

To begin with, I show and explain, on pages 56 and 57, a method of *dancing* the treads around the well-holes of stairs obtained by computation, but which, as I stated at the time, is not the best way to obtain the width of the inner ends of the winders in order to secure a graceful line of rail. At Fig. 91, I show a graphi-

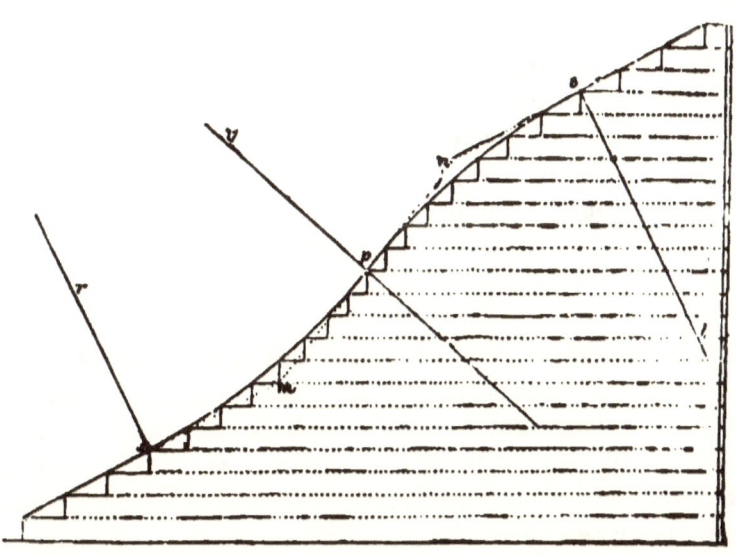

Fig. 91.

cal method of determining the widths of the inner ends of the winders so that a rail having a graceful and smooth sweep may be obtained:

Let the dotted line *s m p*, Fig. 91, represent the kneed line made by the first division of the stairs in the lower part, corresponding to the nosing of the fliers, and the upper part, *m n*, to that of the winders. Bisect the line of the winders *m n* in *p*, and raise a perpendicular, *p i*. Then set off *m s* equal to *m p*, and make *s r* perpendicular to *s m*. The intersection of these two perpendiculars, *s r* and *p i*, gives the centre of the arc of a circle, tangential in *s* and *p* to the sides of the angle *s m p*. In like manner is found the arc to which *p n*, *n o*, are tangents, and a species of cyma is formed by the two arcs, which is a graceful double curve line without knees. This line is met by the horizontal lines, which indicate the surface of the treads, the point *p* being always the fixed point of the centre step, the twelfth in this example. Therefore, the heights of the risers are drawn from the story rod to meet the curved line of development, *s p o*, and are thence transferred to the baluster line on the plan.

By adopting this method a handsome rail will always be the result.

It frequently happens that the stair-builder will be called upon to reduce or enlarge some moulding or bracket in connection with the stairs he is building, and to provide for an emergency of this kind, I herewith show, at Fig. 92, a method by which a reduction or enlargement may be accomplished without changing the actual shape or *contour* of the the moulding or bracket.

The manner of making the reduction or enlargement will be seen at once.

If A is the original, then make the line B twice the length—if twice the size is desired—or one and a half the length, if only one and a half enlargement is wanted; run the lines at the members as shown until they cut the line A. Then on the line B, prick off, with the compasses the points shown 1½ or 2, or 2½, or as much larger as you want the enlarged moulding, then join by lines the points on B to the lines on A; then square over from the line B, touching all the points, and give those lines raised on B the same length as the corresponding lines on A, and this work is complete.

In ordinary stairs the rail runs into a cap on the top of the newel post, and this cap is sometimes made as much as 8 or 10 inches in diameter. When this is the case, the face or moulding on the edge of the cap requires to be a little different in outline. The turner who makes the cap will of course know nothing of this,

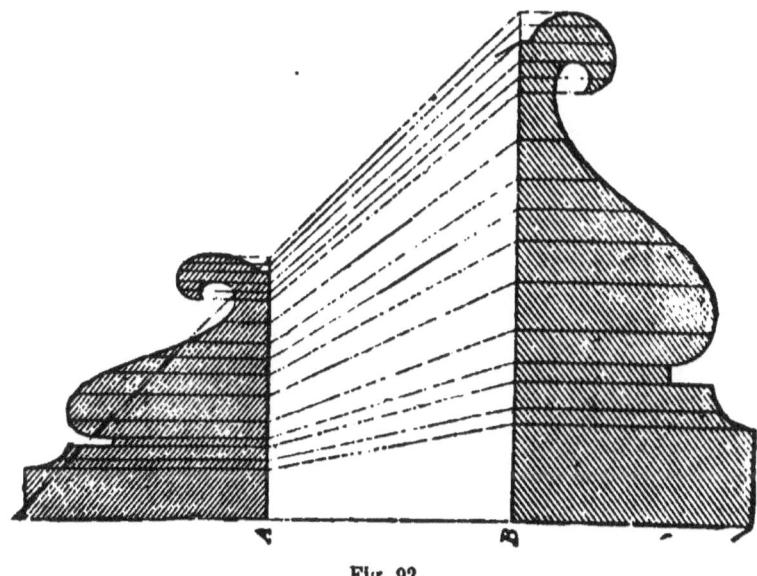

Fig. 92.

therefore it will devolve upon the man who builds the stairs to make patterns for the cap.

Fig. 93 shows the manner by which the correct shape of the cap may be obtained, or by which different sizes of the rail may be made which will mitre into each other without over wood. The divisions A, B, C, D, E, F and G, on the rail correspond to the figures 1, 2, 3, 4, 5, 6, etc., on the cap. These latter divisions may be made greater or smaller, according to the size of cap or rail desired. The manner of finding the points to describe the semi-circles, is obvious and requires no further description.

Many times the workman will find that he has to cut a thin string or skirting board over a rough wall string, or perhaps to fit in against a plastered wall where there has been no string left to show above the treads and risers. This is always a troublesome piece of work, and requires great care and exact workmanship to make anything like a good job.

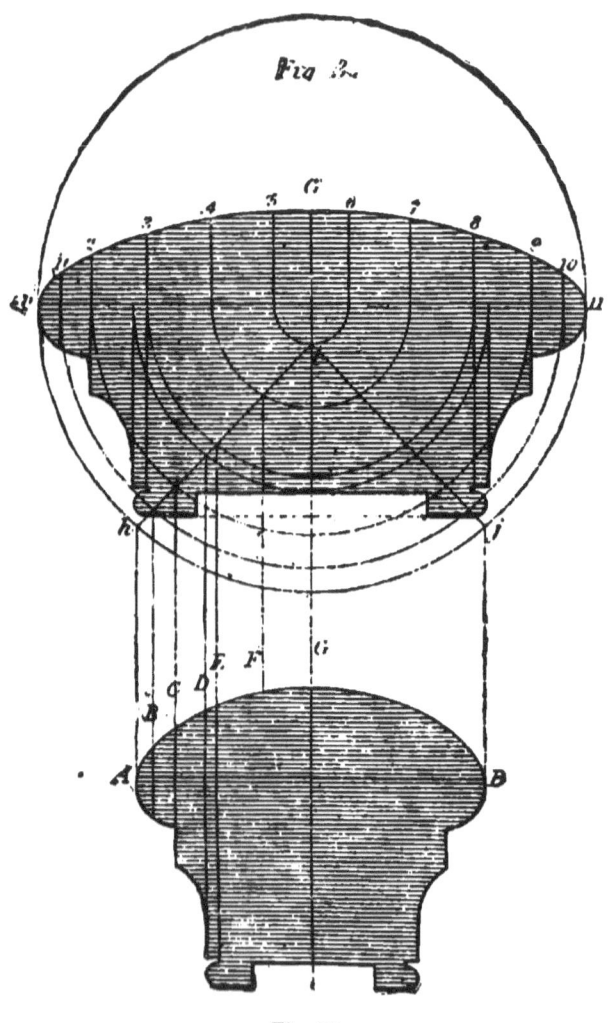

Fig. 93.

At Fig. 94, I show an instrument, in two positions, A and B, that has been especially designed for this purpose. In the cut is shown a bevel made to the rake of the skirting, and the other perpendicular to the stair, and a sliding piece to be applied to the perpendicular

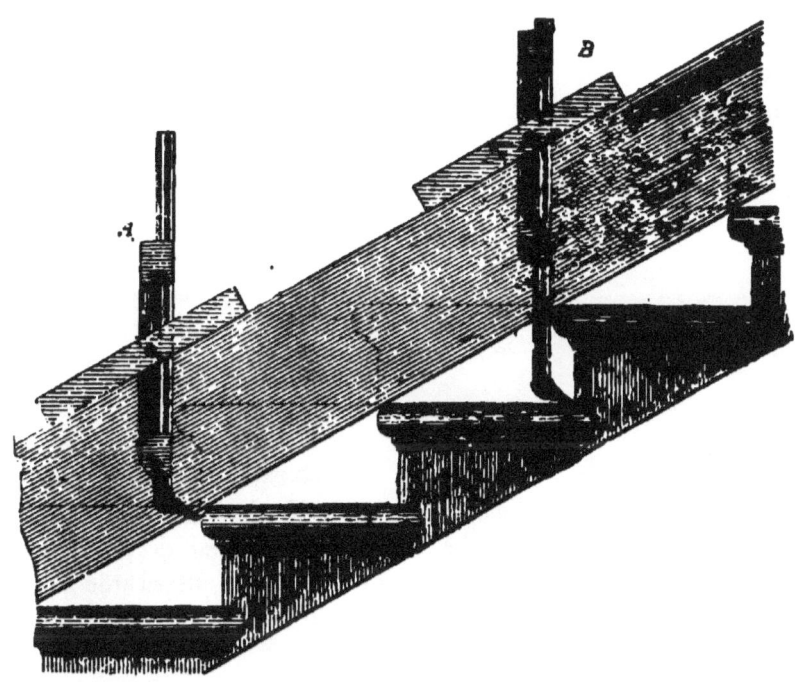

Fig. 94.

side of the bevel with a hooked point of iron or steel, to stand forward at the bottom so much that the sliding piece may clear the nosing of the step. I shall proceed to show its application. Lay the skirting over the top of the steps, as shown, and let a very fine notch be made on the front edge of your sliding piece to the height of a step or rather higher; then apply the point of the sliding piece to the internal corner of a step and prick your skirting in the notch, the bevel being supposed to be brought close to the slider; again, supposing you want to take a point at the nosing as at A, where you see the bevel applied under, apply the point of your sliding piece to the nosing at A; then prick your skirting in the notch, that will give the point which is to correspond, and by this means you may take as many pricks as will be sufficient until the whole is completed. Hence it is evident, that, by the same method, one thing may be correctly marked on another point, and by sliding the instrument up or down the edge of the skirting, each of the treads and risers may be lined out. To form the nosings complete, these "pricks" or points will be all that will be required, as these points will give the correct position to place the template or pattern against. If the nosings are all exact, let a mould be made to fit one of them, and your nosings on the skirtings be drawn by this mould, which will likewise be exact.

Fig. 95 shows the manner in which the instrument is made. Any joiner should be able to make one, as they are very simple, and their construction is obvious.

Fig. 95.

The foregoing illustration is taken from Newland's "Carpenters' and Joiners' Assistant," but the instrument was first described by Payne in 1786, and then by Langly in 1790, and afterwards illustrated and described by Peter Nicholson in 1812, so that it will be seen that the tool is a very old one.

At Fig. 96 I show a scheme for connecting a small cylinder to the strings, in order to make a good and strong joint. It will be noticed that the cylinder is notched out on the back, and the two blocks shown at the back of the offsets are wedges driven in to secure the cylinder in place, and to drive it up tight to the strings. This will be better shown at Fig. 97, where the dotted lines show the

Fig. 96.

position of the wedge. The scheme is so very clearly shown in the engravings that further description is unnecessary.

With respect to bending or glueing up stuff for sweep work, much judgment is necessary; and as the methods are various, I shall mention a few, that the workman may apply them as occasion requires, one method being preferable to another, according to the nature of the work on hand.

The first and most simple method is, that of sawing kerfs or notches on one side of the board, thereby giving it liberty to bend in that direction; but this method though very ready and useful for many purposes, is still very weak where any strain may be on the piece. Still, in this instance, we may in some measure make a tolerably strong sweep, if after sawing the kerfs, and being particular to make them regular and even, and sawing them at equal depths, we rub

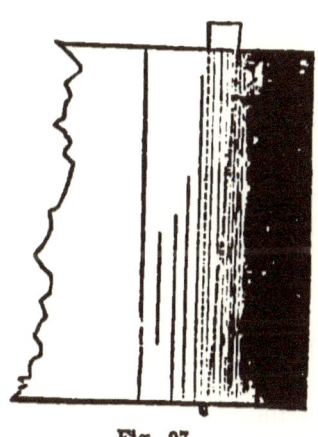

Fig. 97.

some strong glue into each kerf, then bend it to the required sweep, and glue a piece of strong canvas over the kerfs themselves, leaving the glue to harden in the position which we have bent our stuff to.

The next method is, that of glueing up our stuff in thin thicknesses, in a caul or mould made with two pieces of thick wood cut into the required sweep; and this method, if done with care—that is, making the several pieces of equal thickness throughout, and free from knots, is perhaps the best that can be devised for strength and accuracy. It is also a practice sometimes to glue up a sweep in three thicknesses, making the middle piece the contrary way of the grain to the outside and inside pieces, which run length-ways. This method, though frequently used for expedition, is much inferior to the above, as it does not allow the different pieces to shrink together, and consequently the joint between them is apt to give way. Again, in many instances, a solid piece, if not too thick, may be bent into the form required; if we soak well the outside of the curve with hot water, and hold the inside to the fire, when having formed the curve to your mind, you retain it in that position till cold and dry, it will retain the curvature given to it.

The last method I shall here mention is that of forming a curve by means of cutting out solid pieces to the required sweep, and glueing them upon one another till you have attained the thickness required, taking care the joints are alternately in the centre of each piece below it, something in the manner of a course of bricks above each other; in this case it will be necessary, if the work is not to be painted, to veneer the whole with a thin piece after the first has been thoroughly dry and and planed level, and also made somewhat rough with either a rasp or toothing plane.

By scribing is meant, generally, the method of making one piece of stuff fit against another when the joint is irregular; thus the plinth of a room is made to meet or correspond with the unevenness of the floor; in this manner, by opening your compasses to the greatest distance the plinth is from the floor where some parts touch it, and letting one leg run along upon the floor or uneven surface, the other leg will leave a mark on the plinth, which, if we cut away the stuff to that mark, it will then make a good joint with the floor; but the great use of scribing to the joiner is, that of joining moulding of panels or cornices that shall, when placed together, seem a regular mitre joint; and it has this advantage over the common method of mitering—that if the stuff should shrink, it will scarcely alter the appearance of it, whilst that of the mitre, under the same circumstances, causes a gap to show itself, and the joint to appear bad. The method is this: to cut one piece of the moulding to the required mitre, and then, instead of cutting the other to correspond to it, cut away the parts of the first piece, till we come to the edge of the moulding, which will then fit as the other moulding, and appear as a regular mitre.

It may sometimes happen that the stair-builder may wish to

order the rail from some factory; when such is the case, always send the following dimensions: Height of riser from top of one step to top of another; the exact number of risers from floor to floor; the width of step, without projecting nosing; the length of rail on levels, and where measured from. If the stairs have winding steps, make a diagram and figure exact width of each winder on the line of front string-piece and cylinder; also, width of cylinder, and whether the stairs turn to the right or left on the landings. Follow these directions closely, and there will be no trouble about getting the rail to fit properly when it is set up.

GLOSSARY.

Apron-piece.—*In carpentry*, a horizontal piece of timber in a wooden double-flighted stair supporting the carriage pieces and joistings in the half spaces of landings.

Arch.—A construction of bricks, wood, or stone, disposed in the form of a curve. There are several parts, as the keystone, which enters the top of the arch like a wedge, binding the work. Springers, the bottom stones which rest on the supports; and span, which is the distance across the arch.

Architecture.—The art or science of building; especially the art of constructing houses, bridges, and other buildings, for the purposes of civil life.

Architrave.—1. The lower division of an entablature, or that part which rests immediately on the column. 2. Also, the ornamental moulding around the exterior of an arch. 3. A moulding above a door or window, and the like. 4. This term is also applied to door and window casings.

Arris.—The edges formed by two surfaces meeting together, whether plain or curved. In stucco work, when two surfaces meet, as the corner of a beam or cornice, this term applies.

Arris Fillet.—A triangular piece of wood laid against a chimney or wall, to raise shingles or slates, to throw off the rain.

Astragal.—A small semicircular moulding, sometimes plain and sometimes ornamented.

Astragal.—1. A little round moulding, which surrounds the top or bottom of a column. 2. Also, often used in the capital of the Ionic column. And it is also used for various purposes in common work.

Axis.—*In architecture*, an imaginary line through the centre of a column, etc., or its geometrical representation: where different members are placed over each other, so that the same vertical line, on the elevation, divides them equally, they are said to be on the same axis, although they may be on different planes: thus, triglyphs and modillions are so arranged, that one coincides with the axis or line of axis of each column: in like manner, the windows or other openings in the several stories of a façade must all be in the same respective axis, whether they are all of the same breadth or not. *In geometry*, the straight line in a plane figure, about which it revolves to produce or generate a solid. *In mechanics*, the axis of a balance is the line upon which it moves or turns. *In turning*, an imaginary line passing longitudinally through the middle of the body to be turned, from one point to the other of the two cones, by which the work is suspended, or between the back centre and the centre of the collar of the puppet which supports the end of the mandril at the chuck.

Axis of a circle or sphere.—Any line drawn through the centre, and terminated at the circumference on both sides. *Of a cone*, the line from the vertex to the centre of the base. *Of a cylinder*, the line from the centre of the one end to that of the other. *In peritrochio*, a wheel and axle, one of the five mechanical powers, or simple machines; contrived chiefly for the raising of weights to a considerable height, as water from a well, etc. *Of rotation*, of any solid, the line about which the body really revolves when it is put in motion.

In every possible change of position of a rigid body relatively to a fixed centre, there is a line traversing that centre whose direction is not changed; that is the axis of rotation.

Back.—The side opposite to the face or breast of any piece of architecture. In a recess on a quadrangular plane, the face is that surface which has the two adjacent planes, called the sides, elbows, or gables. When a piece of timber is fixed in a horizontal or in an inclined position, the upper side is called the back, and the lower the breast. Thus the upper side of the hand-rail of a staircase is properly called the back. The same is to be understood with regard to the curved ribs of a ceiling and the rafters of a roof, whose story edges are always called the back.

Back.—When a piece of timber is placed in position, the upper side is called the back and the lower the breast.

Baluster.—A small column or pillar used in a balustrade. Balusters are generally placed round the gallery in the stern and the quarter gallery of large ships. (See pages 14, 46, 47, 84, 85; and Figs. 98–107).

Balustrade.—A series or row of balusters, joined by a rail, serving for a rest to the arms, or as a fence or enclosure to balconies, altars, staircases, etc. Balustrades, when intended for use, or against windows, on flights of steps, terraces, and the like, should not be more than three feet six inches, nor less than three feet in height. When used for ornament, as on the summit of a building, their height may be from two-thirds to four-fifths of the entablature whereon they are employed; and this proportion is to be taken exclusive of their zoccolo or plinth, so that from the proper point of sight the whole balustrade may be exposed to view. There are various species of balusters; if single bellied, the best way is to divide the total height of the space allotted for the balustrade into thirteen equal parts, the height of the baluster to be eight, of the base three, and of the cornice two of those parts; or divide the total height into fourteen parts, making the baluster eight, the base four, and the cornice two. If double-bellied, the height should be divided into fourteen parts, two of which are to be given to the cornice, three to the base, and the remainder to the baluster.

The distance between two balusters should not be more than half the diameter of the baluster in its thickest part, nor less than one-third of it; but on inclined planes the intervals should not be quite so wide.

Band.—A flat or square member or moulding, smaller than the facia.

Basement.—The lower part of a building.

Base Mouldings.—The mouldings immediately above the plinth of a wall, pillar or pedestal.

BALUSTERS.

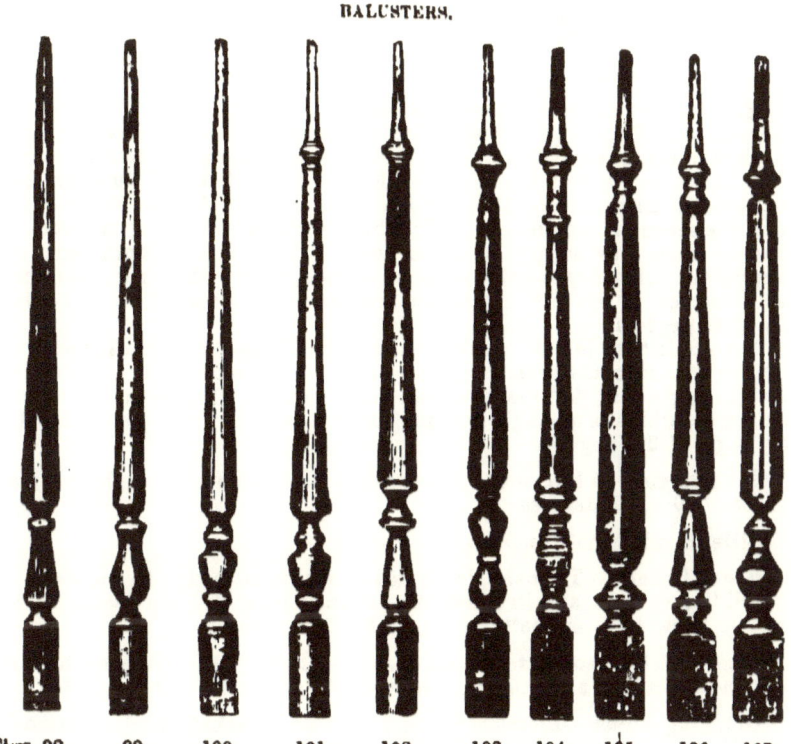

Figs. 98.   99.   100.   101.   102.   103. 104. 105. 106. 107.

Bearing of a piece of timber.—That part of a piece of timber which is unsupported, or is between two or more props.

Bearing.—The length between bearers or walls; thus, if a bearer rests on walls twenty feet apart, the bearing is said to be twenty feet.

Bearing Wall, or partition.—A wall which is built upon the solid, and made to support another wall or partition, either in the same or a transverse position. When the supported wall is built in the same direction as the wall it supports, it is said to have a solid bearing, but when built in a transverse direction, or not supported throughout its length, a false bearing.

Beak.—A small fillet in the under edge of a projecting cornice, intended to prevent the rain from passing between the cornice and fascia.

Belfry.—That part of a steeple in which the bells are hung.

Bell.—*Of the Corinthian and Composite Orders.* It is used to denote the body of the capital by reason of its shape to an inverted bell.

Bell-roof.—Somewhat similar in its curves to a bell.

Belt.—A course of stones projecting from a brick or stone wall, generally placed in a line with the sills of the first floor window, it is either moulded fluted, plane or enriched with patras at regular intervals. Sometimes called stone string.

Belvedere or Look out.—A turret or lantern raised above the roof of an observatory for the purpose of enjoying a fine prospect.

Benda.—*See Fuscia.*

Bevel.—An instrument used by artificers, one leg whereof is frequently curved according to the sweep of an arch or vault. It is movable upon a pivot or centre so as to render it capable of being set at any angle. The make and use of it are much the same as those of the common square and mitre, except that those are fixed, the first at an angle of 90° and the second at an angle of 45°; whereas the bevel being movable, it may in some way supply in some measure the office of both; and yet supply the deficiency of both, which is, indeed, its principal use, inasmuch as it serves to set off or transfer angles either greater or less than 95 or 45 degrees.

Any angle that is not square is called a *bevel angle*, whether it be more obtuse or more acute than a right angle, but if it be one-half as much as a right angle, viz., 45°, the workmen call it a *mitre*. They have also a term *half mitre*, which is an angle one-quarter of a quadrant or square, that is, an angle of 22½ degrees.

Bevel angle.—A term used by workmen to denote any angle besides those of 90 or 45 degrees.

Billet moulding.—*See Moulding.*

Bond-timbers.—Timbers placed in a horizontal direction in the walls of a building in tiers, and in which the battens, laths, etc., are secured. In rubble work, walls are better plugged for this purpose.

Bonds.—This general term includes the whole of the timbers that are disposed in a wall as bond-timbers, wall plates, lintels and templates.

Bridging-joists.—Pieces of timber, or joists in naked flooring, extending in a direction parallel with the girder and supported by bearers called binding joists which lie in a transverse direction.

Brackets in Gothic architecture are usually of very elegant design, and are mostly sculptured to represent angels, heads, foliage, and many other beautiful devices. They are used to support statues under niches, pillars which have their bases at a height above the ground, and for various other purposes.

Brackets for stairs are sometimes used under the ends of wooden steps, next to the well-hole, by way of ornaments, for they have only the appearance of support.—*Nicholson.* (See Figs. 26, 108, 109, 110, 111, 112, 113, 114 and 115).

Fig. 108.   Fig. 109.   Fig. 110.

Fig. 111.   Fig. 112.   Fig. 113.   Fig. 114.

Bracket-stairs.—The same method must be observed, with regard to taking the dimensions and laying down the plan and section, as in dog-ling-stairs. In all stairs whatever, after having ascertained the number of steps, take a rod the height of the story, from the surface of the lower floor to the surface of the upper floor; divide the rod into as many equal parts as there are to be risers; then if you have a level surface to work upon below the stairs, try each one of the risers as you go on: this will prevent any defect. (See Figs. 116 and 117).

Canting.—The cutting away a part of an angular body at one of its angles, that the section may form a parallelogram, whose edges are parallel from the intersection of the adjoining planes.

Carriage.—The timber work which supports the steps of a wooden stair. (See pages 43, 45, 54, 64, 65, 66, 67, 68, 69 and 71).

Cased.—A term which signifies that the outside of a building is faced or covered with materials of a better quality.

Cavetto.—A concave ornamental moulding, opposed in effect to the ovolo—the quadrant of a circle.

Chamfer.—To channel or make indentures in stones, pillars, or other ornamented parts of a building.

Chamfer.—The arris of anything originally right angled, cut aslope, or bevel, so that the plane it then forms is inclined less than a right angle to the other planes with which it intersects. If it is not carried the whole extent of the piece, it is returned, and then it is said to be stop chamfered. (See page 47).

Chase Mortise.—The mode of inserting or mortising inclined transverse joists into parallel timbers in ceilings.

Close String.—In dog-leg stairs, a stair-case without an open newel. (See pages 46 and 47).

Cockle Stairs.—A winding staircase.

Common.—A line, angle surface, etc., which belongs equally to several objects. Common centering is a centering without trusses, having a tie beam at bottom. Common joists are the beams in naked flooring to which the joists are fixed. Common rafters in a roof are those to which the laths are attached.

Cross-banded.—A term applied to a veneer on a hand-rail, the grain of which crosses that of the rail.

Cross-beam.—A large beam going from wall to wall, or a girder that holds the side of the house together.

Curtail step.—The first step by which a stair is ascended finishing at the end in a form of a scroll following the plan of the hand-rail.—*Nicholson.*

Fig. 116.   Fig. 115.

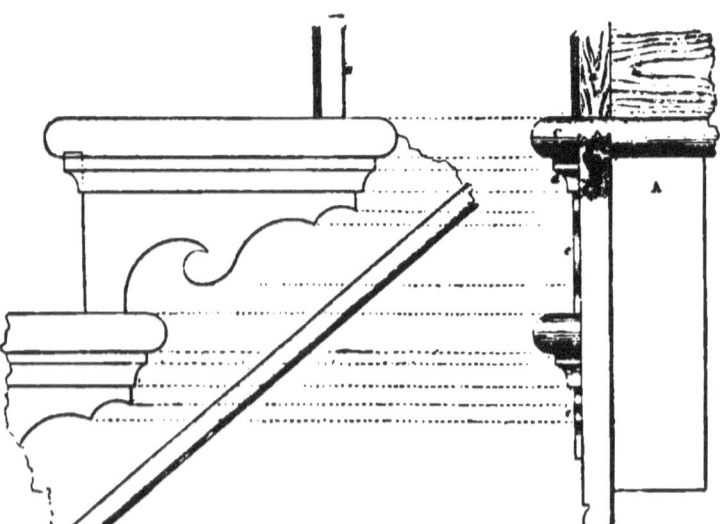

Fig. 117.

Cyma.—A moulding with an undulating or waved profile, partly convex and partly concave, called by workmen an ogee. When the hollow part is uppermost, it is called a cyma-recta; when the convex part is above, a cyma-reversa; when it is the upper moulding of a cornice it is called cymatium.

Cylinder.—A *cylinder* is a solid, described by geometricians as generated by the rotation of a rectangle about one of its sides, supposed to be at rest; this quiescent side is called the *axis* of the *cylinder*, therefore the base and top of the cylinder are equal or similar circles.

A *prism* is a solid, whose base and top are similar right line figures, with sides formed in planes, and rising perpendicularly from the base to the top.

The *cylinder*, so called by *joiners*, is a solid figure, compounded of the two last-mentioned figures; its base is composed of a *semicircle* joined to a *right-angled parallelogram*. This last compound figure is intended whenever the word *cylinder* occurs in the preceding work, unless the word *geometrical* be prefixed. (See pages 14, 63 and 98).

Definitions in Geometry.—1. A point is that which hath no parts, or which hath no magnitude.

2. A line is length without breadth.

3. A superficies has length and breadth.

4. A solid is a figure of three dimensions, having length, breadth, and thickness. Hence surfaces are extremities of solids, and lines the extremities of surfaces, and points the extremities of lines.

If two lines will always coincide however applied, when any two points in the one coincide with the two points in the other, the two lines are called straight lines, or otherwise right lines.

A curve continually changes its direction between its extreme points, or has no part straight.

Parallel lines are always at the same distance, and will never meet, though ever so far produced. Oblique right lines change their distance, and would meet, if produced.

One line is perpendicular to another when it inclines no more to one side than another.

A straight line is a tangent to a circle when it touches the circle without cutting, when both are produced.

An angle is the inclination of two lines towards one another in the same plane, meeting in a point.

Angles are either right, acute, or obtuse.

A right angle is that which is made by one line perpendicular to another, or when the angles on each side are equal.

An acute angle is less than a right angle.

An obtuse angle is greater than a right angle.

A plane is a surface with which a straight line will everywhere coincide; and is otherwise called a straight surface.

Plane figures, bounded by right lines, have names according to the number of their sides, or of their angles, for they have as many sides as angles: the least number is three.

An equilateral triangle is that whose three sides are equal.

An isosceles triangle has only two sides equal.

A scalene triangle has all sides unequal.

A right-angled triangle has only one right angle.

Other triangles are oblique-angled, and are either obtuse or acute.

An acute-angled triangle has all its angles acute.

An obtuse-angled triangle has one obtuse angle.

A figure of four sides, or angles, is called a quadrilateral or quadrangle.

A parallelogram is a quadrilateral, which has both pairs of its opposite sides parallel, and takes the following particular names:

A rectangle is a parallelogram, having all its angles right ones.

A square is an equilateral rectangle, having all its sides equal, and all its angles right angles.

A rhombus s an equilateral parallelogram whose angles are oblique.

A rhomboid is an oblique-angled parallelogram, and its opposite sides only are equal.

A trapezium is a quadrilateral, which has neither pair of its sides parallel.

A trapezoid has only one of its sides parallel.

Plane figures having more than four sides, are in general called polygons, and receive other particular names according to the number of their sides or angles.

A pentagon is a polygon of five sides, a hexagon of six sides, a heptagon seven, an octagon eight, an enneagon nine, a decagon ten, an undecagon eleven, and a dodecagon twelve sides.

A regular polygon has all its sides and its angles equal; and if they are not equal, the polygon is irregular.

An equilateral triangle is also a regular figure of three sides, and a square is one of four; the former being called a trigon, and the latter a tetragon.

A circle is a plane figure, bounded by a curve line, called the circumference, which is everywhere equidistant, from a certain point within, called its centre.

The radius of a circle is a right line drawn from the centre to the circumference.

A diameter of a circle is a right line drawn through the centre, terminating on both sides of the circumference.

An arc of a circle is any part of the circumference.

A chord is a right line joining the extremities of an arc.

A segment is any part of a circle bounded by an arc and its chord.

A semicircle is half a circle, or a segment cut off by the diameter.

A sector is any part of a circle bounded by an arc, and two radii drawn to its extremities.

A quadrant, or quarter of a circle, is a sector having a quarter part of the circumference for its arc, and the two radii perpendicular to each other.

The height or altitude of any figure is a perpendicular let fall from an angle or its vertex to the opposite side, called the base.

The measure of any right-lined angle is an arc of any circle contained between the two lines which form the angle, the angular point being the centre.

A solid is said to be cut by a plane when it is divided into two parts, of which the common surface of separation is a plane, and this plane is called a section.

Definitions of solids.—A prism is a solid, the ends of which are similar and equal parallel planes and the sides parallelograms.

If the ends of the prism are perpendicular to the sides, the prism is called a right prism.

If the ends of the prism are oblique to the sides, the prism is called an oblique prism.

If the ends and sides are equal squares, the prism is called a cube.

If the base or ends are parallelograms, the solid is called a parallelopiped.

If the bases and sides are rectangles, the prism is called a rectangular prism.

If the ends are circles, the prism is called a cylinder.

If the ends or bases are ellipses, the prism is called a cylindroid.

A solid, standing upon any plane figure for its base, the sides of which are plane triangles, meeting in one point, is called a pyramid.

The solid is denominated from its base, as a triangular pyramid is one upon a triangular base, a square pyramid one upon a square base, etc.

If the base is a circle or an ellipsis, then the pyramid is called a cone.

If a solid be terminated by two dissimilar parallel planes as ends, and the remaining surfaces joining the ends be also planes, the solid is called a prismoid.

If a part of a pyramid next to the vertex be cut off by a plane parallel to the base, the portion of the pyramid contained between the cutting plane and the base is called the frustum of a pyramid.

A solid, the base of which is a rectangle, the four sides joining the base plane surfaces, and two opposite ones meeting in a line parallel to the base, is called a cuneus or wedge.

A solid terminated by a surface which is everywhere equally distant from a certain point within it is called a sphere or globe.

If a sphere be cut by any two planes, the portion contained between the planes is called a zone, and each of the parts contained by a plane and the curved surface is called a segment.

If a semi-ellipsis, having an axis for its diameter, be revolved round this axis until it come to the place whence the motion began, the solid formed by the circumvolution is called a spheroid.

If the spheroid be generated round the greater axis, the solid is called a prolate spheroid.

If the solid be generated round the lesser axis, the solid is called an oblate spheroid.

A solid of any of the above structures, hollow within, so as to contain a solid of the same structure, is called a hollow solid.

These terms are frequently used in stair-building.

Dog-legged stairs.—Such as are solid between the upper flights, or those that have no well-hole; and the rail and balusters of both the progressive and retrogressive flight, fall in the same vertical plane. The steps are fixed to strings, newels, and carriages; and the ends of the steps of the inferior kind terminate *only* on the side of the string.—*Nicholson.* (See pages 43 and 45).

Dove-tailing.—The method of fastening one piece of wood to another, by projecting pins, cut in the form of dove-tails in one piece, and let into hollows of the same form in the other. Dove-tailing is either exposed or concealed; concealed dove-tailing is of two kinds, lapped and mitered.

Draught, or Drawing.—Architectural composition or design, is understood to be a necessary mode of conveying instructions to the practical builder and the workmen, by exhibiting a comprehensive view of a projected building; drawings for this purpose must be executed with clearness and precision, conformable to a regular scale of proportions. Plans, elevations, and sections are to represent the internal features of the apartments, halls, passages, and various arrangements for ornament or convenience, and the external façades, porticos, domes, and other outward appendages. Drawings of the smaller parts of an edifice will be required numerous in proportion to their extent and variety of form. Where the façades of a building differ considerably, elevations of each of them will be required, and more than one general view of the projected building will be necessary to give satisfaction to the proprietor.

Ellipse.—That curve called by workmen an oval.

Face Mould.—The pattern for marking the plank or board out of which ornamental hand-railings for stairs and other works are cut.

Face Mould.—In the preparation of the hand-rail of a stair, a mould for drawing the proper figure on both sides of the plank; so that when cut by a saw held at a certain inclination, the two surfaces of the rail piece will be everywhere perpendicular to the plan, when laid in their intended position.—*Nicholson.*

Fascia.—A flat broad member in the entablature of columns or other parts of buildings but of small projection. The architraves in some of the orders, are composed of three bands or fascia; the Tuscan and the Doric ought to have only one. Ornamental projections from the walls of brick buildings over any of the windows, except the uppermost are called *fascia.*

Feather-edged Boards, are narrow boards made thin at one edge, like shingles or some kinds of clapboarding.

Fox-tail wedging, is a peculiar mode of mortising, in which the end of the tenon is notched beyond the mortise and is split, and a wedge inserted which being forcibly driven in, enlarges the tenon and renders the joint firm and immovable.

Flight of stairs.—In a staircase is the series of steps from one landing place to another. Thus the same staircase between one floor and another may consist of more than one flight of steps; the flight being reckoned from one landing to another.

Floor.—The pavement or boarded lower horizontal surface of an apartment. It is constructed of earth, brick, stone, wood, or other materials. Carpenters include in the term the frame timber work on which the boarding is laid, as well as the boards themselves. In carpentry, it denotes the timbers which support the boarding, called also *naked flooring* and *carcass flooring.*

The term floor is, moreover, applied to the stories of a building, as *basement floor, ground floor,* etc. When there is no sunk story, the ground story becomes the basement floor, and the next floor the principal floor, containing the principal rooms; in many country houses they are on the ground floor, but in those of the town mostly on the one pair floor. The expressions one pair, two pair, etc., imply a story above the first flight of stairs from the ground, and so on.

Frame.—The name given to the woodwork of windows, doors, etc.; and in carpentry, to the timber works, supporting floors, roofs, etc.

Furring.—The furring of those scantlings or laths upon the edges of any number of timbers in a range, when such timbers are out of the surface they were intended to form, either from their gravity, or in consequence of an original deficiency of the timbers in their depth. Thus the timbers of a floor, though level at first, oftentimes require to be furred; the same operation is frequently necessary in the reparation of old roofs, and the same work is required sometimes in new as well as old floors.—*Papworth.*

Geometrical Stair.—A flight of stairs, supported only by the wall at one end of the steps.

Geometrical Elevation.—A drawing of the front or side of a building, the projection of a vertical plane of the front or side of a building or other object.

Ground-joists, are joists supporting the floor immediately above the ground.

Ground floor.—The lowest story of a building.

Half-space, or resting place. The interval between two flights of steps in a staircase.

Hall.—The first large apartment on entering a house. The public room of a corporative body. A manor-house.

Hall.—A name applied indifferently to the same large apartment on entering a house, to the public room of a corporative body; a court of justice or a manor-house.

Vitruvius mentions three sorts of halls; the Tetrastyle, which has four columns supporting the ceiling; the Corinthian, which has columns all around, and is vaulted; and the Egyptian, which has a peristyle of Corinthian columns, bearing a second order with a ceiling. These were called *œci.* In magnificent edifices, where the hall is larger and loftier than ordinary, and is placed in the middle of the house, it is called a saloon; and a royal apartment consists of a hall or chamber of guards, a chamber, an antechamber, a cabinet chamber, and a gallery.

Halving.—The junction of two pieces of timber, by inserting one into the other.

Hand-rail, of a stair, a rail raised upon slender posts, called *balusters,* intended to assist persons in ascending and descending, and to protect them from falling down the well-hole. (See sections at Figs. 118, 119, 120, 121, 122 and 123).

Fig. 118.   Fig. 119.

Hollow-newel.—An opening in the middle of the staircase. The term is used in contradistinction to *solid newel,* into which the ends of the steps are built. In the hollow newel, or well-hole, the steps are only supported at one end by the surrounding wall of the staircase, the ends next the hollow being unsupported.—*Nicholson.*

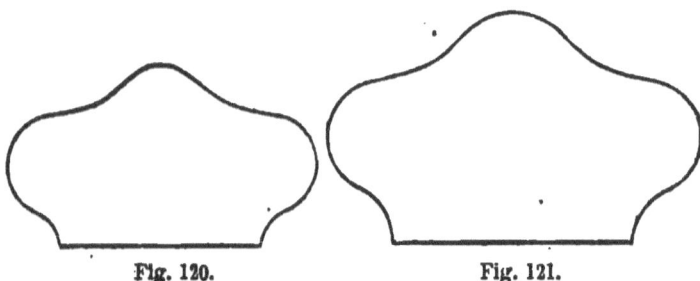

Fig. 120.   Fig. 121.

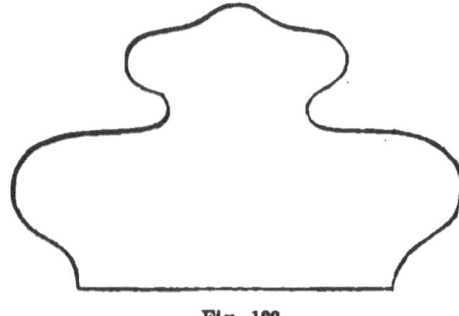

Fig. 122.

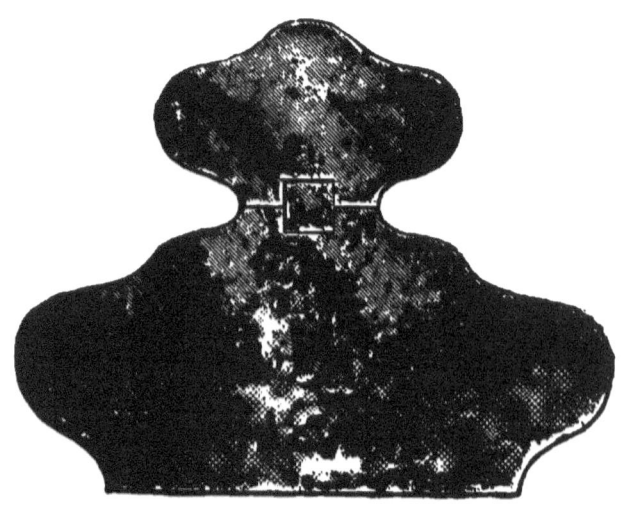

Fig. 123.

Housing.—The space excavated out of a body, for the insertion of some part of the extremity of another, in order to fasten the two together: thus the string-board of a stair is most frequently excavated, or notched out for the reception of steps. The term is also applied to a niche for containing a statue.—*Nicholson.*

Joinery.—That branch in building confined to the nicer and more ornamental parts of carpentry.

Joinery.—The practice of framing or joining wood for the internal and external finishings of houses; thus the covering and lining of rough walls, the covering of rough timbers, the manufacture of doors, shutters, sashes, stairs, and the like are classed under this head.

Joint.—The surface of separation between two bodies brought into contact and held firmly together, either by some cementing medium, or by the weight of one body lying upon another. A joint is not merely the contact of two surfaces, though the nearer they approach the more perfect the joint. In masonry, the distances of the planes intended to form the joint is comparatively considerable because of the coarseness of the particles which enter into the composition of the cement.

Joists.—The timbers to which the boards of a floor or the laths of a ceiling are nailed.

Kerf.—A slit or cut in a piece of timber or in a stone, usually applied to that made by a saw or axe.

Keys.—In naked flooring are pieces of timber fixed in between the joists by mortise and tenon; when these are fastened with their ends projecting against sides, they are termed strutting pieces.

Keys.—Pieces inserted in boards to prevent warping.

Knee.—A convex bend in the back of a hand-rail.

Knee.—A part of the back of a hand-railing of a convex form, the reverse of a *ramp*, which is a back of a hand-rail and is concave; also, any piece of timber bent to an angular joint.

Landing.—The terminating floor of a flight of stairs, either above or below.—*Papworth.*

Members.—The different parts of a building, the different parts of an entablature, the different mouldings of a cornice, etc.

Mortise.—*In carpentry*, a hole cut in a piece of wood, to receive a corresponding projection formed upon another piece.

The labor of making deep mortises, in hard wood, may be lessened, by first boring a number of holes with the auger in the part to be mortised, as the compartments between may then more easily be cut away by the chisel.

Before employing the saw to cut the shoulder of a tenon in neat work, if the line of its entrance be correctly determined by nicking the place with a paring chisel, there will be no danger of the wood being torn at the edges by the saw.

As the neatness and durability of a juncture depend entirely on the sides of the mortise coming exactly in contact with the sides of the tenon, and as this is not easily performed when a mortise is to pass entirely through a piece of stuff, the space allotted for it should be first correctly ganged on both sides. One half is then to be cut from one side, and the other half from the opposite side; and as any irregularities which may arise from an error in the direction of the chisel will thus be cou-fined to the middle of the mortise, they will be of very little hindrance to the exact fitting of the sides of the mortise and tenon. Moreover, as the tenon is expanded by wedges after it is driven in, the sides of the mortise may, in a small degree, be inclined towards each other, near the shoulders of the tenon.

Mouldings.—A term applied to all the varieties of outline or contour given to the angles of the various subordinate parts and features of buildings, whether projections or cavities, such as cornices, capitals, bases, door or window jambs, and heads, etc. There are eight sorts of regular mouldings, viz., the Ovolo, the Talon, the Cyma, the Cavetto, the Torus, the Astragal, the Scotia, and the Fillet.

Nails, used in building, are small metallic spikes serving to bind or fasten the parts together. There are several kinds of nails, called by numerous names. In the middle ages, nails were frequently used much ornamented, of which there are several very beautiful existing specimens, particularly in church doors and the gates of large mansions.

Naked.—This term is applied, in architecture, to a plain surface, or that which is unfinished; as the naked walls, the naked flooring, that is, uncovered; the word is sometimes applied to flat surfaces before the mouldings and other ornaments have been fixed.

Newel.—In architecture, the upright post or central column, round which the steps of a circular staircase are made to wind; being that part of the staircase by which they are sustained.

The newel is, properly, a cylinder of stone which bears on the ground, and is formed by the ends of the steps of the winding-stairs.

There are also newels of wood, which are pieces of wood placed perpendicularly, receiving the tenons of the steps of wooden stairs into their mortises, and wherein are fitted the shafts and rests of the staircase, and the flight of each story. In some of the Tudor and Elizabethan residences, some very fine examples may be seen of the newel richly ornamented, and adding much to the beauty of the staircase.—*Nicholson.*

Newel.—The central column round which the steps of a circular staircase wind; the principal post at the angles and foot of a staircase. In the Tudor and Elizabethian residences very beautiful examples exist, adding much to the beauty of the staircase.

Pedestal.—The square support of a column, statue, etc.; and the base or lower part of an order of columns: it consists of a plinth for a base; the die; and a talon crowned for a cornice. When the height and width are equal, it is termed a square pedestal; one which supports two columns, a double pedestal; and if it supports a row of columns without any break, it is a *continued pedestal.* The lowest and most simple kind of pedestal is the Tuscan, which is about three modules in height by one authority, and five by another.

Pitching-piece.—A horizontal timber, with one of its ends wedged into the wall at the top of a flight of stairs, to support the upper end of the rough strings.

Plan.—The draught of a building taken on the ground floor, showing the distribution, form and extent of its several rooms, passages, etc. In *plans of buildings,* the massive parts, as walls, etc., are generally distinguished by a dark shade, or shade of tints approaching the color of brick or stone. In a *geometrical plan,* the parts are represented in their natural proportions. *The raised plan* of a building is the elevation.

Plancere.—The underpart of the roof of a corona, which is the superior part of the cornice between two cymatia.

Platband.—Any square moulding with little projection; the fascia of an architrave; the list between the flutings, etc.

Platform.—A row of beams which support the timber work of a roof, lying at the top of a wall; a terrace or open walk on the top of a building.

Plinth.—The solid support or base of a column, or pedestal. In a wall, the term *plinth* is applied to two or three rows of bricks which project from it to any flat moulding in a front wall, to make the floors sustain the eaves, or the larmier of a chimney.

Plug and Feather.—A mode of dividing large stone by means of a large tapering wedge, or key, and wedged-shaped pieces of iron, called feathers, driven into holes, previously drilled, into the rock to forcibly split it.

Ramp.—A concave bend in the back of a hand-rail.

Recess.—A cavity in a wall, left either for ornament or use when it is to receive some furniture, as a sideboard, or to add to the quantity of room; and for ornament when made in the form of a niche, to give beauty and variety to the building.

Sagging.—The bending of a body in the middle by its own weight.

Scantling.—The measure to which a piece of timber is to be or has been cut.

Scantling.—The dimensions of a piece of timber in breadth and thickness; also, quarterings for a partition, when under five inches square, also applied to stone in a cubical form.

Scarfing.—The joining of two pieces of timber by bolting or nailing transversely together, so that the two appear but one.

Scarfing.—The joining and bolting of two pieces of timber together transversely, so that the two appear as one.

Scenography.—The representation of solids in perspective.

Scotia.—The hollow moulding in the base of a column, between the fillets of the tori.

Scotia.—A semi-circular concave moulding in the bases of Ionic columns. Also, the groove or channel cut in the projecting angle of the Doric corona.

Scroll.—A carved curvilinear ornament, somewhat resembling in profile the turnings of a ram's horus.—*Hatfield.*

Skeleton.—*In carpentry,* a shell or framing. *In surveying,* the outline of a trigonometrical survey. *In artillery,* a light shell for projecting combustibles. *In cotton-spinning,* a kind of case frame. *A skeleton key,* a key constructed to fit almost any set of wards in a lock.

Sliding rule.—A rule constructed with logarithmic lines, formed upon a slip of wood, brass or ivory, inserted in a groove, in a rule made to slide longitudinally therein, so that by means of another scale upon the rule itself the contents of a surface or solid may be known.

Soffit.—*In architecture,* the internal concave surface of the arch. Any timber ceiling formed of cross-beams or flying cornices, the square compartments or panels of which are enriched with sculpture, painting, or gilding.

Solids are all bodies that have three dimensions; and among geometricians those that are terminated by regular planes are called regular solids, such as the tetrahedron, hexahedron, octahedron, dodecahedron, and icosahedron.

Spandril.—The angle formed by a stairway.

Spandril bracketing.—A cradling of brackets fixed between one or more curves, each in a vertical plane, and in the circumference of a circle whose plane is horizontal.

Spherical bracketing.—Brackets of such a form that the surface of lath and plaster will form a spherical surface.

Spiral.—A curve line of a circular kind which in its progress recedes from its centre.

Spiral.—*In geometry*, a curve-line of the circular kind, which in its progress always recedes more and more from its centre. *In architecture*, a curve that ascends winding about a cone or spire, so that all its points continually approach its axis.

Spirit-level.—A cylindrical glass tube, filled with spirit of wine, except a small bubble of air. In whatever position the tube may be placed, the bubble of air will always tend to the highest part of it; but when placed in a perfectly horizontal position, the bubble will remain stationary at the centre of the tube.

Splay.—A slanting or bevelling in the sides of an opening to a wall for a window or door, so that the outside profile of the window is larger than that of the inside; it is done for the purpose of facilitating the admission of light. It is a term applied to whatever has one side making an oblique angle with the other: thus, the heading joists of a boarded floor are frequently splayed in their thickness. The word *fluing* is sometimes applied to an aperture, in the same sense as *splayed*.

Spring Bevel of a Rail.—The angle made by the top of the plank, with a vertical plane touching the ends of the rail piece, which terminates the concave side.

Squaring a Hand-rail.—The method of cutting a plank to the form of a rail for a staircase, so that all the vertical sections may be right angles.

Stairs, (from the Saxon stæger) in a building, the steps whereby to ascend and descend from one story to another.

The breadth of the steps of stairs in general use in common dwelling-houses, is from 9 to 12 inches, or about 10 inches medium. In the best staircases of noblemen's houses, or public edifices, the breadth ought never to be less than 12 inches, nor more than 18. It is a general maxim, that the greater breadth of a step requires less height than one of less breadth; thus, a step of 12 inches in breadth will require a rise of 12½ inches, which may be taken as a standard by which to regulate those of other dimensions; so that multiplying 12 inches by 5½, we shall have 66; then supposing a step to be 10 inches in breadth, the height should be 66 ÷ 10 = 6 3-5 inches, which is nearly, if not exactly, what common practice would allow. The proportion of steps being thus regulated, the next consideration is the number requisite between two floors or stories which will be ascertained by supposing the breadth of the steps given, say 10 inches each, as depending on the space allowed for the staircase, and this, according to the rule laid down, will require a rise of 7 inches nearly; suppose, then, the distance from floor to floor to be 13 feet

4 inches, or 160 inches, $160 \div 7 = 22$ 3-7, which would be the number required, but as all the steps must be of equal heights, we should rather take 23 risers, provided the staircase room would allow it, and so make the height of each somewhat less than 7 inches.

The most certain method of erecting a staircase is, to provide a rod of sufficient length to reach from one floor to another, divided into as many equal parts as the intended number of risers, and try every step as it is set, to its exact height. The breadth of the staircase may be from 6 to 20 feet, according to the use or application of the building, or the form or proportions of the plan.

If the steps be less than 3 feet in length, the staircase becomes inconvenient for the passing of furniture, as is frequently the case in small houses.

Though it is desirable to have such rules as are here laid down for regulating the proportions of the heights, breadths, and lengths, of steps, architects and workmen cannot be so strictly tied to them, but that they may vary them as circumstances may demand.—*Nicholson.*

Stairs are constructions composed of horizontal planes elevated above each other, forming steps; affording the means of communication between the different stories of a building.

In the distribution of a house of several stories, the stairs occupy an important place. In new constructions their form may be regular, but in the reparation or remodelling of old buildings, the first consideration is generally to make the distribution suitable for the living and lodging rooms, and then to convert to the use of the stairs the spaces which may remain; giving to them such forms in plan as will render them agreeable to the sight, and commodious in the use.

When houses began to be built in stories, the stairs were placed from story to story in straight flights like ladders. They were erected on the exterior of the building, and to shelter them when so placed, great projection was given to the roofs. To save the extent of space required by straight flights, the stairs were made to turn upon themselves in a spiral form, and were inclosed in turrets. A newel, either square or round, reaching from the ground to the roof, served to support the inner ends of the steps, and the outer ends were let into the walls, or supported on notched boards attached to the walls.

At a later period the stairs came to be inclosed within the building itself, and for a long time preserved the spiral form, which the former situation had necessitated.

DEFINITIONS.—The apartment in which the stair is placed, is called the *staircase.*

The horizontal part of a step is called the *tread*, the vertical part the *riser*, the breadth or distance from riser to riser the *going*, the distance from the first to the last riser in a flight the *going of the flight.*

When the risers are parallel with each other, the stairs are of course *straight.*

When the steps are narrower at one end than the other, they are termed *winders.*

When the bottom step has a circular end, it is called a *round-ended step;* when the end is formed into a spiral, it is called a *curtail step.*

The wide step introduced as a resting-place in the ascent is *a landing*, and the top of a stair is also so called.

When the landing at a resting place is square, it is designated a *quarter space.*

When the landing occupies the whole width of the staircase it is called a *half space*.

So much of a stair as is included between two landings is called a *flight*, especially if the risers are parallel with each other: the steps in this case are *fliers*.

The outward edge of a step is named the *nosing*; if it project beyond the riser, so as to receive a hollow moulding glued under it, it is a *moulded nosing*.

A straight-edge laid on the nosings represents the angle of the stairs, and is denominated the *line of nosings*.

The raking pieces which support the ends of the steps are called *strings*. The inner one, placed against the wall, is the *wall string*; the other the *outer string*. If the outer string be cut to mitre with the end of the riser, it is a *cut and mitered string*; but when the strings are grooved to receive the ends of the treads and risers, they are said to be *housed*, and the grooves are termed *housings*.

Stairs in which the outer string of the upper flight stands perpendicularly over that of the lower flight are called *dog-legged stairs*, otherwise *newel stairs*, from the fact of a piece of stuff called a *newel*, being used as the axis of the spiral of the stair; the newel is generally ornamented by turning, or in some other way. The outer strings in such stairs are tenoned into the newel, as also are the first and last risers of the flight.—*Newland*.

Staircase.—A term applied to the whole set of stairs, with the walls, supporting the steps, leading from one story to another. The same staircase frequently conducts to the top of the building, and thus consists of as many stories as the building itself.

When the height of the story is considerable, resting places become necessary, which go under the name of *quarter-paces* and *half-paces*, according as the passenger has to pass a right angle, or two right angles; that is, as he has to describe a quadrant or a semi-circle. In very high stories that admit of sufficient head-room, and where the space allowed for the staircase is confined, the staircase may have two revolutions in the height of one story, which will lessen the height of the steps; but in grand staircases, only one revolution can be admitted, the length and breadth of the space on the plan being always proportioned to the height of the building, so as to admit of fixed proportions.

In contriving a grand edifice, particular attention must be paid to the situation of the space occupied by the stairs, so as to give them the most easy command of the rooms.

With regard to the lighting of a grand staircase, a skylight or rather lantern, is the most appropriate; for the light thus admitted, is powerful, and the design admits of greater elegance; indeed, where the staircase does not adjoin the exterior walls, this is the only method by which light can be admitted.

In small buildings, the position of the staircase is indicated by the general distribution of the plan; but in large edifices, this is not so obvious, but must at last be determined by considering naturally its connection with other apartments.—*Nicholson*.

Staircases.—It was in the reign of Elizabeth that staircases first became features in English houses. Hand-rails and balustrades, unlike the rickety contrivances of modern days, were of gigantic proportions, and presented at once a bold, picturesque, and secure appearance; yet so variously and fancifully decorated, that their effect was always pleasing and free from clumsiness. In the middle of Verulam House was a delicate staircase of wood, which was curiously carved; and on the posts of every interstice was fixed some figure, as a grave divine with his book and spectacles, a mendicant friar, etc. In two of the principal chambers of Wressil Castle are small beautiful staircases, with octagon screens, embattled at the top, and covered with very bold sculpture, containing double flights of stairs, winding round each other, after the design of Palladio. The east stairs at Wimbledon House lead from the marble parlor to the great gallery and the dining-room, and are richly adorned with wainscot of oak round the outsides thereof, all well gilt with fillets and stars of gold. The steps of these stairs were in number 33, and 6 feet 6 inches long, adorned with 5-foot paces, all varnished black and white, and chequer-work; the highest of which foot-pace is a very large one, and benched with a wainscot bench, all garnished with gold.

Staircases, in ordinary modern practice, should be light, spacious, and easy, seeming to invite people to ascend. Principal staircases should not be narrower than 4 feet, so that if two persons meet thereon, they may pass each other with convenience; but they may be extended in breadth to 10 or 12 feet, according to the importance of the building. The steps should never exceed 6 inches in height, nor be less than 4 inches; but this latter height is only allowable in very wide staircases. The breadth, or the flat horizontal part, which is called the tread of the step, should not be less than a foot, nor exceed 15 inches.—*Weale.*

Staves.—*In joinery,* the boards that are joined together laterally, in order to form a hollow cylinder, cylindroid, cone, or conoid, or any frustum of these bodies. The shafts of columns, in joinery, are frequently glued up in staves.

Steps, (from the Saxon, stæp), the degrees of a staircase, by which we rise, consisting of two parts, one horizontal, called *treads,* the other vertical called *risers.* When steps are placed round the circumference of a circle, or an ellipsis, or any segments of them, they are called *winders;* but when the sides are straight, they are called *flyers.* The first or lower step, with a scroll wrought upon its end, according to the plan of the hand-rail is called *the curtail step.*

Stretched out.—A term applied to a surface that will just cover a body so extended that all its parts are in a plane, or may be made to coincide with a plane.

Striking.—A term used to denote the draught of lines on the surface of a body; the term is also used to denote the drawing of lines on the face of a piece of stuff for mortises, and cutting the shoulders of tenons. Another application of the word occurs in the practice of joinery, to denote the act of running a moulding with a plane. The *striking of a centre* is the removal of the timber framing upon which an arch is built, after its completion.

String or String Piece.—That part of a flight of stairs which forms its ceiling or sofite. *See Carriage.*

String Board.—In wooden stairs, the board next the well-hole which receives the ends of the steps; its face follows the direction of the well-hole, whatever the form: when curved, it is frequently formed in thicknesses glued together, though sometimes it is got out of the solid, like a hand-rail.

String-board.—In wooden stairs, a board placed next to the well-hole, and terminating the ends of the steps. The face of string-boards follows the direction of the well-hole, whether it be prismatic or an in-verted cone. String-boards are sometimes glued in several thicknesses, with the fibres of the wood running in the direction of the steps; some-times they are wrought out of solid, like a hand-rail, the grain of the wood being in the same direction; and they are also glued up like columns, viz., having the fibres vertical. Brackets are most frequently placed upon the string-boards, and mitered into the risers.—*Nicholson.*

Tangent.—*In geometry,* a right line perpendicularly raised on the ex-tremity of a radius, which touches a circle so that it would never cut it, although infinitely produced, or, in other words, it would never come within its circumference.

Templet.—A mould used in masonry and brickwork, for the purpose of cutting or setting the work. When great nicety is required, two temp-lets should be used, one for moulding the end of the work, and its re-verse for trying the face. Where many stones or bricks are required to be done with the same mould, the templets ought to be be made of copper.—*Nicholson.*

Tenon.—*In carpentry,* the square end of a piece of wood or metal di-minished to one-third of its thickness, to be received into a hole in an-other piece, called the mortise, for the joining or fastening of the two together.

Tread of the step of a stair.—The horizontal part of the step.

Trimmed.—When a piece of work is fitted between two others pre-viously executed, it is said to be *trimmed in* between them; thus, a parti-tion wall is said to be trimmed up between the floor and the ceiling; a post between two beams, a trimmer between joists, etc.—*Nicholson.*

Trimmed, is also applied to the putting of anything into shape, by cutting it away by degrees until it be of the proposed form.—*Nicholson.*

Trimmed-out.—An expression applied to the trimmers of stairs, when brought forward to receive the rough strings.

Trimmer.—A small beam into which the ends of several joists are framed. Beams of this kind are either stair-trimmers, hearth-trimmers, or tail-trimmers.—*Nicholson.*

Trimming Joists.—The two joists into which each end of the trimmer is framed.

The distance of the trimming-joists, when employed in fire-places, must be such as to take in not only the fire-place, but the flues on each side of it. Trimming-joists ought to be stronger than the other joists, on account of the support they have to give.—*Nicholson.*

Veneer.—A very thin leaf of wood, of a superior quality, for covering doors or articles of furniture, made of an inferior wood.—*Nicholson.*

Vestibule.—The place before the entrance to Roman houses; it was surrounded by a wall. In modern houses the small ante-room which leads from the outside to the principal hall.

Vitruvian Scroll.—A peculiar pattern, consisting of convolved undu-lations, used in classical architecture.

Volute.—The characteristic ornaments and judicial marks of the Ionic capital formed by circumvolving spiral mouldings are termed volutes. The small circle in which the spiral or springs terminate is called the eye of the volute. The introduction of volutes is said by Vitruvius to have arisen from an imitation of the mode in which women were formerly accustomed to ornament their hair; but they are thought, with greater probability, to have represented the horns of the Ammonian Jupiter.

Wedge.—The wedge is a solid piece of wood or metal, generally made in the form of a triangle prism, of which the two ends or bases are equal and similar plane triangles and the three sides rectangular parallelograms: and it is called rectangular, isosceles, or scalene, according as its equal and similar bases are composed of right-angled, isosceles, or scalene triangles. As a mechanical power, the wedge performs its office, sometimes in raising heavy bodies, but more frequently in dividing or cleaving them; hence all those instruments which are used in separating the parts of bodies, such as axes, adzes, knives, swords, coulters, chisels, planes, saws, files, nails, spades, etc., are only different modifications that fall under the general denomination of the wedge.

Wedging.—The insertion of triangular prisms into the end of a tenon, to make it fill the mortise so completely as to prevent its being withdrawn.

Well.—The place occupied by the flight of stairs. The space left beyond the ends of the steps is called the well-hole.

Well-Staircase.—A winding staircase of ascent, or descent, to different parts of a building, so called from the walls enclosing it resembling a well; called frequently a geometrical staircase.

Winders.—Stairs, steps not parallel to each other.

The winders are supported by rough pieces called *bearers*, wedged into the wall, and secured to the strings.

When the front string is ornamented with brackets, it is called a *bracketed stair*.

DESCRIPTIVE CATALOGUE

OF

Practical Books

AND

PERIODICALS,

PUBLISHED AND FOR SALE BY

THE INDUSTRIAL PUBLICATION CO.

"KNOWLEDGE IS POWER."

☞ Any of these Books may be obtained from any Bookseller or Newsdealer, or will be sent free by mail to any part of the United States or Canada ON RECEIPT OF PRICE.

Remittances should be made in Bank Drafts, Postal Orders, or Registered letters. Fractional parts of a dollar may be sent in postage stamps of small denominations, but we will not receive postage stamps to the amount of $1.00 or over. Postage stamps of large denominations, and Canadian postage stamps are of no use to us. Canadian currency and British postage stamps will be received in any quantity, *but only from foreign correspondents.*

New Editions of this catalogue, containing descriptions of New Books, are issued from time to time, and will be sent free to any address on application. Address all orders to

INDUSTRIAL PUBLICATION CO.,

294 Broadway, New York.

TWO NEW BOOKS.

STAIR-BUILDING MADE EASY.

BEING A FULL AND CLEAR DESCRIPTION OF THE

ART OF BUILDING THE BODIES, CARRIAGES, AND CASES FOR ALL KINDS OF STAIRS AND STEPS.

Together with Illustrations showing the Manner of Laying Out Stairs, Forming Treads and Risers, Building Cylinders, Preparing Strings,

With Instructions for Making Carriages for Common, Platform, Dog-Legged, and Winding Stairs.

To which is added an Illustrated Glossary of Terms used in Stair-Building, and Designs for Newels, Balusters, Brackets, Stair-Mouldings, and Sections of Hand-Rails.

* ◆ *

By FRED. T. HODGSON.

* ◆ *

☞ This work takes hold at the very beginning of the subject, and carries the student along by easy stages, until the entire subject of Stair-Building has been unfolded, so far as ordinary practice can ever require. This book, and the one on HAND-RAILING, described below, cover nearly the whole subject of STAIR-BUILDING.

A NEW SYSTEM OF

HAND-RAILING,

Or, How to Cut Hand-Railing for Circular and other Stairs, Square from the Plank, without the aid of a Falling Mould.

THE SYSTEM IS NEW, NOVEL, ECONOMIC, AND EASILY LEARNED.

Rules, Instructions, and Working Drawings for Building Rails for Seven Different Kinds of Stairs are given.

* ◆ *

BY AN OLD STAIR-BUILDER.

* ◆ *

Edited and Corrected by FRED. T. HODGSON.

The Steel Square

AND ITS USES.

By FRED. T. HODGSON.

This is the only work on THE STEEL SQUARE AND ITS USES ever published. It is Thorough, Exhaustive, Clear, and Easily Understood. Confounding terms and scientific phrases have been religiously avoided where possible, and everything in the book has been made so plain that a boy twelve years of age, possessing ordinary intelligence, can understand it from end to end.

The New Edition is Illustrated with over Seventy-five Wood-cuts, showing how the Square may be used for solving almost every problem in the whole Art of Carpentry.

The following synopsis of the contents of the work will give some idea of its character and scope.

—History of the "Square."—Description, with Explanations of the Rules, Figures, Scales, and Divisions shown on good Squares.

—Brace Rules, Octagonal Scale, Board, Plank and Scantling Rules, fully explained and described.

—How to lay out Rafters, Hips, Jack-Rafters, Purlins, Bevel Works, etc., etc.

—Backing for Hips, Lengths and Bevels of Valley Rafters. Laying out Stairs and Strings.

—How to describe Circles, Ellipses, Parabolas and other figures, with the Square.

—How to obtain Bevels for Hoppers and all kinds of Splayed Work and Spring Mouldings, by the Square.

—Bisecting Circles, Proportion of Circles, Division of Widths, Bisection of Angles, Diminishing Stiles, Centering Circles, etc., etc.

—Theoretical Rafters, Cuts for Mitre Boxes, Measurement of Surfaces, including Painting, Plastering, Shingling, Siding, Flooring, Rough Boarding, Tinning and Roofing.

—Rules for describing Octagons and Polygons of every description, and how to find their angles and areas.

—Rules for finding the lengths of Rafters and Hips of Irregular Roofs, Cuts for Equal and Unequal Mitres, Trusses and Bevel Timber Work.

—The Development of Hip and Curved Roofs; Veranda Rafters, Straight and Curved; Hopper Cuts of all kinds, Angle Corner-pieces, Splayed Work for Gothic Heads, etc., etc., and many other things useful to the Operative Mechanic.

Handsomely Bound in Cloth with Gilt Title.

Price ONE DOLLAR,

The Carpenter's Steel Square,

AND HOW TO USE IT.

OPINIONS OF THE PRESS.

" This little work consists of a republication of some papers contributed by its talented author some time ago to the *American Builder*, and which were received with so much favor by artisans, for whom they were written, as to induce their author to collect them into the present volume." * * * * * * " The work is well illustrated by upwards of fifty cuts which have been well engraved, and can hardly fail to give any one an idea of the capabilities of the steel square, and what can be accomplished from it when in skilful hands."—*Journal of Franklin Institute, Phila.*

"A most valuable little treatise of 70 pages upon that commonplace subject, the ' steel square,' being a description of that useful tool, and its uses in obtaining the lengths and bevels of rafters, hips, groins, braces, brackets, purlins, collar beams and jack rafters, and its application in obtaining the bevels and cuts for hoppers, spring moldings, octa-gons, stairs, diminished stiles, etc., illustrated by over 50 wood cuts. Mr. Hodgson has succeeded admirably in demonstrating that the study of the value and use of the square is by no means the dry subject one would suppose, and that as a tool in the hands of an intelligent workman, its possibilities are far beyond the standard usually conceded to it. It is a valuable book for the use of the carpenter, and should be upon the office desk of every retailer of lumber, from the valuable hints it will give him as a guide to his negotiations with his customers in figuring out their wants. It is, in fact, well adapted to the wants of every man who has a shed or fence to erect upon his premises, or who wishes to keep a check upon his builder."—*Northwestern Lumber-man, Chicago, Ill.*

"This is a little book that no carpenter, joiner, cabinetmaker, or amateur wood-worker, can do without, if they wish to keep up with the times in their several branches of trade.

"We believe this is the first and only book that has been written on this subject alone, and we must say, that the duty of writing it fell into good hands, as the author has handled his subject in a masterly manner. One is struck with astonishment at the number of difficult and apparently intricate problems this simple instrument—the square—is made to solve, and in such a manner that any mechanic who can read the figures on the tool can work out the solutions. The lengths and bevels of rafters, hips, braces, trusses, purlins, collar beams, and jack rafters are obtained as if by magic, and without thought or calculation.

"The work is handsomely gotten up, printed on heavy white paper, substantially bound, and cleanly turned out. The some fifty odd wood cuts are almost equal to steel engravings, and the whole get-up is a credit to both author and publisher, and the low price at which it is sold, (75 cents), places it within reach of every wood-worker, no matter how poor he may be."—*Enterprise, Collingwood, Ont.*

" It is a timely book on the subject in hand, and we can safely recommend it as com-petent to fill a long felt vacancy in the mechanics' library. The work presents a valu-able collection of rules and data connected with the framing square, to the solution of roofing problems, braces, hoppers, etc., etc."—*Orillia Packet, Ont.*

" Some fifty engravings aid in the description of the square and its uses in obtaining lengths and bevels of all kinds ; also, its application in obtaining the bevels and cuts for all conceivable shapes used in the wood shops. Any wood-worker possessing this book will find its cost, seventy-five cents, is not to be compared with its real value, and usefulness in the shop."—*The Carriage Monthly, Phila.*

" The work is a very valuable one, and should be in the hands of every carpenter."—*Messenger, Collingwood, Ont.*

" The work will be of very great service to carpenters and builders."—*Bulletin, Collingwood, Ont.*

PRACTICAL CARPENTRY.

BEING A GUIDE TO THE

Correct Working and Laying Out of all kinds of Carpenters' and Joiners' Work.

With the Solutions of the Various Problems in Hip-Roofs, Gothic Work, Centering, Splayed Work, Joints and Jointing, Hinging, Dovetailing, Mitering, Timber Splicing, Hopper Work, Skylights, Raking Mouldings, Circular Work, Etc., Etc.

TO WHICH IS PREFIXED A THOROUGH TREATISE ON

"CARPENTER'S GEOMETRY."

ILLUSTRATED BY OVER 300 ENGRAVINGS.

By FRED. T. HODGSON,

AUTHOR OF "THE STEEL SQUARE AND ITS USES," "THE BUILDER'S GUIDE AND ESTIMATOR'S PRICE BOOK," "THE SLIDE RULE AND HOW TO USE IT," ETC., ETC.

Handsomely Bound in Cloth, Price $1.00.

This is the most complete book of the kind ever published. It is Thorough, Practical and Reliable, and at the same time is written in a style so plain that any workman or apprentice can easily understand it. The annexed table of contents will give a better idea of its scope and value than can be had from any amount of notices or descriptions :

TABLE OF CONTENTS.

PART I.

GEOMETRY.—Straight Lines.—Curved Lines.—Solids.—Compound Lines. —Parallel Lines.—Oblique or Converging Lines.—Plane Figures.— Angles.—Right Angles.—Acute Angles.—Obtuse Angles.—Right-angled Triangles.—Quadrilateral Figures.—Parallelograms.—Rect-angles.—Squares.—Rhomboids.—Trapeziums.—Trapezoids.—Diagonals.—Polygons.—Pentagons.—Hexagons.—Heptagons.—Octagons.—Circles.—Chords.—Tangents.—Sectors.—Quadrants.—Arcs.— Concentric and Eccentric Circles.—Altitudes.—Problems I. to XXIX. —Drawing of Angles.—Construction of Geometrical Figures.—Bisection of Lines.—Trisection of Lines and Angles.—Division of Lines into any Number of Parts.—Construction of Triangles, Squares and Parallelograms.—Construction of Proportionate Squares.—Construction of Polygons.—Areas of Polygons.—Areas of Concentric Rings and Circles.—Segments of Circles.—The use of Ordinates for Obtaining Arcs of Circles.—Drawing an Ellipse with a Trammel. —Drawing an Ellipse by means of a String.—Same by Ordinates.— Raking Ellipses.—Ovals.—Sixty-two Illustrations.

PART II.

ARCHES, CENTRES.—Window and Door Heads.—Semi-circular Arch.—Segmental Arches.—Stilted Arches.—Horseshoe Arch.—Lancet Arch.—Equilateral Arch.—Gothic Tracery.—Wheel-Windows.—Equilateral Tracery.—Square Tracery.—Finished Leaf Tracery.—Twenty-two Illustrations.

PART III.

ROOFS.—Saddle Roof.—Lean-to or Shed Roof.—Simple Hip-Roof.—Pyramidal Roof.—Theoretical Roof.—Roof with Straining Beam.—Gothic Roof.—Hammer-Beam Roofs.—Curved Principal Roofs.—Roofs with Suspending Rods.—Deck Roofs.—King-post and Principal Roof.—Queen-post and Principal Roof.—Roofs with Laminated Arches.—Strapped Roof Frames.—Tie-beam Roofs.—Roofs for Long Spans.—Theatre Roof.—Church Roof.—Mansard Roof.—Slopes of Roofs.—Rules for Determining the Sizes of Timbers for Roofs.—Acute and Obtuse Angled Hip-Roofs.—Development of Hip-Roofs.—Obtaining Lengths and Bevels of Rafters.—Backing Hip-Rafters.—Lengths, Bevels and Cuts of Purlins.—Circular, Conical and Segmental Roofs.—Rafters with Variable Curves.—Veranda Rafters.—Development of all kinds of Rafters.—Curved Mansard Rafters.—Framed Mansard Roofs.—Lines and Rules for obtaining various kinds of Information.—Thirty-four Illustrations.

PART IV.

COVERING OF ROOFS.—Shingling Common Roofs.—Shingling Hip-Roofs.—Method of Shingling on Hip Corner.—Covering Circular Roofs.—Covering Ellipsoidal Roofs.—Valley Roofs.—Four Illustrations.

PART V.

THE MITERING AND ADJUSTING OF MOULDINGS.—Mitering of Spring Mouldings.—Preparing the Mitre-box for Cutting Spring Mouldings.—Rules for Cutting Mouldings, with Diagrams.—Mitre-boxes of various forms.—Lines for Spring Mouldings of various kinds.—Seven Illustrations.

PART VI.

SASHES AND SKYLIGHTS.—Raised Skylights.—Skylights with Hips.—Octagon Skylights with Segmental Ribs.—Angle-bars, with Rules and Diagrams, showing how to obtain the Angles, Forms, etc.—Sash-Bars, Hints on their Construction.—Twelve Illustrations.

PART VII.

MOULDINGS.—Angle Brackets.—Corner Coves.—Enlarging and Reducing Mouldings.—Irregular Mouldings.—Raking Mouldings, with Rules for Obtaining.—Mouldings for Plinths and Capitals of Gothic Columns.—Mouldings around Square Standards.—Mitering Circular Mouldings with each other.—Mitering Circular Mouldings with Straight ones.—Mitering Mouldings at a Tangent.—Mitering Spring Circular Mouldings.—Description of Spring Mouldings.—Lines for Circular Spring Mouldings.—Seventeen Illustrations.

PART VIII.

JOINERY.—Dovetailing.—Common Dovetailing.—Lapped Dovetailing.—Blind Dovetailing.—Square Dovetailing.—Splay Dovetailing.—Regular and Irregular Dovetailing.—Lines and Cuts for Hoppers and Splayed Work.—Angles and Mitres for Splayed Work.—Nineteen Illustrations.

PART IX.

MISCELLANEOUS PROBLEMS.—Bent Work for Splayed Jambs.—Development of Cylinders.—Rules and Diagrams for Taking Dimensions.—Angular and Curved Measurements.—Eight Illustrations.

PART X.

JOINTS AND STRAPS.—Mortise and Tenon Joints.—Toggle Joints.—Hook Joints.—Tongue Joint.—Lap Splice.—Scarfing.—Wedge Joints.—King-bolts.—Straps, Iron Ties, Sockets, Bearing-plates, Rings, Swivels and other Iron Fastenings.—Straining Timbers, Struts and King-pieces.—Three Plates, Sixty-five Illustrations.

PART XI.

HINGING AND SWING JOINTS.—Door Hinging.—Centre-pin Hinging.—Blind Hinging.—Folding Hinging.—Knuckle Hinging.—Pew Hinging.—Window Hinging.—Half-turn Hinge.—Full-turn Hinge.—Back Flap Hinging.—Rule-joint Hinging.—Rebate Hinging.—Three Plates, Fifty-one Illustrations.

PART XII.

USEFUL RULES AND TABLES —Hints on the Construction of Centres.—Rules for Estimating.—Form of Estimate.—Items for Estimating.—Remarks on Fences.—Nails: sizes, weights, lengths and numbers.—Cornices, Proportions and Projections for Different Styles of Architecture; and Tall and Low Buildings, Verandas, Bay Windows and Porches.—Proportion of Base-boards, Dados, Wainscots and Surbases.—Woods, Hard and Soft, their Preparation, and how to Finish.—Strength and Resistance of Timber of various kinds.—Rules, showing Weight and other qualities of Wood and Timber.—Stairs, Width of Treads and Risers; their Cost; how to Estimate on them, etc.—Inclinations of Roofs.—Contents of Boxes, Bins and Barrels.—Arithmetical Signs.—Mensuration of Superficies.—Areas of Squares, Triangles, Circles, Regular and Irregular Polygons.—Properties of Circles.—Solid Bodies.—Gunter's Chain.—Drawing and Drawing Instruments.—Coloring Drawings.—Coloring for Various Building Materials.—Drawing Papers.—Sizes of Drawing Papers.—Table of Board Measure.—Nautical Table.—Measure of Time.—Authorized Metric System.—Measures of Length.—Measures of Surfaces.—Measures of Capacity.—Weights.—American Weights and Measures.—Square Measure.—Cubic Measure.—Circular Measure.—Decimal Approximations.—Form of Building Contract.

A NEW BOOK

FOR

CABINET MAKERS, UPHOLSTERERS, FURNITURE MEN, AMATEUR WOOD FINISHERS, ETC., ETC.

HINTS

AND

Practical Information

FOR

CABINET-MAKERS, UPHOLSTERERS, AND FURNITURE MEN GENERALLY.

TOGETHER WITH

A DESCRIPTION OF ALL KINDS OF FINISHING, WITH FULL DIRECTIONS THEREFOR—VARNISHES—POLISHES—STAINS FOR WOOD—DYES FOR WOOD—GILDING AND SILVERING—RECEIPTS FOR THE FACTORY—LACQUERS, METALS, MARBLES, ETC.—PICTURES, ENGRAVINGS, ETC.—MISCELLANEOUS.

This work contains an Immense Amount of the most Useful Information for those who are engaged in Manufacture, Superintendence, or Construction of Furniture or Wood Work of any Kind. It is one of the Cheapest and Best Books Ever Published, and contains

Over 1,000 Hints, Suggestions, Methods,

And Descriptions of Tools, Appliances, and Materials.

All the Recipes, Rules and Directions have been carefully Revised and Corrected by Practical Men of great experience, so that they will be found thoroughly trustworthy.

Price, Bound in Cloth, with Side Title in Gold, $1.00.

SENT TO ANY ADDRESS ON RECEIPT OF PRICE.

HAND SAWS.

THEIR USE, CARE AND ABUSE.

HOW TO SELECT, AND HOW TO FILE THEM.

Being a Complete Guide for Selecting, Using and Filing all kinds of Hand-Saws, Back-saws, Compass and Key-hole Saws, Web, Hack and Butcher's Saws ; showing the Shapes, Forms, Angles, Pitches and Sizes of Saw-Teeth suitable for all kinds of Saws, and for all kinds of Wood, Bone, Ivory and Metal ; together with Hints and Suggestions on the Choice of Files, Saw-Sets, Filing Clamps, and other Matters pertaining to the Care and Management of all Classes of Hand and other Small Saws.

The work is intended more particularly for Operative Carpenters, Joiners, Cabinet-Makers, Carriage Builders, and Wood-Workers Generally, Amateurs or Professionals.

ILLUSTRATED BY OVER SEVENTY-FIVE ENGRAVINGS.

By FRED. T. HODGSON,

AUTHOR OF "THE STEEL SQUARE AND ITS USES," "THE BUILDER'S GUIDE AND ESTIMATOR'S PRICE BOOK," PRACTICAL CARPENTRY," ETC., ETC.

Price   -   -   -   -   -   - $1.00.

TABLE OF CONTENTS.

PART I.

History of the Saw.—Saws of the Greeks.—Invention of the First Saws.—Eygptian Bronze Saws in the British Museum.—Antiquity of Saws.—Mention of Saws in Holy Writ.—Saws of the Stone Age.—Saws of the South-sea Islanders.—Saws for Cutting Stone.—Japanese Saws.—Different Varieties of Saws.—Manner of Using Saws by the Ancients.—Assyrian Saws.—Invention of Circular and Band-Saws.—First Circular-Saws in America.

PART II.

Philosophy or the Cutting Qualities of Saw-Teeth.—The " Why and Wherefore " of the Cutting Pitch and Angles of Rip-Saw Teeth.—The Round Gullet-Tooth.—Chisel-Teeth and their Action on the Wood.—On the Various Angles Required for Cutting Hard and Soft Woods, with Explanations of Space, Pitch, Gullet, Gauge, Set, Rake and Points.—Names of Saws, with Dimensions, Form of Teeth, Descriptions and Explanations.—How to Choose a Saw ; with Hints as to Form, Quality, Make and " Hang " of a Saw, with Remarks Concerning Different Makers—Sash-Saws. Dovetail-Saws, Rip-Saws, Panel-Saws, Cross-cut Saws, Bow-Saws, Web-Saws, Key-hole Saws, Compass-Saws and Tenon-Saws.

PART III.

How to Use Hand-Saws.—How to Saw Well and Easily.—Hints for Sawing Straight.—Rules for New Beginners.—French, German and American Workmen.—Saws Filed to Work on the Pull-Stroke.—Changeable Key-hole Saws.—Use of Back-Saws.—Use of Web-Saws.—Care of Buck-Saws.—The Buck-Saw; the Terror of Boyhood, and Why.—The Butcher's-Saw, the Hack-Saw, and the Surgeon's-Saw with Description of Each, and Hints as to their Management,

TABLE OF CONTENTS (*Continued*).

PART IV.

Filing and Setting Hand-Saws.—The Qualities Required to make a Good Filer.—Rules in some Old-time Joiner Shops.—Careless Filing and its Consequences.—Clamping Saws for Filing.—The Line of Teeth.—Angular Groove on Cutting Edge of Saw.—Filing Backs of Teeth.—Jointing the Sides of Teeth.—Shape of Teeth for Cross-cutting Hard Wood, Medium and Soft Wood.—Cutting Angles Required for Various Degrees of Hardness in Woods.—Angle to Hold the File.—The True Theory of Saw-Filing.—Buckling and Twisting Saws; How Done and How Avoided.—"Hook and Pitch."—Careless Use of Saws, and the Injuries Done to them in Consequence.—The Filing of Different Saws, and why One Class of Saws Require Different Treatment from Another. The Saw that Scrapes, and the Saw that Cuts; the "Why" of this Difference.—Why Some Men do Much More Work than Others, and with Greater Ease, when Sawing.

PART V.

Miscellaneous Saws; their Uses, How to Care for Them, and How to Use Them.—The **M** Tooth, Teeth that Cut Both Ways, Crenate Teeth, Brier Teeth, Gullet Teeth, Parrot-bill Teeth. Hog Teeth, the Lancet and other Fancy Forms of Teeth, Described and Explained.—The Old-style "Peg Tooth," for Two-handed Cross-cut Saws.—Various Examples of the "Peg-Tooth Saw.—Hack-Saws; How to Use and How to Keep in Order.—Butcher's-Saws, Surgeon's-Saws, Saws for Cutting Combs, Ivory, Brass, Gold, and Silver.—Circular-Saws for Cutting Metal, Ivory, Tortoise-shell, and other Hard Materials.—Jig-Saws, Band-Saws; their Uses and How to Keep them in Order.—Scroll-Saws; their Uses and Care.—Progress of the Band-Saw; its Future; How to Make them do Clean Work.—Heating Saws; Rules for their Management.—Why Circular-Saws Burst.

PART VI.

Remarks on Saws, Files, Sets, and other Appliances.—Saw-Files; what Constitutes a Good One, and How to Select.—Different Qualities of Saw-Files, and How to Know the Various Grades.—Why there are Different Grades.—Hints on the Use of Files.—Circular-Saws that are not Circular.—How to Become an Expert Sawyer.—Speed of Circular-Saws; Table of Same.—Speed of Reciprocating-Saws, or Jig-Saws, Speed of Feed for Same.—Working Action of Band-Saws.—How Band-Saws Became Possible.—French and American Band-Saw Blades.—Inside Sawing with Band-Saws.—Detachable Band-Saws.—Aids to Saw-Filing. — Saw-Clamps. — Saw-Filers. — Saw-Sets. — Hand-Setting with Punch and Hammer.—Setting with "Sets."—Machine Band-Saw Setters.—Devices for Holding Saws while being Set and Filed.

PART VII.

Notes and Memoranda.—Saw-Gauges.—Comb-Saw Gauges.—Saw-Guides. Mitre-Boxes.—Circular *vs.* Band-Saws.—Emery Sharpeners.—Small Saws.—Machine-Saws.—Narrow Saws.—Brazing Band-Saws.—Remarks on Circular-Saws.—Power Required to Drive Circular-Saws.—Mill-Saws.—Saws with Few Teeth.

Plaster and Plastering.

MORTARS AND CEMENTS.

HOW TO MAKE, AND HOW TO USE.

BEING A COMPLETE GUIDE FOR THE PLASTERER IN THE PREPARATION
AND APPLICATION OF ALL KINDS OF PLASTER, STUCCO, PORTLAND
CEMENT, HYDRAULIC CEMENTS, LIME OF TIEL, ROSENDALE AND
OTHER CEMENTS, WITH USEFUL AND PRACTICAL INFORMA-
TION ON THE CHEMISTRY, QUALITIES AND USES OF THE
VARIOUS KINDS OF LIMES AND CEMENTS. TO-
GETHER WITH RULES FOR MEASURING,
COMPUTING, AND VALUING PLASTER
AND STUCCO WORK.

TO WHICH IS APPENDED

AN ILLUSTRATED GLOSSARY OF TERMS

USED IN PLASTERING, ETC.

Besides numerous Engravings in the text, there are three Plates, giving some
forty figures of Ceilings, Centrepieces, Cornices, Panels and Soffits.

By FRED. T. HODGSON,

Price - - - - - - - $1.00.

INDEX.

	PAGE
Description of Plates,	1
Preface,	3
Preliminary,	9

TOOLS AND MATERIALS.

	PAGE		PAGE
The Hoe or Drag,	10	The Operator,	12
The Hawk,	10	The Scratcher,	13
The Mortar-Board,	11	The Hod,	13
Trowels,	11	The Sieve,	13
Floats,	11	Sand Screens,	13
Moulds,	11	Mortar-Beds,	14
Centre Moulds,	12	The Slack Box,	14
The Pointer,	12	Lath,	14
The Paddle,	12	Lather's Hatchet,	15
Stopping and Pricking out Tool,	12	Nail Pocket,	15
Mitering Rods,	12	Cut off Saw,	15

MATERIALS EMPLOYED IN PLASTERING.

	PAGE		PAGE
Internal Plastering,	16	Substitutes for Sand,	23
Coarse Stuff,	16	Marble Dust,	24
Fine Stuff,	16	Hair,	24
Putty,	16	Colors,	24
Stucco,	16	Whitewash,	24
Lime,	17, 18, 20	Whiting,	25
Plaster-of-Paris,	17, 18	Saylor's Portland Cement,	25
Laths,	17	Cellar Floors,	25
Cements,	17	Mastic for Plastering,	25
Calcination,	18	Stable Floors,	25
Quicklime,	18	Concrete for Foundations,	26
Slaking,	18	Keene's Cement,	27
Air Slaking,	19	Metallic Cement,	27
Hydraulicity,	19	Portland-Cement Stucco,	28
Hydraulic Limes,	20	Lias Cement,	28
Sand,	22	Rough Cast,	29

OPERATIONS.

	PAGE		PAGE
General Instructions,	30	External Plastering,	35–41
Floating the Work,	31	Scagliola,	41
Trowelling and Rendering,	32	Carton Pierre,	42
Running Cornices,	32	Papier Mache,	42
Ornamental Cornices,	34	Stamped Leather,	42
Flowers and Cast Work,	35	Stearate of Lime,	42–43

PLASTERER'S MEASUREMENT.

	PAGE		PAGE
Measuring and Valuation,	44	Measuring Cornices,	47
Mensuration of Superfices,	44	Measuring Stucco,	48
Taking Dimensions,	44	Coloring,	48
Specifications,	46	Summary,	48–50
Rendering to Walls,	46	Pugging,	50
Lath and Plaster Work to Ceilings,	47	Whitewashing and Coloring,	51–53
Lath and Plaster Work to Partitions,	47		

MISCELLANEOUS MEMORANDA.

	PAGE		PAGE
Hard Hydraulic Cement,	54	To Take Wax Moulds from Plaster,	59
Colored Cements,	54	Cement for Mouldings,	60
Brick-Dust Cement,	54	Cement Floors for Cellars,	60
Hardening Plaster,	54	Wash,	60
Mastic Cement,	54	Coloring in Distemper,	61
Cement for Outside Brick Walls,	55	Mortar,	61
To Mend Plaster Models,	55	Caution,	61
Cheap Concrete Flooring,	55	Concrete Walls,	62
To Make Moulds,	55	External Stucco,	62
Artificial Building Stone,	56	Proportions of Materials,	62
Artificial Marble,	56	Puzzolana,	62
Hard Mortar,	56	Grout,	63
Marble-Worker's Cement,	56	Weights of Materials,	64
Mason's Cement,	57	Items,	64
Whitewash,	57	Cisterns,	64
Red Wash for Bricks,	57	Blackboards,	65
To Whiten Internal Walls,	57	Measuring Plasterer's Work,	66
Concrete,	58	Notes,	67
Papier Mache,	58	Mortars and Cements,	67–74
Plaster Ornaments,	59	Concrete Houses,	74–77
Fibrous Plaster,	59	Strength of Different Mortars,	77–78
Staining Marble,	59	Form of Agreement,	78–81
Cleaning Marble,	59		

GLOSSARY OF TERMS. A to Z, ... 83–101

IMPORTANT ANNOUNCEMENT

TO ARCHITECTS, CONTRACTORS AND BUILDERS.

For many years past there has been a want by the building fraternity of a good and reliable book on ESTIMATING, one that will give prices of materials and labor for every department of building, so far as this is possible. Such a book, the publishers believe, has at last been produced, and is now offered to those interested.

THE BUILDER'S GUIDE,

AND ESTIMATOR'S PRICE BOOK.

By FRED. T. HODGSON.

HANDSOMELY BOUND IN CLOTH, GILT TITLE.   PRICE, - $2.00.

Current Prices of Lumber, Hardware, Glass, Plumbers' Supplies, Paints, Slates, Stones, Limes, Cements, Bricks, Tin and other Building Materials; also, Prices of Labor, and Cost of Performing the Several Kinds of Work Required in Building. Together with Prices of Doors, Frames, Sashes, Stairs, Mouldings, Newels, and other Machine Work. To which is appended a large number of Building Rules, Data, Tables and Useful Memoranda, with a Glossary of Architectural and Building Terms.

This is an entirely new work, and gives Prices of Labor and Materials down to a recent date, and is, therefore, the most reliable book in the market on the subject of prices of labor and materials required for building. The work contains, besides Prices, Data, Rules, and Several Hundred Tables and Hints on Building, a blank column where the prices of Labor or Material may be written in pencil, where such prices differ from those given in the book. There is also a very complete Glossary of Building and Architectural Terms appended to the work, which is a useful and valuable addition for practical builders.

The work is really a Cyclopædia of Prices and Builder's Tables, Data and Memoranda, and is necessarily a large work, having over 330 pages, each page being 7¼ x 4¾, and covered with closely printed matter.

In order to give an idea of what the work contains, we give the following brief

SYNOPSIS OF CONTENTS:

PART I.—Contains Hints and Rules for Correct Estimating.—Forms for Taking Estimates, Quantities, Prices, and Manner of Computation.—General Memoranda of Items for Estimates.—Excavations.—Foundations.—Drains.—Iron Work.—Baths and Water Closets.—Brick Walls.—Carpenter's Work.—Joiner's Work.—Mantels, Grates, Stove Fittings, etc.—Pantry, Closets, Kitchens and Appurtenances.—Bell Hanging, Gas Fixing and Fixtures.—Stairs and Staircases.—Roofs, Gutters and Conductors.—Porches, Verandas and Fences.—Framing; Cost of same.—Cost of Painting, Plastering, Shingling, Slating, Tinning, Finishing. Glazing, Building Chimneys, and other Brick Work.—Rules for Measuring all kinds of Hip and other Roofs, with Cost of same.—Rough Boarding, Shingling, Siding, Laying Floors, and other Work.—Cost of Material and Labor for Stairs, Newels, Balusters, Rails, Doors, Mouldings, Sliding and Folding Doors, Windows of all kinds, Blinds, Wainscoting, Baseboards, Finials, Cresting, Plumbing, Flooring, and everything else used about a Building.

PART II.—Contains an Extensive Schedule of Builder's Prices, for Digging, Shovelling, Ramming in Loose Earth, Clay and Gravel.—Cost of Masonry, Rubble, Hammer-Dressed Work, Rough Rock Work, Reveals, Ashler Work, Be-pairs, Arches, Plain Work, Rubbed Work, Beaded Work, Fluting, Reeding, Throating, Grooving, Rebating, Leading in Work, Sunken Work, Mortising, etc.—Prices of all kinds of Native Stones per Cubic Foot.—Prices of Cements; Portland, Rosendale, Keene's, Lime of Teil. Lime, Lath, Slate, etc.—Bricklaying; Price per 1,000, Laborer's Wages, Prices of Bricks of Different Grades, Circular and Elliptical Work, Brick Paving of all kinds, Laid Dry or in Mortar.—Drain Pipes, Cost and Quality; Terra-Cotta Chimney Tops, Cresting, Tiles and Mouldings, etc.—Colored Bricks, Tuck Pointing, Setting in Sash and Door Frames, Taking Down Old Work, Rebuilding with Old Bricks, Firebricks, Tile Work, Quality and Prices of Bricks from Various Localities, Prices of Peerless Brick Company's Colored Bricks, Colored Mortars and Cements, Odd-Shaped Bricks.—Plasterer's Work, Scaffolding, Lathing, Mortars for all kinds of Work, Cements for Walls and Ceilings, Cornices and Stucco Work, Plaster-of-Paris Flower and Ornamental Work, Kalsomining and Washes of all Kinds.—Carpenter's and Joiner's Work ; Wages, Prices of Lumber, Prices of Made-up Stuff of all Kinds.—Hard-wood Work, Nails, Screws, Locks, Butts and other Hardware.—Stairs of all Kinds, Table for Finding the Run and Rise of Treads and Risers, Turned Work for Stairs and other Work.—Painting, Colors, Prices for Different Kinds of Work, Ladders, Scaffolding, Tools, Graining, Painting Iron Work, Staining, Repairing Old Work. Numerical Work, Varnishing, Lettering, Oiling, Sash and Door Painting, Mixing Colors, Prices of Colors, Miscellaneous Remarks.—Roofing Materials of all Kinds, with Prices and Cost of Laying ; Bell-Hanging Materials, Skylights, Tubs, Sinks, Sheet Iron, Pumps, Tanks, Registers, Ventilators, Wire Ropes, and other matters required in Building.

PART III.—Contains Rules for Builder's Bookkeeping, Form of Balance Sheet, Rules for Measuring Artificer's Work, including Excavation, Drains, Shoring, Concreting, and Labor in General : also Methods of Measuring all Kinds of Materials for Brick, Stone, or Wood Work.—Elements of the Mechanics of Architecture, Strength of Materials, Rules for Obtaining Same ; Iron, Wood, Stone and Brick, Crushing Loads for Various Building Materials, Columns, Iron, Wood, Stone.—Tables for Computing the Strength of Materials, Factors of Safety, Rolled-Iron Beams and Girders.—Bricks and Brick Piers, Terra-Cotta, Strength and Qualities of Cements and Mortars, Fire-Brick, Colored Mortars, Granite and other Stone.

PART IV.—Miscellaneous Tables.—Weight of Iron, Lead, Brass, Copper and Cast Iron, per Foot Superficial or in Bars ; Strength of Round Ropes, Weight of Boiler Iron, Wrought-Iron Pipes, Flat and Round Wire Ropes for Elevators, Iron Roofing, Lead Pipes, Nails, Foreign Weights and Measures, Force of Wind, Square Measure, Long Measure, Equivalents, Arithmetical and other Signs, Expansion by Heat, Force of Explosives, Number of Shingles, Slates, Tiles and other Covering Required for 100 feet of Roofing, Number of Bricks Required for Given Wall, Strength of Woods, Loads for Bridges, Strains on Bridges and Trusses, Specific Gravities.

PART V.—Mensuration of Superfices, Areas of Squares, Cubes, Triangles, Multi-sided Figures, etc.; Measurements of Solids, Cubes, Cones, Cylinders, Spheres, etc.; Squares and Cubes of Numbers, Table of Spherical Contents, Diameters, Circumferences and Areas of Circles, Board and Plank Measure, Scantling Measure, Wages Table, Sizes and Capacities of Cribs, Boxes and Tanks.

PART VI.—Mechanics' Lien Laws of Alabama, Arkansas, Connecticut, California, Colorado, District of Columbia, Delaware, Florida, Georgia, Indiana, Iowa, Illinois, Kansas, Kentucky, Maine, Louisiana, Massachusetts, Maryland, Mississippi, Michigan, Missouri, New Jersey, Nevada, Nebraska, New Hampshire, North Carolina, New York, Oregon, Ohio, Pennsylvania, Rhode Island, South Carolina, Texas, Tennessee, Vermont, Virginia, West Virginia, Wisconsin, Ontario.

PART VII.—Schedule of Architect's Charges, Drawings, Superintendence, Percentage on Public Buildings.—Architect's Rules and Methods of Charging for Services Rendered.—Leading Architectural and Building Journals.—Glossary of Architectural and Building Terms. (This "Glossary" covers some fifty-seven pages, and deals with over One Thousand Terms used in Architecture and Building).

THE WORKSHOP COMPANION.

A Collection of Useful and Reliable Recipes, Rules, Processes, Methods, Wrinkles, and Practical Hints,

FOR THE HOUSEHOLD AND THE SHOP.

CONTENTS.

Abyssinian Gold;—Accidents, General Rules;—Alabaster, how to work, polish and clean;—Alcohol;—Alloys, rules for making, and 26 recipes;—Amber, how to work, polish and mend;—Annealing and Hardening glass, copper, steel, etc.;—Arsenical Soap;—Arsenical Powder;—Beeswax, how to bleach;—Blackboards, how to make;—Brass, how to work, polish, color, varnish, whiten, deposit by electricity, clean, etc., etc.;—Brazing and Soldering;—Bronzing brass, wood, leather, etc.;—Burns, how to cure;—Case-hardening;—Catgut, how prepared;—Cements, general rules for using, and 56 recipes for preparing;—Copper, working, welding, depositing;—Coral, artificial;—Cork, working;—Crayons for Blackboards;—Curling brass, iron, etc.;—Liquid Cuticle;—Etching copper, steel, glass;—Eye, accidents to;—Fires, to prevent;—Clothes on Fire;—Fireproof Dresses;—Fly Papers;—Freezing Mixtures, 6 recipes;—Fumigating Pastils;—Gilding metal, leather, wood, etc.;—Glass, cutting, drilling, turning in the lathe, fitting stoppers, removing tight stoppers, powdering, packing, imitating ground glass, washing glass vessels, etc.;—Grass, Dry, to stain;—Guns, to make shoot close, to keep from rusting, to brown the barrels of, etc., etc.;—Handles, to fasten;—Inks, rules for selecting and preserving, and 34 recipes for;—Ink Eraser;—Inlaying;—Iron, forging, welding, case-hardening, zincing, tinning, do. in the cold, brightening, etc., etc.;—Ivory, to work, polish, bleach, etc.;—Javelle Water;—Jewelry and Gilded Ware, care of, cleaning, coloring, etc.;—Lacquer, how to make and apply;—Laundry Gloss;—Skeleton Leaves;—Lights, signal and colored, also for tableaux, photography, etc., 25 recipes;—Lubricators, selection of, 4 recipes for;—Marble, working, polishing, cleaning;—Metals, polishing;—Mirrors, care of, to make, pure silver, etc., etc.;—Nickel, to plate with without a battery;—Noise, prevention of;—Painting Bright Metals;—Paper, adhesive, barometer, glass, tracing, transfer, waxed, etc.;—Paper, to clean, take creases out of, remove water stains, mount drawing paper, to prepare for varnishing, etc., etc.;—Patina;—Patterns, to trace;—Pencils, indelible;—Pencil Marks, to fix;—Pewter;—Pillows for Sick Room, cheap and good;—Plaster-of-Paris, how to work;—Poisons, antidotes for, 12 recipes;—Polishing Powders, preparation and use of (six pages);—Resins, their properties, etc.;—Saws, how to sharpen;—Sieves;—Shellac, properties and uses of;—Silver, properties of, oxidized, old, cleaning, to remove ink stains from, to dissolve from plated goods, etc., etc.;—Silvering metals, leather, iron, etc.;—Size, preparation of various kinds of;—Skins, tanning and curing, do with hair on;—Stains, to remove from all kinds of goods;—Steel, tempering and working (six pages);—Tin, properties, methods of working;—Varnish, 21 recipes for;—Varnishing, directions for;—Voltaic Batteries;—Watch, care of;—Waterproofing, 7 recipes for;—Whitewash;—Wood Floors, waxing, staining, and polishing;—Wood, polishing;—Wood, staining, 17 recipes;—Zinc, to pulverize, black varnish for.

164 closely-printed pages, neatly bound. Sent by mail for 36 cents (postage stamps received).

WORK MANUALS.

The intention of the publishers is to give in this Series a number of small books which will give Thorough and Reliable Information in the plainest possible language, upon the

ARTS OF EVERYDAY LIFE.

Each volume will be by some one who is not only practically familiar with his subject, but who has the ability to make it clear to others. The volumes will each contain from 50 to 75 pages, will be neatly and clearly printed on good paper and bound in tough and durable binding. The price will be *25 cents each, or five for One Dollar.*
The following are the titles of the volumes already issued. Others will follow at short intervals.

I. Cements and Glue.

A Practical Treatise on the Preparation and Use of All Kinds of Cements, Glue and Paste. By JOHN PHIN, Editor of the *Young Scientist* and the *American Journal of Microscopy.*
Every mechanic and householder will find this volume of almost everyday use. It contains nearly 200 recipes for the preparation of Cements for almost every conceivable purpose.

II. The Slide Rule, and How to Use It.

This is a compilation of Explanations, Rules and Instructions suitable for mechanics and others interested in the industrial arts. Rules are given for the measurement of all kinds of boards and planks, timber in the round or square, glaziers' work and painting, brickwork, paviors' work, tiling and slating, the measurement of vessels of various shapes, the wedge, inclined planes, wheels and axles, levers, the weighing and measurement of metals and all solid bodies, cylinders, cones, globes, octagon rules and formulæ, the measurement of circles, and a comparison of French and English measures, with much other information, useful to builders, carpenters, bricklayers, glaziers, paviors, slaters, machinists and other mechanics.
Possessed of this little Book and a good Slide Rule, mechanics might carry in their pockets some hundreds of times the power of calculation that they now have in their heads, and the use of the instrument is very easily acquired.

III. Hints for Painters, Decorators and Paperhangers.

Being a selection of Useful Rules, Data, Memoranda, Methods and Suggestions for House, Ship, and Furniture Painting, Paperhanging, Gilding, Color Mixing, and other matters Useful and Instructive to Painters and Decorators. Prepared with Special Reference to the Wants of Amateurs. By an Old Hand.

IV. Construction, Use and Care of Drawing Instruments.

Being a Treatise on Draughting Instruments, with Rules for their Use and Care, Explanations of Scales, Sectors and Protractors. Together with Memoranda for Draughtsmen, Hints on Purchasing Paper, Ink, Instruments, Pencils, etc. Also a Price List of all materials required by Draughtsmen. Illustrated with twenty-four Explanatory Illustrations. By FRED. T. HODGSON.

V. The Steel Square.

Some Difficult Problems in Carpentry and Joinery Simplified and Solved by the aid of the Carpenters' Steel Square, together with a Full Description of the Tool, and Explanations of the Scales, Lines and Figures on the Blade and Tongue, and How to Use them in Everyday Work. Showing how the Square may be Used in Obtaining the Lengths and Bevels of Rafters, Hips, Groins, Braces, Brackets, Purlins, Collar-Beams, and Jack-Rafters. Also, its Application in Obtaining the Bevels and Cuts for Hoppers, Spring Mouldings, Octagons, Diminished Styles, etc., etc. Illustrated by Numerous Wood-cuts. By FRED. T. HODGSON, Author of the " Carpenters' Steel Square."

Note.—This work is intended as an elementary introduction for the use of those who have not time to study Mr. Hodgson's larger work on the same subject.

POCKET MANUAL NUMBER ONE ; OR, THE

Writers' and Travellers' Ready Reference Book

FOR EVERY DAY USE.

Rev. JOHN M. HERON, A. M., Editor.

CONTENTS.

1. Title Page.
2. Dedication and Copyright.
3. Editor's Preface.
4. Contents.
5. Over 20,000 Synonymous Words.
6. Foreign Words and Phrases in general use.
7. Domestic and Foreign Postage Rates and Laws and Stamp Duties.
8. Value Foreign Coins as per authorized standard U. S. Mint.
9. Use of Capital Letters.
10. Rules for Punctuation.
11. Abbreviations and their use.
12. A Perpetual Calendar.
13. An Interest Table.

14. A Table showing distance of the principal American Cities from New York, the difference in Time, and the present Population of Each.
15. Our Country and Government; the Area of the U. S., how acquired; Population of States and Territories, Number of Electoral Votes each is entitled to, Representatives, etc.; The Executive and Judicial Branches of the Government, duties of officials, their salaries; American Progress, etc., etc.
16. Our Deportment.
17. A Complete Index.

Thousands of people have long felt the need of such a work as this. The correspondent, student, literary worker, or any person who has any writing to do, is constantly annoyed to think of just the right words to use in order to convey the idea intended and make a smooth and finished sentence. The Writers' and Travellers' Ready Reference Book contains 20,000 synonymous words, alphabetically arranged, and this feature of it not only supplies this often much needed word, but it at the same time EDUCATES the searcher and enables him to express himself verbally with grace and ease. To the writer this list of Synonymous Words is second only to the Spelling Book. The use of Capitals, rules for Punctuation and use of Abbreviations are all-important, and frequently a lack of their observance or an ignorance of their proper use turns what " might have been " *a successful life* into another channel because such things as these caused some person to reject the application which otherwise would have been the successful turning point in the career of the writer. We cannot always carry a Spelling Book or Dictionary with us, and nowhere is information on these points so concisely given and so handy for reference as in the Writers' and Travellers' Ready Reference Book. We often spend considerable time and go to lots of trouble to ascertain something about Postage Rates. There are but few of us who do not need a list to give us the meaning of Foreign Words and Phrases which we constantly come across in reading. A Calendar, Interest Table, and table showing the value of Foreign Coins, are all eminently practical and useful. All these this little book contains. The *one* table showing at a glance the population of the principal American cities, the distance of each from New York City, and the difference in time, is a *marvel of condensation,* and is worth more than the price of the book to any traveller. Under the head of " Our Country and Government " is given *the pith* of a large volume. JUST SUCH facts as every American ought to possess, and they can be obtained nowhere else for less than *four times the money.*

Good manners and an observance of a few simple Rules of Etiquette often *do more* towards winning friends and making one happy, than wealth, or the most classic education. They *always* go further than either or both towards making a *gentleman or lady.* Such Gems of Deportment as are of value to all, will be found in the " Pocket Manual."

IF YOU would perfect and educate yourself in these matters, by all means, GET IT. IF YOU would save yourself from many annoyances and much loss of time and money, GET IT. IF YOU would make an inexpensive, appropriate and useful present to any person, GET IT.

The Pocket Manual is printed from *new and perfect* plates, on fine tinted paper, *made expressly for it,* bound in Silk Cloth, Flexible Covers, with Ink and Gold Side Stamp, Red Edges. **Price 50 cents.**

THE
POCKET MANUAL
NUMBER TWO,
OR, A
KEY TO A PROFITABLE OCCUPATION FOR ANY PERSON,
REV. JOHN M. HERON, A.M., EDITOR.

TWENTY-FIVE DOLLARS WORTH OF INFORMATION IN THE POCKET.

CONTENTS.

How to Become a Short-Hand Writer, or complete and practical instruction in Phonography, by CURTIS HAVEN, Pres't Phila. College of Phonography, etc.

How to Become a Proof-reader, by JOSEPH JOHNSON, experienced proof-reader.

How to Become a Telegraph Operator, by J. W. CROUSE, Ex Supt. Pa. R. R. Wires, Eastern Division.

How to Use a Type-Writer, or simple instructions for operating with a Writing Machine. By J. W. EABLE, Phila. Manager Remington Type-Writer Co.

How to Get a Farm from U. S. By ARTHUR BRADLEY, Attorney.

How to Manufacture Super-phosphate of Lime and Guano. By M. FRANZ, Scientist.

How to Raise Poultry or Poultry and Eggs as a Business. By M. H. PENDLETON, editor "Poultry Messenger."

How to Become a Dressmaker. Plain directions for learning to do finished work for one's self or as a business, by MISS ISABEL CRAWFORD, Practical Dressmaker.

How to Draw and Paint Flowers, etc., from nature or otherwise. By PROF. JOHN COLLINS, Artist.

The Subscription Book Business. Its Influence, Growth, Desirability, etc., by W. H. THOMPSON, Publisher.

How to Become a Book-keeper and Practical Instructions for Book-keepers. By THOMAS MAY PEIRCE, M.A., of the Peirce College of Business, Phila.

How to Make out Reports and Audit Acc'ts of Building Associations, what Building Associations are and how conducted. By THOMAS GAFFNEY, Practical Accountant and Building Association Expert.

Directions for Silk Culture, with instructions for raising Worms, spinning Cocoons, etc., by MRS. M. E. CUNNINGHAM, assisted by the silk Culture Association.

Collecting Old Coins. Tables of different coins with market prices, etc. By G. L. FANCHER, Numismatist.

Stamps Collecting, and How to Buy and Sell Stamps. By L. W. DURBIN, Philatelist and Stamp Dealer.

How to Make Soap. By FRANK P. HARMED, Chemist of the Penn Chemical Works.

Ambition, Enterprise and Integrity. By REV. JOHN M. HERON, A.M.

Table of Wages by the Month. From the American Home and Farm Cyclopædia.

EVERY ARTICLE, with the exception of one or two of the less important ones, is ORIGINAL, and has been prepared with the UTMOST CARE by a person of particular experience, reputation and ability for the subject. So much original matter and so able a corps of writers was never before presented in a book of the size and price.

ILLUSTRATIONS. Several articles have been illustrated at a heavy expense. The lessons in short hand were produced by photo-engraving from pen drawings 16 TIMES the size. There are some 25 of these. Prof. Collins' and Attorney Bradley's articles are most tastily and beautifully illustrated.

The skill of the engraver has been required in rendering complete several other features.

The Pocket Manual is printed on the finest rose tint paper, made expressly for it, from new and perfect plates, with a rule around each page, contains 234 pages.

Price, Bound in Finest English Cloth, Red Edges. Gold Side Stamp, 50 cents.

RECENT ISSUES.

Collodio-Etching.

A Guide to Collodio-Etching. By Rev. Benjamin Hartley. Illustrated by the Author. 12mo., Cloth, Neat, - - - - - - - $1.00.

This volume gives complete and minute instructions for one of the most delightful of Amateur Arts. It is fully illustrated by wood-cuts of all the apparatus used (which is very simple and easily made), and also by actual photo prints of the etchings themselves.

Scientific Experiments.

Easy Experiments in Chemistry and Natural Philosophy. For Educational Institutions of all Grades, and for Private Students. By G. Dallas Lind, Author of "Methods of Teaching in Country Schools," and "Normal Outlines of the Common School Branches." Paper, - - - - - - 40 cents.

This book, besides being a valuable guide for the teacher and student, will afford scientific amusement sufficient to brighten the evenings of a whole winter.

The Builder's Guide and Estimator's Price Book.

Being a Compilation of Current Prices of Lumber, Hardware, Glass, Plumbers' Supplies, Paints, Slates, Stones, Limes, Cements, Bricks, Tin, and other Building Materials; also, Prices of Labor, and Cost of Performing the Several Kinds of Work Required in Building. Together with Prices of Doors, Frames, Sashes, Stairs, Mouldings, Newels, and other Machine Work. To which is appended a large number of Building Rules, Data, Tables, and Useful Memoranda, with a Glossary of Architectural and Building Terms. By Fred. T. Hodgson, Editor of "The Builder and Wood-Worker," Author of "The Steel Square and Its Uses," etc., etc. 12mo., Cloth, - - - - - - $2.00.

Celestial Objects for Common Telescopes.

By the Rev. T. W. Webb, M.A., F.R.A.S. Fourth Edition, Revised and Greatly Enlarged. Fully Illustrated with Engravings and a large Map of the Moon.

Cloth, -   -   -   -   -   -   - $3.00

This edition has been made for us by the English publishers, and is in every respect the same as the English edition. The work itself is too well known to require commendation at our hands. No one that owns even the commonest kind of a telescope can afford to do without it

"Many things, deemed invisible to secondary instruments, are plain enough to one who 'knows how to see them.'"—SMYTH.

"When an object is once discerned by a superior power, an inferior one will suffice to see it afterwards."—SIR. W. HERSCHEL.

Chemical History of the Six Days of Creation.

By John Phin, Editor of the "American Journal of Microscopy" and the "Young Scientist."

12 mo., Cloth,   -   -   -   -   75 cents.

In this volume an attempt is made to trace the evolution of our globe from the primeval state of nebulous mist, "without form and void," and existing in "darkness," or with an entire absence of the manifestations of the physical forces, to the condition in which it was fitted to become the habitation of man. While the statements and conclusions are rigidly scientific, it gives some exceedingly novel views of a rather hackneyed subject.

Ponds and Ditches.

A Work on Pond Life and Kindred Objects. By M. C. Cooke, M.A., LL.D. Cloth, 12mo.,   -   -   75 cents.

This is a most interesting volume by a well-known author and microscopist. It is very freely illustrated with engravings of the objects usually found in pond water.

Microscopical Examination of Drinking Water.

A Guide to the Microscopical Examination of Drinking Water. By J. D. McDonald.

8vo., Cloth, 24 plates,   -   -   -   - $2.75

How to Put Up a Lightning Rod.

Plain Directions for the Construction and Erection of Lightning Rods. By John Phin, C.E., editor of the "Young Scientist," author of "Chemical History of the Six Days of the Creation," etc. Second Edition. Enlarged and Fully Illustrated. 12 mo., Cloth, Gilt Title, - - - - - - 50 cents.

This is a simple and practical little work, intended to convey just such information as will enable every property owner to decide whether or not his buildings are thoroughly protected. It is not written in the interest of any patent or particular article of manufacture, and by following its directions, any ordinarily skilful mechanic can put up a rod that will afford perfect protection, and that will not infringe any patent. Every owner of a house or barn ought to procure a copy.

Lectures in a Workshop.

By T. P. Pemberton, formerly Associate Editor of the "Technologist;" Author of "The Student's Illustrated Guide to Practical Draughting." With an appendix containing the famous papers by Whitworth "On Plane Metallic Surfaces or True Planes;" "On an Uniform System of Screw Threads;" "Address to the Institution of Mechanical Engineers, Glasgow;" "On Standard Decimal Measures of Length." 12 mo., Cloth, Gilt, $1.00

We have here a sprightly fascinating book, full of valuable hints, interesting anecdotes and sharp sayings. It is not a compilation of dull sermons or dry mathematics, but a live, readable book. The papers by Whitworth, now first made accessible to the American reader, form the basis of our modern systems of accurate work.

Mechanical Draughting for Self-Taught Students.

The Student's Illustrated Guide to Practical Draughting. A series of Practical Instructions for Machinists, Mechanics, Apprentices, and Students at Engineering Establishments and Technical Institutes. By T. P. Pemberton, Draughtsman and Mechanical Engineer. Illustrated with Numerous Engravings. Cloth Gilt, - - - - - - - $1.00

This is a simple but thorough book by a draughtsman of twenty-five years' experience. It is intended for beginners and self-taught students, as well as for those who pursue the study under the direction of a teacher.

Cements and Glue.

A Practical Treatise on the Preparation and Use of all Kinds of Cements, Glue, and Paste. By John Phin, Editor of the "Young Scientist" and the "American Journal of Microscopy."

Stiff Covers, - - - - - - 25 cents.

This is the first of a Series of 'Work Manuals," which are intended to be thoroughly trustworthy and practical. They are not mere reprints of old matter, but fresh presentations of valuable material, representing the latest developments of science. Every mechanic and householder will find the volume on Cements of almost everyday use. It contains nearly 200 recipes for the preparation of cements for almost every conceivable purpose.

The Amateur's Hand-Book of Practical Information.

For the Workshop and the Laboratory. Second Edition. Greatly Enlarged. Neatly Bound, - - 15 cents.

This is a handy little book, containing just the information needed by Amateurs in the Workshop and Laboratory. Directions for making Alloys, Fusible Metals, Cements, Glues, etc.; and for Soldering, Brazing, Lacquering, Bronzing, Staining and Polishing Wood. Tempering Tools, Cutting and Working Glass, Varnishing, Silvering, Gilding, Preparing Skins, etc., etc.

The New Edition contains extended directions for preparing Polishing Powders, Freezing Mixtures, Colored Lights for tableaux, Solutions for rendering ladies' dresses incombustible, etc. There has also been added a very large number of new and valuable receipts.

Five Hundred and Seven Mechanical Movements.

Embracing all those which are Most Important in Dynamics, Hydraulics, Hydrostatics, Pneumatics, Steam Engines, Mill and Other Gearing, Presses, Horology and Miscellaneous Machinery; and including Many Movements never before published, and several of which have only recently come into use. By Henry T. Brown, editor of the "American Artisan." Eleventh Edition. $1.00

This work is a perfect Cyclopædia of Mechanical Inventions, which are here reduced to first principles, and classified so as to be readily available. Every mechanic that hopes to be more than a rule-of-thumb worker ought to have a copy.

The Engineer's Slide Rule and Its Applications.

A Complete Investigation of the Principles upon which the Slide Rule is Constructed, together with the Method of its Application to all the Purposes of the Practical Mechanic. By William Tonkes. - - 25 cents.

Rhymes of Science: Wise and Otherwise.

By O. W. Holmes, Bret Harte, Ingoldsby, Prof. Forbes, Prof. J. W. McQ. Rankine, Hon. R. W. Raymond, and others. With Illustrations. Cloth, Gilt Title, 50 cents.

We advise all our readers into whose souls the sunlight of fun ever enters to purchase this little book. "Making light of *cereous* things" has been said, by a high authority, to be "a *wicked* profession," but the genius which can balance the ponderosity of an ichthyosaur upon the delicate point of a euphonious rhyme, or bear aloft a bulky leptorhyncus on the sparkling foam of a soul-stirring love ditty, is worthy—worthy of a purchaser.—*Philadelphia Medical News.*

Instruction in the Art of Wood Engraving.

A Manual of Instruction in the Art of Wood Engraving; with a Description of the Necessary Tools and Apparatus, and Concise Directions for their Use; Explanation of the Terms Used, and the Methods Employed for Producing the Various Classes of Wood Engravings. By S. E. Fuller. Fully Illustrated with Engravings by the author, separate sheets of engravings for transfer and practice being added. New Edition, Neatly Bound, - - - - - - 30 cents.

What to Do in Case of Accident.

What to Do and How to Do It in Case of Accident. A Book for Everybody. 12mo., Cloth, Gilt Title, 50 cents.

This is one of the most useful books ever published. It tells exactly what to do in case of accidents, such as Severe Cuts, Sprains, Dislocations, Broken Bones, Burns with Fire, Scalds, Burns with Corrosive Chemicals, Sunstroke, Suffocation by Foul Air, Hanging, Drowning, Frost-Bite, Fainting, Stings, Bites, Starvation, Lightning, Poisons, Accidents from Machinery and from the Falling of Scaffolding, Gunshot Wounds, etc., etc. It ought to be in every house, for young and old are liable to accident, and the directions given in this book might be the means of saving many a valuable life.

A New Book for Bee-Keepers.

A Dictionary of Practical Apiculture, giving the correct meaning of nearly Five Hundred Terms, according to the usage of the best writers. Intended as a Guide to Uniformity of Expression amongst Bee-Keepers. With Numerous Illustrations, Notes, and Practical Hints. By John Phin, Author of "How to Use the Microscope," etc. Editor of the "Young Scientist." Price, Cloth, Gilt, 50 cts.

This work gives not only the correct meaning of five hundred different words, specially used in bee-keeping, but an immense amount of valuable information under the different headings. The labor expended upon it has been very great, the definitions having been gathered from the mode in which the words are used by our best writers on bee-keeping, and from the Imperial, Richardson's, Skeat's, Webster's, Worcester's and other English Dictionaries. The technical information relating to matters connected with bee-keeping has been gathered from the Technical Dictionaries of Brande, Muspratt, Ure, Wagner, Watts, and others. Under the heads *Bee, Comb, Glucose, Honey, Race, Species, Sugar, Wax* and others, it brings together a large number of important facts and figures which are now scattered through our bee-literature, and through costly scientific works, and are not easily found when wanted. Here they can be referred to at once under the proper head.

How to Become a Good Mechanic.

Intended as a Practical Guide to Self-taught Men; telling What to Study; What Books to Use; How to Begin; What Difficulties will be Met; How to Overcome them. In a word, how to carry on such a Course of Self-instruction as will enable the Young Mechanic to Rise from the Bench to something higher. Paper, - - - - - - - 15 cts.

This is not a book of "goody-goody" advice, neither is it an advertisement of any special system, nor does it advocate any hobby. It gives plain, practical advice in regard to acquiring that knowledge which alone can enable a young man engaged in any profession or occupation connected with the industrial arts to attain a position higher than that of a mere workman.

The Horse.

A Treatise on the Horse and his Diseases. By J. B. Kendall, M.D. 76 Engravings. Paper, - - - - - 20 cts.

A Treatise giving an index of diseases, and the symptoms; cause and treatment of each, a table giving all the principal drugs used for the horse, with the ordinary dose, effects and antidote when a poison; a table with an engraving of the horse's teeth at different ages, with rules for telling the age of the horse; a valuable collection of recipes, and much valuable information.

Section Cutting.

A Practical Guide to the Preparation and Mounting of Sections for the Microscope; Special Prominence being given to the Subject of Animal Sections By Sylvester Marsh. Reprinted from the London edition. With Illustrations. 12mo., Cloth, Gilt Title.   ·   75 cents.

This is undoubtedly the most thorough treatise extant upon section cutting in all its details. The American edition has been greatly enlarged by valuable explanatory notes, and also by extended directions, illustrated with engravings, for selecting and sharpening knives and razors.

A Book for Beginners with the Microscope.

Being an abridgment of "Practical Hints on the Selection and Use of the Microscope." By John Phin. Fully illustrated, and neatly and strongly bound in boards. 30 cts.

This book was prepared for the use of those who, having no knowledge of the use of the microscope, or, indeed, of any scientific apparatus, desire simple and practical instruction in the best methods of managing the instrument and preparing objects.

How to Use the Microscope.

"Practical Hints on the Selection and Use of the Microscope." Intended for Beginners. By John Phin, Editor of the "American Journal of Microscopy." Fourth Edition. Greatly enlarged, with over 80 engravings in the text, and 6 full-page engravings, printed on heavy tint paper. 12mo., cloth, gilt title,   - $1.00

The Microscope.

By Andrew Ross. Fully Illustrated. 12mo., Cloth, Gilt Title.   -   -   -   -   -   75 cents.

This is the celebrated article contributed by Andrew Ross to the "Penny Cyclopædia," and quoted so frequently by writers on the Microscope. Carpenter and Hogg, in the last editions of their works on the Microscope, and Brooke, in his treatise on Natural Philosophy, all refer to this article as the best source for full and clear information in regard to the principles upon which the modern achromatic Microscope is constructed. It should be in the library of every person to whom the Microscope is more than a toy. It is written in simple language, free from abstruse technicalities.

The Microscopist's Annual for 1879.

Contains List of all the Microscopical Societies in the country, with names of officers, days of meeting, etc.; etc.; Alphabetical and Classified Lists of all the Manufacturers of Microscopes and Objectives, Dissecting Apparatus, Microscopic Objects, Materials for Microscopists, in Europe and America, etc., etc.; Postal Rates, Rules and Regulations, prepared expressly for microscopists; Weights and Measures, with tables and rules for the conversion of different measures into each other; Custom Duties and Regulations in regard to Instruments and Books; Value of the Moneys of all Countries in U. S. Dollars; Value of the Lines on Nobert's Test Plates; Table of Moller's Probe Platte, with the number of lines to inch on the several diatoms, etc., etc.; Focal Value of the Objectives of those makers who Number their Objectives (Hartnack, Nachet, etc.); Focal Value of the Eye-pieces of different makers; Magnifying Power of Eye-pieces and Objectives, etc., etc. The whole forming an indispensable companion for every working microscopist. Limp Cloth, Gilt - - - 25 cents.

Microscope Objectives.

The Angular Aperture of Microscope Objectives. By Dr. George E. Blackham. 8vo., Cloth. Eighteen full page illustrations printed on extra fine paper. $1.25. Sold only by Subscription.

This is the elaborate paper on Angular Aperture, read by Dr. Blackham before the Microscopical Congress, held at Indianapolis.

Kutzing on Diatoms.—Nearly ready.

The Siliceous Shelled Bacillariæ or Diatomaceæ; the History of their Discovery and Classification; their Distribution, Collection, and Life-History. By Friedrich Traugott Kutzing. Translated from the German by Prof. Hamilton L. Smith, of Geneva, N. Y. 12mo., Cloth, Gilt, - - - - - - 50 cents.

FOURTH EDITION. Greatly Enlarged, with over 80 illustrations in the Text and 6 full page Engravings, printed on Heavy Tint Paper. 1 *Vol.* 12mo., 240 *pages. Neatly Bound in Cloth, Gilt Title. Price* $1.00.

HOW TO USE THE MICROSCOPE.

A SIMPLE AND PRACTICAL BOOK, INTENDED FOR BEGINNERS.

By JOHN PHIN,

Editor of " The American Journal of Microscopy."

CONDENSED TABLE OF CONTENTS.

THE MICROSCOPE.—What it Is; What it Does: Different Kinds of Microscopes: Principles of its Construction; Names of the Different Parts.

SIMPLE MICROSCOPES.—Hand Magnifiers; Doublets; Power of Two or More Lenses When Used Together; Stanhope Lens; Coddington Lens; Achromatic Doublets and Triplets; Twenty-five Cent Microscopes—and How to Make Them; Penny Microscopes, to Show Eels in Paste and Vinegar.

DISSECTING MICROSCOPES.—Essentials of a Good Dissecting Microscope.

COMPOUND MICROSCOPES.—Cheap Foreign Stands; The Ross Model; The Jackson Model; The Continental Model; The New American Model; Cheap American Stands; The Binocular Microscope; The Binocular Eye-piece; The Inverted Microscope; Lithological Microscopes; The Aquarium Microscope; Microscopes for Special Purposes; "Class" Microscopes.

OBJECTIVES.—Defects of Common Lenses; Spherical Aberration; Chromatic do.; Corrected Objectives; Defining Power; Achromatism; Aberration of Form; Flatness of Field; Angular Aperture; Penetrating Power; Working Distance; Immersion and "Homogeneous" Lenses; Duplex Fronts; French Triplets, etc., etc.

TESTING OBJECTIVES.—General Rules; Accepted Standards—Diatoms, Ruled Lines, Artificial Star; Podura; Nobert's Lines; Möller's Probe Platte, etc., etc.

SELECTION OF A MICROSCOPE.—Must be Adapted to Requirements and Skill of User; Microscopes for Botany; For Physicians; For Students.

ACCESSORY APPARATUS.—Stage Forceps; Forceps Carrier; Plain Slides; Concave Slides; Watch-Glass Holder; Animalcule Cage; Zoophyte Trough; The Weber Slide; The Cell-Trough; The Compressorium; Gravity Compressorium; Growing Slides; Frog Plate; Table; Double Nose-piece.

ILLUMINATION.—Sun-Light; Artificial Light—Candles, Gas, Lamps, etc., etc.

ILLUMINATION OF OPAQUE OBJECTS.—Bulls-Eye Condenser; Side Reflector; The Lieberkuhn; The Parabolic Reflector; Vertical Illuminators.

ILLUMINATION OF TRANSPARENT OBJECTS.—Direct and Reflected Light; Axial or Central Light; Oblique Light; The Achromatic Condenser; The Webster Condenser, and How to Use it; Wenham's Reflex Illuminator, and How to Use it; The Wenham Prism; The "Half-Button;" The Woodward Illuminator; Tolles' Illuminating Traverse Lens; The Spot Lens; The Parabolic Illuminator; Polarized Light.

HOW TO USE THE MICROSCOPE.—General Rules; Hints to Beginners.

HOW TO USE OBJECTIVES OF LARGE APERTURE.—Collar-Correction, etc.

CARE OF THE MICROSCOPE.—Should be Kept Covered; Care of Objectives; Precautions to be Used when Corrosive Vapors and Liquids are Employed; To Protect th Objectives from Vapors which Corrode Glass; Cleaning the Objectives; Cleaning th Brass Work.

COLLECTING OBJECTS.—Where to Find Objects; What to Look for; How to Capture Them.

THE PREPARATION AND EXAMINATION OF OBJECTS.—Cutting Thin Sections, of Sof Substances; Valentine's Knife; Sections of Wood and Bone; Improved Section Cutter; Sections of Rock; Knives; Scissors; Needles; Dissecting Pans and Dishes; Dissecting Microscopes; Separation of Deposits from Liquids; Preparing Whole Insects; Feet, Eyes, Tongues, Wings, etc., of Insects; Use of Chemical Tests; Liquids for Moistening Objects; Refractive Powers of Different Liquids; Iod-Serum. Artificial-od-Serum; Covers for Keeping Out Dust; Errors in Microscopic Observations.

PRESERVATIVE PROCESSES.—General Principles; Preservative Media.

APPARATUS FOR MOUNTING OBJECTS.—Slides; Covers; Cells; Turn-Tables, etc.

CEMENTS AND VARNISHES.—General Rules for Using.

MOUNTING OBJECTS.—Mounting Transparent Objects Dry; in Balsam; in Liquid; Whole Insects; How to Get Rid of Air-Bubbles; Mounting Opaque Objects.

FINISHING THE SLIDES.—Cabinets; Maltwood Finder; Microscopical Fallacies.

NEW DESIGNS

FOR

Fret or Scroll Sawyers.

———

MR. F. T. HODGSON, whose admirable series of articles on the USE OF THE SCROLL SAW are now in course of publication in the YOUNG SCIENTIST, has prepared for us a series of

SEVENTEEN DESIGNS,

of which the following is a list:

No. 1.—This shows one side, back, and bottom, of a pen rack. It may be made of ebony, walnut, or other dark wood.

No. 2.—Design for inlaying drawer fronts, table tops, box lids, and many other things. It is a sumach leaf pattern.

No. 3.—Design for a thermometer stand. It may be made of any hard wood or alabaster. The method of putting together is obvious.

No. 4.—This shows a design for a lamp screen. The open part may be covered with tinted silk, or other suitable material, with some appropriate device worked on with the needle, or, if preferred, ornaments may be painted on the silk, etc.

No. 5.—A case for containing visiting cards. Will look best made of white holly.

No. 6.—A placque stand, it may be made of any kind of dark or medium wood.

No. 7.—A design for ornaments suitable for a window cornice. It should be made of black walnut, and overlaid on some light colored hard wood.

No. 8—A design for a jewel casket. This will be very pretty made of white holly and lined with blue velvet. It also looks well made of ebony lined with crimson.

No. 9.—Frame. Will look well made of any dark wood.

No. 10.—Frame. Intended to be made in pairs. Looks well made of white holly, with leaves and flowers painted on wide stile.

No. 11.—Horseshoe. Can be made of any kind of wood and used for a pen rack. When decorated with gold and colors, looks very handsome.

No. 12.—Design for a hinge strap. If made of black walnut, and planted on a white or oaken door, will look well.

No. 13.—Design for a napkin ring. May be made of any kind of hard wood.

No. 14.—Hinge strap for doors with narrow stiles.

No. 15.—Centre ornament for panel.

No. 16.—Corner ornament for panel.

No. 17.—Key-hole escutcheon.

These designs we have had photo-lithographed and printed on good paper, so that the outlines are sharp, and the opposite sides of each design symmetrical. Common designs are printed from coarse wooden blocks, and are rough and unequal, so that it is often impossible to make good work from them.

The series embraces over forty different pieces, and designs of equal quality cannot be had for less than five, ten or fifteen cents each. We offer them for twenty-five cents for the set, which is an average price of only one cent and a half each.

Mailed to any address on receipt of price.

INDUSTRIAL PUBLICATION CO.,

New York.

SHEET NO. 1.

VISITING CARDS

SHEET NO. 2.

REDUCED FIGURES OF
NEW DESIGNS FOR FRET OR SCROLL SAWYERS.
SIZE OF SHEETS 28 BY 22 INCHES.
(For description see preceding page.)

www.ingramcontent.com/pod-product-compliance
Lightning Source LLC
Chambersburg PA
CBHW021117020726

47500CB00003B/804